The Diagnosis

written by

Conor Murray

Cover Art by Ben McLeod

Results

The examination room was small, cold, and clinical. Cheap-looking turquoise tiles adorned the walls. The floor was the same shade but made of hard, worn linoleum. A small wooden desk with an old computer and telephone sat in the corner for the doctors and nurses to use. Light from the early morning sun spilled in through the cheap metal blinds, making sharp lines on the floor. The place smelled like all hospitals do, of harsh disinfectant masking the smell of blood and feces.

Olivia Thompson sat on the edge of an examination table in an ugly patterned gown, her long brown hair framing the sharp features of her face. Expression blank, she stared across the room at nothing, nervously swinging her long legs back and forth as she waited for her results.

Come on. What the hell is taking so long? It's gonna be something minor. The other thing is rare, super rare, one in a million rare. Nothing to worry about.

A nurse entered the room wearing a blue surgical facemask and latex gloves, a clipboard of documents under her arm. She shut the door with her leg. Olivia sat up straight at her entrance, eager for news. A quick glance at the nurse's nametag read 'Ramirez.'

Short, with jet-black hair streaked with gray, to Olivia's eyes, the woman looked a little younger than her mother, late thirties or early forties. Although most of her face was obscured by the mask, the bags under her eyes told a tale of a thousand nightshifts.

“Olivia Thompson, seventeen years old. Is that correct?” the nurse's tone was flat, businesslike, nothing resembling emotion.

“Yes,” Olivia responded.

"I'm Nurse Ramirez. I'll be taking over for Doctor Clark. She's busy.”

"But you're just a nurse," Olivia's voice was slightly condescending. The nurse either didn't notice or didn't care.

"Yes, well, some patient care tasks are delegated to nursing staff," the nurse answered through her surgical mask.

"Oh, OK…that's cool…it's not an STD," Olivia blurted out without much explanation.

The nurse's eyes looked a little surprised at Olivia's unusual declaration. "Ah, yes. I've read through your file, and we've ruled out that possibility."

"Good. I had to say because the nurse at school always assumes it's an STD, even if you just go in with a damn cold."

"You haven't been sleeping well. Poor appetite, significant nausea, and some vomiting. This is all correct?"

"Yeah, but I barely eat anyway. I'm not anorexic or anything, I'm just not hungry most of the time," Olivia rambled.

"My mom says I need to put some meat on my bones, that I'd look better—"

"But this recent loss of appetite is more aggressive, is that correct?"

"Yeah, but don't worry, I'm not pregnant or anything. That's another thing the nurse at school always assumes."

"Yes, we've also ruled out that possibility."

"The eating thing is fine. As I said, I barely eat anyway. I just need the nausea and vomiting dealt with."

"I understand."

The nurse took a deep breath as if to say something important, but Olivia cut in before she could open her mouth.

"Doctor Clarke said it's something viral, probably something minor, but still worth checking out," Olivia told the nurse before joking, "So, what did the blood tests say? Am I a vampire or something?"

The joke hung in the air. No laughter came from the nurse, no sudden denial, nothing. She just stared at Olivia in silence, a silence that continued for an uncomfortably long time. Olivia's face lost its chipper expression. Her lips tightened, mouth dried up, and a sudden fear rushed through her with a wave of heat. The nurse's eye widened in pity for a moment. It was just long enough for Olivia to know the truth even before the words were spoken.

"You tested positive for both genetic mutations of the HMBS gene, and blood analysis shows evidence of V1 prion disease."

Delivery of the news in a somber and respectful tone didn't make it any easier to digest. Olivia opened her mouth to speak but couldn't form any words. Frightened and confused, like nothing the nurse was saying made any sense as if she referred to some other person who wasn't in the room.

It's a mistake. This doesn't happen to good people. It's a mistake, It's a mistake. Dr. Clarke will know, she knows me.

"Now, I must inform you at this point—" the nurse eventually spoke.

"I wanna speak to Doctor Clarke. She knows me, this is a mistake," Olivia's voice shook as she spoke.

"There's no mistake—"

"Yes, there is, and if you don't get Doctor Clarke to come down here, I'm gonna call my father, and he's gonna have your ass fired."

Olivia's voice steadied as she barked the instruction at the nurse. The woman was clearly taken aback by her sudden transition from deer in the headlights to cornered dog. The nurse rolled her chair back toward the desk and reached her hand underneath it.

"Olivia, I'm trying to help you."

"Just call Doctor Clarke then."

Jumping onto the floor, Olivia approached the nurse with a snarl on her face. It clearly wasn't Nurse Ramirez's first rodeo, not the first entitled demand from a possibly violent patient.

"I need you to take a couple of steps back, Olivia."

Cold, clear, concise, it was a demand not a suggestion. It was only then Olivia realized the nurse reached for a panic button. She looked at the woman with utter incredulity. How could a grown woman be intimidated by her?

"Please," the nurse insisted, hand hovering under the desk.

Olivia laughed at what she perceived to be an utterly comical situation. She backed away from the nurse by about four steps, holding her hands out in mock surrender.

"Better?"

"Yes, thank you," the nurse answered. "Now, I need you to understand something, I'm here to help you and, right now, I'm the only friend you've got."

"Then please call Doctor Clarke. She can straighten this whole thing out."

The nurse paused for a moment before responding, "Even if I call her, she won't come. She's the one who offloaded your case to me. It's procedure."

Olivia was shaken by the revelation. Her face lost its color. She stumbled backward unsteadily and fell into a small plastic chair like a ton of bricks, face expressionless.

"Procedure? My life is fucking over, and you wanna talk about procedure." Olivia's voice had lost its anger. Now, she just sounded broken.

"This topic is supposed to be covered in your health education classes at school."

"I go to a religious school."

"They're still supposed to teach you, it's the law."

"There was pressure from a parents committee at school," Olivia said in a faraway voice.

Nurse Ramirez pulled her surgical mask down. Her face was soft, rounded, and friendly, not the sharp features Olivia had pictured in her head. The nurse suddenly seemed more human. A small smile cracked in the corner of her mouth and her dark eyes widened a little in sympathy. Olivia offered a sad little smile in return.

"So, you know nothing about how this works?" the nurse asked her.

"Only what I see on the news, and the only news my family watches says all the vampires should be burned along with the peace treaty."

Nurse Ramirez ran her hand down her face in exasperation at the information.

"And you've never read any of the information online?"

"Why would I?"

The nurse took a small pause before speaking, "OK, look. Once a patient receives this diagnosis, doctors are prohibited from treating them. It's the law. Doctor Clarke would lose her license."

"So, why are you able to talk to me?"

"Every hospital has a designated nurse with special training for these situations."

"How did you get the shitty end of that stick?"

"I volunteered."

For the first time, Olivia looked at the nurse with some degree of respect and nodded in recognition. The woman had put herself forward for this work, work most people wouldn't touch with a ten-foot pole. The kind of work that made your neighbors stop talking to you and your kids friendless at school.

"OK…OK. So, what happens next?" Olivia asked.

"Do you know about the three-day rule?" the nurse asked.

"Yeah, I know about the three-day rule. Everyone knows about the three-day rule. You don't need a health-ed class to know about that."

The nurse looked at Olivia's file. "Good. It's Thursday the 20th, so, you have until 8 AM on Sunday the 23rd to present yourself at the border of the Vampire Union, or—"

Olivia raised her hand to silence the nurse. "I know what the *or* is."

"Either way, I need to explicitly say it."

"Let me guess, it's the law," Olivia said.

The nurse nodded in grim confirmation and took a deep breath before speaking. "Or…you present yourself for euthanization at any of the sanctioned medical facilities."

Olivia's face was now a pale white. She looked gaunt, hollowed out. A torrent of thoughts splashed around in her head. She had a thousand questions, and they all seemed pointless, but she asked one anyway.

"And if I don't do either?" she asked.

The nurse's face sharpened, warmth seemed to drain out of it, like a sunny day suddenly turned dark. "Then they'll come for you and bring you to a facility by force."

"To murder me," Olivia could barely speak the words. Her voice broke as she uttered them.

"They wouldn't see it that way but, yes, that's what it is."

Olivia broke down and sobbed uncontrollably. Tears rolled down her face and made soft pattering sounds as they hit the fabric of her hospital gown.

"How will they know?" Olivia asked through tears.

"Once your results came back positive from the lab, they got put in a medical database. After three days, the data gets uploaded to a law enforcement database automatically. If you're not already over the border, they start looking, and they don't stop."

"But can't you—" Olivia started.

"The databases are read-only from our side. Once the initial entry is made at the lab, not even a judge can overturn it. It's to stop the very thing you were about to ask me to do."

"Oh…" Olivia looked dumbstruck. The last sliver of hope her father's connections might have been able to save her had just been extinguished.

"I'm sorry," the nurse only spoke to fill the void.

"I'm supposed to go to college next year. I was gonna apply to Lakeshore," Olivia rambled. "My grades might not be good enough, but my dad went to college with an admissions officer there, and he was going to put in a good word for me…"

The nurse tried to break into Olivia's rambling by holding out a tissue to her. She barely noticed.

"Olivia."

"…and I have to go to a party at Sara's on Saturday night…" Olivia continued through the tears.

"Olivia!" the nurse shouted at her.

She was broken out of her babbling story. The nurse stared directly into her eyes with conviction.

"Forget about all those things. Get them out of your head, they don't matter anymore. Focus on the next three days," the nurse told her.

"Why, what's the point?" Olivia asked, body slumped, face ashen.

"Because you could still have a life. But first, you have to make it through these next three days."

Olivia took the tissue from the nurse and wiped her eyes dry. The brash young woman who walked into the examination room was gone. Only a frail-looking frightened girl remained, hunched over in a chair like some creature. Olivia looked into the nurse's eyes, big and brown, warm, reassuring, like a mother's. Olivia searched for some kind of comfort.

As she stared into the deep brown cauldrons of Nurse Ramirez's eyes, Olivia wondered how many people she'd had this conversation with over the years. She'd clearly danced this dance before, Olivia could tell. Her words well-chosen, practiced.

Maybe the others had different questions, maybe they took the news better than her, or maybe some couldn't accept it at all, became violent. It would explain the panic button. Olivia wouldn't become violent. She couldn't afford to. She needed information more than anything.

"What kind of life would it be up there?"

The nurse spoke, her voice softer than before, "In truth, I don't know. They're a closed society. From what I do know, it's certainly not the horror show they portray it as on the news."

"Amber at school says they have forced marriages, and you have to kill a child before they accept you as one of their own."

Nurse Ramirez cocked her eyebrow at the dubious story.

"I don't think those stories are true. The vampires are like us…more or less."

The words *more or less* caught Olivia's attention. She looked at the shafts of sunlight pouring in through the window blinds, illuminating dust particles before they hit the green laminate floor.

"More or less? When does the more or less kick in?"

"The physical transformation takes about twelve weeks, give or take," the nurse began. "Your symptoms and bloodwork indicate you're in the early stages. The nausea should ease up soon. You shouldn't have a serious aversion to sunlight till about midway through the process."

Olivia paused for a moment to digest the information. Again, the words seemed alien, as if they were for someone else who wasn't in the room, some girl from the next town over you heard rumors about in school.

"Is it contagious?" Olivia asked.

"No, not in the sense of it passing from person to person, and there's a wealth of research on the subject. I wouldn't have lowered my mask if it was a risk," the nurse responded.

"Then why bother with the mask at all?"

"There's plenty of other things you can catch around a hospital, Olivia."

"Guess I don't have to worry about things like that anymore," Olivia said.

“No, I suppose not.”

"The other thing," Olivia asked, voice trembling. “You know…”

Olivia couldn’t form the words to finish the question, but the nurse correctly guessed where she was going.

"If you're lucky, you won't need to…feed in that manner for another few weeks yet. You should try to continue to eat regular food as long as you can keep it down."

The nurse explained the horrors of Olivia's new existence in as simple and straightforward a fashion as possible, like she described something mundane, as though how to take a medication or maintain good hygiene habits.

"If I'm lucky, if I'm lucky…"

Numb now, some of the grim details of her new existence laid bare, her new existence sounded more like that of an animal than a person. A disgusting creature living in the shadows of a frozen shit-hole country far to the north. An unspeakable abomination you saw snatching children from their beds in a horror movie. A monster, unholy, irredeemable.

The nurse broke through Olivia's thoughts. "I understand they give you more detailed information on these subjects when you cross the border into the Vampire Union."

Olivia couldn't listen to much more. "Oh, that's good. Look, I'm gonna be late for school."

The nurse looked at Olivia with concern but not surprise. Perhaps she'd seen this unusual reaction in others before. Panic, then flat nothingness.

"You're going back to school?"

"Yeah, I only have a sick note for the morning. If I don't show up, people will think something's wrong."

"I understand. This is a natural reaction I've seen in others before, but remember, time is not a luxury you have much of. We live about as far south as you can get—" The nurse tried to give her advice, but it was cut off.

"I know…I know," Olivia said, clearly becoming exasperated.

"OK, I understand your frustration. I can't imagine what you're going through, but you need to be gone by early tomorrow morning at the latest, or you won't make it."

"OK, OK. I understand. Can I call my dad to have him come pick me up, at least?" Olivia asked.

Pausing for a moment, the nurse looked at Olivia. Her dark brown eyes surveyed the young girl hunched forward in the chair, clearly trying to get the measure of her, trying to see if any of the information she provided was truly getting through.

"You mentioned you go to a religious school," the nurse began. "What are your parents' opinions on this…subject?"

Olivia was upset at the suggestion her father would be called into disrepute.

"My dad's my dad. He'll understand," Olivia responded, trying to convince the nurse but also herself, doubt creeping into every facet of her mind.

"And your mother?"

There was a lengthy pause, clearly long enough for the nurse to sense the danger even before Olivia had a chance to open her mouth.

"She's a bit over the top on the religious stuff…but I mean…"

The nurse had heard enough. "I strongly recommend you do not tell your family."

"But…"

"It's illegal for them to help you get to the border anyway, and you need to get there under your own steam. It's the law."

Confused and frightened, Olivia was overwhelmed with information. Could she really not speak to her family? Her first port of call if she was ever in any real danger would be to go to her father. He'd always understand, even if it was serious, even if she'd fucked up beyond belief. Her father could fix things. He was that kind of man.

"But if I told them, they can't stop me from going, right?" Olivia asked.

"Legally, no, but…"

Olivia looked vulnerable in her little plastic chair.

"Well, I have to say goodbye at least."

Nurse Ramirez stood up and walked over to Olivia. She hunkered down so she was at eye level and stared deep into Olivia’s blue eyes like she was trying to stare into her very soul.

"Olivia, listen to me, and listen good," the nurse began in a deadly serious tone. "There are people out there, maybe your family included, who will do everything in their power to stop you reaching that border alive. Do you understand?"

"Those are just stories people tell to frighten kids," Olivia responded, looking straight into Nurse Ramirez's gaze.

Unflinching, the nurse responded, "Sadly, those stories are all too real Olivia."

Bowing her head in despair, Olivia sobbed again. The nurse used her hand to hold the girl's chin so she looked directly at her again.

"You tell no one, and beg, steal, or borrow, you make your way to that border. Do you understand me, Olivia?" the nurse's soft warm voice was completely gone, the instruction given like a drill instructor.

She released Olivia's chin. It didn't drop. The two remained staring at each other, eyeball to eyeball.

"Yes…I understand," Olivia responded with as much resolve as she could muster.

The nurse finally looked relieved, like she'd finally gotten through to Olivia the seriousness of her situation. She stood up, walked back over to the desk, and sat down.

Her voice returned to its warmer, friendlier tone. "I have some pamphlets you can take with you if you want them."

"Are they any use?"

"Not really. They're government-issued, but I have to offer them anyway," the nurse responded with a clear hint of disdain for the pamphlets.

"Then they're just evidence that could give me away."

"Good, you're being smart. Keep it up, and you'll survive this." The nurse looked pleased Olivia had passed this small test.

A tiny laugh burst out of Olivia at the direness of her situation. "Yeah…maybe. Look, I better get to school."

“I really have to advise you again, that is not a good idea,” the nurse said.

“If I don’t show up for evening roll call, I’ll be missed. Nothing serious but enough to raise questions. And if I go home straight away my mom’s likely to be there, that leads to even more questions. I have to keep up appearance until this evening at least.”

The nurse held her hands up in surrender, clearly understanding the bind Olivia was in.

"I understand, I'll leave you to get dressed."

Getting up from the desk, the nurse walked toward the door. Olivia watched her as she went.

"I'm guessing I won't see you after this?" Olivia said.

"You're right, this is goodbye. But good luck, Olivia. I'm rooting for you."

"Thanks." Olivia offered the nurse a small smile as she walked out the door.

The door clicked shut, and Olivia sat perfectly still in silence for a time. Her mind was a void again, numb, too much information to process, so it processed nothing, then reality sank in. A wave of panic washed over her, and she cried loudly. The rage she couldn't let out during the meeting with the nurse now sprayed out in a short, sharp scream, then there was silence. She wiped the tears from her face and stood up with purpose.

The Bus

Fulford wasn't a big city. Its downtown area had only a handful of tall buildings that looked dilapidated but were still in use. It was a typical regional city in the Newland Settlers Confederation. Every region had at least three cities like Fulford, and none were remarkable. Maybe they once were but, now, they were hollowed out. People sucked away to larger urban centers on the coast or old industrial cities that still had some life.

Olivia stood blank-faced under a canopy outside a grimy bus terminal. She wore the de facto uniform of her peers: fitted jeans, sneakers, T-shirt, and a hoodie. She could have been a million girls her age, and right at that second, she'd have agreed to swap places with any one of them if she could.

Fulford General Hospital loomed ominously in the background a few streets away. She glanced up at the building. The memory of it would be burned into her consciousness as long as she lived. How long that would be, she didn't know. First, she had to live through the next three days.

A small group of commuters waited with Olivia, all trying to keep warm in the cold winter air, their breath forming large clouds of vapor. A flag clanged as its mounting rings banged against the flagpole in the wind. Olivia looked up at it fluttering in the gusts. The flag was mounted to the side of the terminal, a large blue rectangle with four diagonal green stripes in the corner. It flew at half-mast.

"Did something happen?" a squat elderly woman asked a tall man in a suit nearby, gesturing at the flag.

"Some kid shot up his high school in Wayford. Twelve dead, they say," the man in the suit informed her with some reserved anger in his voice.

"Oh, my." The old woman put her hand over her mouth.

The conversation snapped Olivia out of her trance.

"Why?" Olivia asked almost absently.

"What?" the businessman responded, clearly not expecting such a question.

"Why'd he shoot up the school?" Olivia asked.

"I bet he played those violent videogames," the old woman suggested, nodding to the other waiting passengers. "You'll see, it's always the same."

"No. On the news, they said he was a vampire sympathizer. Fucking scum." The reserved anger was replaced by a more, full-blown sort.

Olivia's heart skipped a beat at the words *vampire sympathizer*. A wave of paranoia washed over her. Like, somehow, all the people at the bus stop secretly knew of her diagnosis and were just waiting for the right time to jump her. Imagination running wild, their faces all suddenly looked accusatory, cruel, sneering.

Another young woman waiting at the stop piped up, "It's not true. He was just an incel, he posted a manifesto online. Something about his arms being too skinny so all women rejected him."

"You wanna believe that crap, go ahead," the man remarked, his lip curled.

Olivia prayed she would not be pulled further into the conversation. She was sorry she entered in the first place, as if simply by speaking she might give herself away somehow.

A dirty inter-city style bus with fogged-up windows pulled into a bay, interrupting the conversation, a digital signboard in the window read:

GREENFIELDS-CARRINGTON-BLAKEVIEW

It was Olivia's bus. She was relieved to be able to escape the conversation and rushed to board. Only a few of the crowd joined her, the rest waiting at an adjacent bay.

The bus doors made a loud hiss, and then swung open. A burst of warm air hit Olivia. Climbing aboard, she handed her ticket to the jolly-looking driver who punched it with a smile. She made her way down the aisle toward the back of the empty bus, eventually taking a seat near the last row on one of the ugly blue and maroon fabric seats.

A few others filed onto the bus but barely enough to half fill it. Olivia was relieved she didn't have to share a seat with anyone. The doors finally closed, and the bus pulled out of the terminal. It was warm and comfortable despite its worn-out look.

She sat staring out the window as buildings flicked past, face set with a frozen expression.

What had she done to deserve this? Nothing, just a random kick in the teeth from life, like cancer. But at least with cancer you got the sympathy of your friends and family. People rallied around you, had fucking fundraisers, and shaved their heads in solidarity. She wished it was cancer.

She imagined telling her friends at school and them all crying and telling her how brave she was and how she's such a fighter. She deliberately banged her head hard against the cold bus window to snap herself out of the daydream.

You don't have cancer, and nobody is going to rally around you unless it's to lynch you.

She settled in for the long journey. The buildings gradually got smaller outside the window as the bus made its way out of the city. Soon, it was in open countryside with rolling green hills. Eventually, it arrived at a sedate-looking town and pulled into a tiny depot.

"Greenfields," announced the driver as the bus came to a halt.

Olivia snapped out of her trance-like state, got out of her seat, and walked to the front of the bus to disembark. As she passed the driver, he spoke, "Cheer up, kid”.

"Yeah, sure ," Olivia responded under her breath. The bus driver scoffed at her muttering as she got off the bus.

School

Olivia stood outside her school, staring at it, desperately trying to will herself to go inside. But what was the point? Maybe she should just go home now and make a run for it. No, finishing the day would raise less suspicion. If she skipped evening roll, they might call home. If she went home now to pack, her mother might be there. That would raise too many questions. No, she had to finish out the day like nothing had changed.

Greenfield's School No.1 was a hideous modern concrete construction with an awning at the front, which covered a path leading up to the door. Ugly and uniform, almost designed to stifle any strong emotion or creative thought that might spring up in its students. There must have been a building like it in every town in the country as if they only had one set of blueprints, and they just made copy after copy of the same shitty school.

Taking out her smartphone, she pressed the button to check the time. The background wallpaper was a picture of herself and a girl with long black hair, both sticking out their tongues, trying to be as edgy as possible.

The time on the phone read: 13:10

She had hoped lunch would have been over by the time she got to school, but like with everything that day, she was out of luck. Putting her phone back in her pocket, she took a deep breath and walked toward the front door.

Olivia made her way through the school halls, past uniform rows of lockers along a well-worn path in the linoleum floor toward the cafeteria. As she approached, the din from inside became louder. She pulled opened the door and slipped into the cafeteria. A hive of activity, a hundred different conversations took place at once. Groups of friends all sat together, with some loners dotted around trying to fly under the radar.

This scene should have been warm and familiar, but it was like a horror show. Everyone obliviously living their lives while hers was collapsing around her. Standing there, she surveyed all their stupid faces with utter contempt.

Fake it, just fake it.

A broad smile widened across Olivia's face as she walked through the cafeteria like a battered wife trying her best to convince the world her life was perfect.

"O!" a voice came calling loudly over the noise.

Turning around to find the source, she still couldn't identify where it was coming from.

"Olivia!" the voice called louder this time, and along with it, a hand waved in the air.

The source of the voice was clear now. She knew its owner well. Sara, her best friend, sat at a table near the end of the room with two other girls. She made her way toward them and sat down. Sara was only a week younger than Olivia, a little shorter than her but with a similar frame. Pretty, with sallow skin and shoulder-length black hair, a mischievous smile adorned her face.

Olivia knew the smile all too well. It had gotten them both into and out of trouble on more than one occasion. The other two other girls rounded out the inner circle of friends. Jasmine was black with perfect skin and curly hair. Olivia always thought she looked like the kind of black girl they put in TV adverts, so as not to scare conservative white people.

Rounding out the group was Amber, peroxide blonde hair and a thick layer of makeup covering harsh acne, which had plagued her since she was twelve years old. None of the other three ever mentioned it, except behind her back.

"Sup?" Jasmine directed toward Olivia.

"Not much. Did I miss anything important?" Olivia asked.

"Jenna Lang and Kevin Adams are dating," Amber responded as if it was critical information.

"What?" came the confused response from Olivia.

"I think she meant in class, Amber. But, by all means, fill us in on who Jenna Lang is giving handjobs to this week," Sara said.

Olivia's face scrunched up, and her eyebrows narrowed, like her brain was having difficulty marrying the conflicting concepts of her current life and death struggle with the usual school gossip.

"Isn't Kevin Adams that guy who organizes those RPG games in the rec room?" Olivia asked.

"Yup," Jasmine responded.

"How the hell did that pairing happen?" Olivia asked.

"Well, Jenna Lang is a total slut who'll give pretty much any guy a handjob. So, statistically speaking, it was bound to happen eventually," Jasmine informed the table authoritatively as if she was quoting a research paper.

The group sniggered over their lunch at Jasmine's analysis. It helped Olivia, who laughed a little, too, almost forgetting her problems.

"So, other than Jenna Lang's nocturnal activities, did I miss anything important?" Olivia asked.

"It's not just nocturnal. She'll give handjobs any time of day," Jasmine joked.

A huge cackle of laughter erupted from the table, so loud other tables looked around to see what was so funny. There were looks of derision from some of the other students. The group piped down so as not to attract too much attention.

"You didn't actually miss any classes. Sucks to be you," Sara informed Olivia as the laughter subsided.

"What? How?" she asked.

"They held an active shooter drill because of what happened in Wayford," Sara told her. "All morning classes were canceled."

"Oh, shit. Yeah, I heard about that," Olivia responded.

"They say he was a vampire sympathizer. Speaking of which…" Amber interjected while nodding her head backward to indicate a girl approaching. "Angie McAvoy coming up."

A girl walked through the main thoroughfare of the canteen and would soon pass their table. Olivia glanced up just long enough to lock eyes for a split-second as she approached. The girl looked through her like she didn't exist. Olivia dropped her gaze in shame.

Angie McAvoy was a redhead about the same age as Olivia. Just shy of six feet and still growing, with broad shoulders, shoulders that suggested she could throw a decent punch, which Olivia knew from experience she was more than capable of. Neatly dressed in pants and a sweater, not a single hair on her head out of place. If you didn't know any better, you'd assume she was a teacher rather than a student. It was all a front.

Olivia knew it, and so did everyone else in the school. Angie used to be more relaxed, wore hoodies and jeans like everyone else…until her brother went missing. They said he ran for the border. People think he made it. A month or so after he went missing, Angie showed up to school dressed like that. As if somehow being dressed like a librarian would convince everyone she was a model citizen coping perfectly with her brother's sudden disappearance.

It didn't fool anyone. Angie was a pariah. It's what happened when a family member got the diagnosis. Most kids transferred schools to avoid the shame of it, but not Angie. Angie was hard as granite. Kids around school said she didn't change school because there were no places that would take her, and her family couldn't afford to move away, but Olivia knew her well enough to know the truth of it.

It was pride that kept Angie in that school. She could have transferred, made it easy on herself, but that wasn't her. Getting dressed up like that, coming into school every day and not batting an eyelid, it was her fuck you to the system. She wasn't gonna let people push her out. She wasn't ashamed.

Angie walked past the table carrying an empty food tray. Olivia's table all avoided her gaze. When she was a few fcet past the table, Amber threw a balled-up piece of aluminum foil at her. It hit its mark perfectly, clocking her in the back of the head. She stopped dead in her tracks but didn't turn around, large frame perfectly still.

There was silence from most of the tables nearby, all waiting on a reaction from the outcast, but they got none, Angie started walking again and pretended like the incident hadn't happened. Several tables erupted into sniggering bouts, including Olivia's, but Olivia herself kept silent.

In three days, your government is going to murder you, and here you are with your retard friends laughing at Angie McAvoy. What the fuck are you doing?

Olivia's face turned pale as her brain reminded her of her dire situation. Noticing the pained expression on Olivia's face, Sara silenced the rest of the table. "Come on, guys. Angie's got enough problems. Leave her be."

"Yeah, well, I just don't wanna get murdered when she goes on a damn shooting spree," Amber said.

"And throwing shit at her is your way of what? Dissuading her? She's gonna shoot your dumb ass first," Jasmine joked to Amber, who seemed utterly oblivious to the perils of poking an angry bear.

"Nah, I'd be the first one getting the bullet," Olivia somberly observed.

The mood at the table darkened at Olivia's declaration, and the collective look on the other girls' faces seemed to signal complete agreement.

"Yeah, probably," Sara said, biting her lip.

They were friends once, all of them, though none of them would fully admit it now. They had a list of stock lines when the subject came up. *'Oh, she just hung around, and we were too nice to tell her to get lost'*, *'She was always a bit of cunt anyway'* and *'I think she's secretly a dyke.'* Anything to avoid the taint of being associated with a social untouchable.

But Olivia and Angie had been close, closer than the rest. Close enough to know how much the betrayal must have hurt, how it must have festered and finally manifested itself in Angie's bizarre formal veneer.

"Shit!" Jasmine declared as she checked her watch and gestured to Amber. "Me and dumbass here have to get over to room fourteen for chemistry. See you guys later."

The group split. Jasmine and Amber got up in a panic and rushed off, forgetting to return their trays. Olivia and Sara sat looking at the trays as if wondering if they should return them before shrugging and abandoning them.

Sara and Olivia made their way out into the halls, snaking down identical corridors, past rows of color-coded lockers. Eventually, they came to a halt at a group that was painted red. They were stacked two high, all with identical dial-type combination locks. The style of lock was mandatory. On the back, there was a hole for a skeleton key so the school could open them any time they wanted.

Olivia remembered the day they opened Angie's locker when she came back to school after her brother went missing. They didn't do it during classes to be subtle, they wanted to make a scene of it. They made her stand there while they rifled through her things, half the school watching, giggling, judging. Angie was smart enough to have removed anything the school could have used as a pretense to expel her. No cigarettes, vape pen, or burner phone. Much like Angie's personal appearance, her locker had been wiped clean, only the veneer of a perfectly happy student remained.

Olivia wondered if they'd do the same to her locker when she disappeared. No, it would be the cops searching her locker. She wasn't just some family member who might be guilty of something. In their eyes, she *was* guilty. It made little to no difference what they found once she was gone.

Sara spun the small dial on the lock attached to her locker like a master safecracker, entering the code 1901. She removed the lock and swung the door open. Olivia slowly unlocked hers and looked inside like she was staring into a void.

"How'd your thing go this morning?" Sara quietly asked.

"Fine."

"Really? So, why'd you have to go all the way to Fullford without telling your parents?" Sara asked.

"I thought it was something more serious, but it wasn't. Turned out to be some stomach bacteria. I have to take like three separate antibiotics," Olivia tried to lie as convincingly as possible. Her uncle had something similar six months before, and it seemed a plausible lie.

"Stomach bacteria, ugh. Coulda been a lot worse, though. Last person who went to Fullford by themselves without telling anyone, well…" Sara didn't finish the thought, her tone becoming somber.

"Simon McAvoy. You think he made it?"

"Yeah, secretly, I kinda hope so," Sara offered an opinion she wouldn't dare give in public.

"You had a crush on him if I remember correctly," Olivia said.

Sara cut Olivia with dagger eyes, a look that said, 'Never say anything like that again.'

"No, I didn't. It's just sad for his sister is all," Sara replied her voice was soft and warm with sincerity, which was rarely if ever-present in her voice.

"So, why'd we stop hanging out with her then?"

"I don't know, Olivia, because we didn't have much choice. It's just what happens," Sara tried to convince her friend.

"Yeah, I guess."

"Look, I'll talk to Amber and Jasmine, tell them to cut out the bullshit of throwing shit at Angie at least. Cool?" Sara suggested.

"Yeah, cool."

Sara took a moment and looked Olivia dead in the eyes. "Olivia, listen. You're my best friend. Even if what happened to Simon McAvoy happened to you, you know you could tell me, right?"

Olivia's brain went into overdrive. Did Sara know, or suspect at least, or was she just paranoid and it was a simple reassurance from a friend? She looked deep into Sara's deep brown eyes and tried to read them. They seemed genuine, warm, and comforting. Olivia wanted to trust her, a part of her brain begging her to confide her secret to someone, anyone, so at least one person knew what she was going through.

The words formed in her head and almost slipped out like water. But then another part of Olivia's brain took over. It told her to shut her mouth, destroying the words of confession that had formed and, in their place, produced an impressive belly laugh.

Sara looked hurt as Olivia broke out laughing.

"Well, the day that happens, you can steal your dad's car and drive me to the border. I'll try and write to you in prison," Olivia lied.

"I was trying to be sincere, dickhead."

"I know," Olivia responded, smiling at her warmly. "Come on, we better get to class."

Both Olivia and Sara slammed their lockers shut, spun the combination locks closed, and wandered off to class.

The evening's classes were a blur to Olivia, she walked from room to room like a ghost, her mind a convoluted jumble of thoughts and fears until the final class of the day. She sat behind a tiny desk in a packed classroom. Sara was at a desk to the right. Two rows behind them, Angie McAvoy stared out the window.

Mr. Jacobs wasn't a particularly engaging teacher at the best of times but, today, his words were just white noise, like static on an old TV. In true geography teacher fashion, he had plastered the walls of his classroom with a vast assortment of flags, charts, diagrams, and maps, which currently held Olivia's attention.

She sat staring at the flag of the NSC hanging on a freestanding wooden flagpole in the corner, a marine blue rectangle with four diagonal green stripes. Warm and familiar, it had always made her feel protected like if she was kidnapped in some foreign country, a fleet of helicopters bearing that very flag would come to the rescue. But now, it would be cars bearing that flag that would come to drag her away if she didn't run.

She turned her attention to the posters and charts. A large, faded poster depicted a massive, interconnected matrix of railway lines, as well as images of several different train types, from old steam trains to newer electric ones, and even a mock-up concept of futurist-looking ones. A slogan on the poster proudly read:

THE RAILROADS, ARTERIES OF THE NSC

Another poster was next to it. This one wasn't just posted in the geography room, some variant of it was posted in every classroom in every school in the land. A photo of a small suburban family home at night. The smiling family can be seen watching TV together through the illuminated windows. A pair of shadowy figures lurk outside, staring in at the unsuspecting family. Superimposed over the photo is a set of vampire fangs engulfing the entire house. Below the image read the following words:

DO YOU SUSPECT A CLASSMATE OF BEING A MEMBER OF AN ILLEGAL ORGANIZATION?

CALL CONFIDENTIAL 555- 41675

IF YOU STAY SILENT, A FAMILY'S BLOOD COULD BE ON YOUR HANDS.

The word *blood* had been printed in a dripping red font for effect. Olivia remembered being terrified the first time she saw the poster. It must have been an effective campaign as it was in circulation since she was about ten years old, the images and lettering burned into the consciousness of every child in the country.

Freedom of speech laws let you express certain vampire sympathies legally, but it only protected you so far. Once you started taking any concrete action or organizing, you were declared an illegal organization and faced heavy penalties. Beside that image was another, much newer propaganda poster. It depicted two abstract figures standing in the rain near a car, one clearly pleading with the other. The text read:

REMEMBER HELPING A PERSON WITH "THE DIAGNOSIS" REACH THE BORDER IS A CRIME. THEY MUST TRAVEL UNDER THEIR OWN STEAM.

JUST SAY NO, OR YOU COULD FACE UP TO 10 YEARS IN PRISON.

Signed well before Olivia's birth, the peace treaty with the Vampire Union included a special law. It allowed any newly diagnosed vampires in the NSC three days to make it to the border. But in the past few years, they'd undercut the law with a series of new laws making it as difficult as possible. The Corvin law was the most severe. It meant anyone who helped someone get to the border was automatically deemed a criminal operative and could be arrested.

Olivia stared at the poster. She had seen it a thousand times, but it was different today. Today, she truly understood the gravity of it for the first time. They wanted to put every roadblock in her way so they could legally kill her. It was that simple. If she could have cried at that moment, she would have. Instead, something else welled up inside her, something resembling resolve.

She turned her attention to a large political map pinned on the wall to the right of Mr. Jacobs. The map was centered around a large country marked in blue. In the center the name was written in large bold letters:

NEWLAND SETTLERS CONFEDERATION (NSC)

To the east of the NSC on the map was a large body of water marked:

WESTERN OCEAN

The people in the old countries to the east had named it before they discovered the New Lands, and so it kept its unusual name even in the NSC. To the west was a country depicted in a dusty brown color:

SIMONIA

It had city names like Tal Ratad and Duro jDuon. Olivia kept her attention on the NSC. The country bore the names of towns and cities she knew well: Fulford, Wayford, Carringham, New Oxbridge, Ashtown. She could even see in a tiny font the name of her hometown, Greenfields. It was far south, a great distance from the border with the Vampire Union.

Her eyes tracked their way up the map, glancing past all the towns and cities, through all the railroad lines and, eventually, reached a borderline marked with thick red Xs. Above the border was an area marked in black, like it was a void rather than a country. It was labeled:

VAMPIRE UNION

Rivers and mountains were marked, but only a few cities were deemed important enough to be named: Bloodvale, Two-Moon City, Dunroe. Every name sounded alien. Visions of inhospitable black industrial cities with plumes of chemical smoke rising from factory chimneys formed in her mind. Olivia's guts twisted at the thought of living in such a place, but she remembered the words of Nurse Ramirez: *'They're like us, more or less.'*

Olivia repeated the mantra over and over in her head, trying to convince herself it was true. Continuing to scan up the map, she spotted a small town just over the border inside the Vampire Union named Vampire's Rest. It sounded quaint, like a village from the old countries, with small stone walls and an old bar that had been there for generations. It seemed to be only marked because it was a border crossing town near Overton. Her eyes tracked a route from Greenfields all the way up to the town.

You can make that journey. If you want to live, you have to. Do you want to live? Then you're going to make that journey.

For the first time, she was truly considering the reality of the journey she would need to make. Adrenaline pumped in her veins, and nausea built in the pit of her stomach. That's what she needed for the next three days, not thought, not contemplation, nor worry about her new life or her condition. Those were problems for later. For now, she needed adrenaline to make that journey.

Eyes burning with zeal, she looked at almost every possible route she could take to the border…then a ball of paper hit her in the side of the head. She looked to her right to see Sara smiling at her.

"Wake up, dumbass. You're staring into space," Sara whispered.

"I feel like crap," Olivia whispered back.

Sara rolled her bottom lip, making a sad face to convey sympathy without seeming overly sincere. The bell rang, and all the students sprang from their desks in a flurry.

"The bell does not dismiss you, I do." Mr. Jacobs attempted to sound authoritative, but the students ignored him and kept packing up their books.

"Why do I even bother?" he muttered to himself, the students already making their way toward the door.

Sara and Olivia shuffled out with the rest. Walking out the door, Olivia took a last sideways glance at the map. The two young women ambled their way to their lockers on the other side of the school. It was the end of the day, and most of the students had already left. The corridors were mostly deserted, only a few students still filtering out.

Sara leaned against her locker as Olivia put books away. She put others into her bag that she needed for homework as if she had any intention of doing it, but it was important to go through the motions to avoid suspicion. Her stomach felt like a washing machine. The nausea of the past few weeks had abated a bit, but it still hit her in waves now and then.

"You coming over later?" Sara asked.

"Nah, I was just gonna go home and rest. My stomach's in knots."

"You know what helps with that?"

"Antibiotics?" Olivia replied, but she knew where Sara was going.

"No, weed," Sara briefed her as if she was a doctor.

"Oh, really?

"And guess who has two thumbs and has some?" Sara replied while pointing toward herself with her thumbs.

"I really can't, I gotta get some rest, Sara, I'm sorry."

"What about tomorrow then?"

An odd look came over Olivia's face at the realization this would be the last time she'd ever see her best friend. She suppressed the thought and faked a smile back at Sara. The front had to be maintained.

"Yeah, tomorrow for sure," Olivia said, stomach-turning as she did.

Pinky finger extended Sara offered it to Olivia in a comical fashion like they were twelve years old on their first summer holiday together.

"Pinky swear?" Sara asked.

"Pinky swear," Olivia said.

The two locked their little fingers together. Olivia couldn't even make eye contact with her friend. Childish as it was, she was promising Sara she'd see her again, discounting some miracle that wasn't going to be the case. In truth, the next time Sara was likely to see Olivia was in one of the national newspapers. They broke the finger lock, and Sara walked away.

"See ya tomorrow," Sara said as she went.

"Yeah, see ya tomorrow," Olivia replied.

Olivia watched her the whole time as Sara walked down the long corridor. She turned at the end and, just like that, she was gone. Heart ready to crack, Olivia held back the tears welling inside.

That's that last time you're ever gonna see her.

The nausea finally got the better of her, and her stomach made a sudden dropping motion, like when an airplane hits turbulence. She sprinted for the nearest bathroom.

The door swung open, and Olivia burst inside. The girls' bathroom was deserted. She vomited violently into the sink, her face turning red with the force of it. When she'd finished, she turned on the faucet and washed her mouth out with water, wiping away bits of vomit and spittle. Her reflection stared back at her from the filthy mirror. She looked exhausted and pale in the flickering halogen light of the bathroom.

"Pull it together," Olivia instructed her mirror image, then she slapped herself across the face three times in rapid succession.

The old halogen bulb flickered as she stared at her reflection. Legs turned to jelly, arms shaking, she had to hold herself up by gripping the side of the washbasin with both hands. Why was this happening to her? There was no rhyme or reason to it, just random cruelty. Every dream she had for her life had turned to ash in the space of a few hours. Worse still, she had to remain silent. She could confide in no one.

"Fake it, just fake it," she ordered her reflection.

She turned on the faucet and tested the water. Winter in full force, the water was ice cold. Hands cupped together, she splashed the frigid water on her face, then ran the sleeve of her hoodie over it. As the sleeve ran down her face, her expression changed to a broad friendly smile.

Fake it.

Body and mind as steady as they were going to get, Olivia picked up her bag and exited the bathroom. Seconds after she left, a set of legs dropped from one of the toilet cubicles. Someone had been listening.

The Car

Waiting at the edge of the empty school car park, Olivia cut a lonely-looking figure. The sun set fast. A deep orange, its last rays low in the sky breaking through some trees nearby, but then it disappeared over the horizon entirely, leaving Olivia in darkness.

Mercury dropping, she stamped her feet to keep warm. She wondered how many sunsets she had left, or sunrises for that matter. Forty, fifty? *Worry about the next three days!* Her advice went unheeded, she continued to concern herself with the long-term physical nature of her condition rather than the immediate danger.

The transformation, how would it be? Images of bones breaking and reforming into some monstrosity were conjured up, hideous, malformed with blood-red eyes. In a silent panic, her heart pounded uncontrollably at the obscene visions, based on nothing but old movies and her own vivid imagination. Two cones of startlingly bright light cut through the darkness, snapping Olivia from her horrific visions.

The xenon lights of her mother's SUV. The sleek black vehicle rolled up and came to a stop. Olivia opened the passenger door and climbed inside, it was warm and comfortable.

Olivia's mother, Marina, was behind the wheel. Forty-one years old with shoulder-length sandy brown hair, conservatively dressed, and with narrow-framed designer glasses. Olivia had once told her she looked like one of the panelists on *The Conversation*, a daytime talk show where menopausal women talked about burning *issues* like teen sex parties that didn't actually exist. Her mother took it as a compliment rather than the slight it was intended as. As Olivia put on her safety belt, her mother gave her a warm smile.

"Sorry I'm late. I got held up with the parents' committee," she said.

"It's fine. It's not like I'm in a hurry to get anywhere. Of course, if I had a car and a driver's license, we wouldn't have this problem," Olivia said.

Her mother sighed at the suggestion. The argument had been done to death, over and over again. Why she wanted to have it again with her mother tonight of all nights, not even Olivia quite knew. Maybe anger. If she had a license and car, she could just drive to the border. Or maybe the habit of the argument just felt familiar, like nothing in life had changed.

"We've had this discussion several times, this country has—" her mother began before being cut off.

"…a public transport system the envy of the free world, blah, blah."

"I see you're in a mood. How was school?" her mother asked with a curled lip while trying to keep her eyes on the road.

"Dull."

"Dull? I got a text from Karen's mother that they had an active shooter drill." Her mother sounded surprised it wasn't the first thing Olivia mentioned.

"Oh, yeah, I guess the constant reminder we might get gunned down at school is kinda exciting."

Marina took her eyes off the road to scowl at her daughter for a moment. "That's not funny, young lady. Children died."

"I just don't think a drill is going to help."

"Rounding up those vampire sympathizers is what would help."

A wave of anger washed over Olivia. Her mother's political and religious opinions were one and the same. Mostly parroting statements she had heard on conservative news channels, which was most of the news channels these days. Ordinarily, Olivia just listened and agreed for an easy life, but today was different.

"I heard it was an incel guy," Olivia said.

"An in-what guy now? What are you talking about?"

"An incel. You know, those…" Olivia took one glance at the confused look on her mother's face and decided it wasn't worth the effort. "Never mind, forget it."

"Well, the parents' committee is taking steps to ensure the safety—"

"Oh, great, the committee. Well, I guess they could tear some more pages out of our textbooks, maybe that'll help."

Her mother was a founding member of PAVS, Parents against Vampire Sympathizers, the Greenfields branch. Until about two years ago, PAVS was just a talking shop where busybody parents wrote pointless recommendations but, recently, the government gave them some minor oversight powers on the school curriculum.

It was an easy win for the ruling party. Give a tiny hint of power to the parents and watch the votes flow in at the next election. Mostly, PAVS tried to stop any reliable information about the Vampire Union or diagnosis as a whole from *corrupting* young minds. There were more extreme groups than PAVS, and Olivia was thankful her mother wasn't a member of one of those.

A perfect example of a tiny bit of power going to someone's head. All her mother rambled on about was 'the committee this' and 'the committee that.' Olivia's eyelid twitched in anger. *Right about now, I could have used those missing textbook pages your committee tore out, you stupid cunt.* Olivia starred out the window at the dark open countryside roll past rather than look at her mother.

"I don't know what's gotten into you these past few months. That Sara Edwards is a bad influence," her mother said.

"Sara's my friend. I wish you'd stop bad-mouthing her. If you'd prefer, I could start hanging out with Angie McAvoy again? You used to like her, and you share the same dress sense, or lack thereof," Olivia said in a dry, dull tone.

This was a step too far for her mother, who instantly slammed her foot on the brake. The car screeched to a halt in the middle of the deserted country road. She put the car in neutral and took a deep breath before turning to Olivia with cold, dead eyes.

"You are never to speak that girl's name. You are never to tell people you were friends with her, or that she visited our home on any occasion. Do you understand?" Her mother had a zealous look burning in her eyes.

"I understand." Olivia held up her hands in surrender.

Her mother put the car back into drive and pressed the accelerator as if nothing had happened. Olivia was shaken. Angie McAvoy didn't exist in their household anymore, history wiped clean. Angie had never sat at their dinner table, their families had never been on a holiday together, she and Olivia had never fallen out of the tree in the back garden. She was a ghost story, a revenant, only made real if you spoke her name.

"This situation with Sara will resolve itself anyway," her mother said. "You'll be going to Lakeshore next year and, with her grades, I very much doubt she'll be doing the same."

"My grades aren't that much better than hers. It's Dad's connections getting me into Lakeshore."

"That's another thing you're not to mention to anyone. Is that clear?" her mother ordered, but less dramatically than before.

"Crystal…" Olivia was done fighting over things she knew were never going to happen.

"I don't understand it. Sara used to be so well-behaved, and she comes from such a good family."

"People change."

Olivia stared out the window. The two sat in awkward silence for a few moments as the night rolled by.

"For once, you're right, though," Olivia said. "Next year, I'll be gone, and Sara will be somewhere else, and I won't see her."

"Well, good. At least you're starting to sound like you are seriously considering your future."

Her mother utterly failed to pick up on the fatalistic tone in Olivia's voice. Being so obsessed with appearances, her brain was probably incapable of even entertaining the idea that one of her children might get diagnosed. That only happened to bad families with low moral standards.

Olivia knew only too well how the cogs in her mother's mind worked, or at least she thought she did. Nurse Ramirez was right. Olivia decided right there, and then she couldn't tell her family. She was alone.

Resting her elbow on the window, she looked at the passing darkness, unable to bear looking at her mother. They drove in silence through the winter night, only the narrow road ahead visible.

Home

With Headlights dipped the black SUV rolled up to the Thompson family home. It was an impressive, modern timber construction spread across two levels with a double garage. The exterior and gardens resembled a show house, perfectly pristine, not a leaf or blade of grass out of place as if you couldn't imagine that real, pissing, shitting humans lived inside.

Olivia's mother dabbled in the garden rose bed, but the heavy lifting was done by cheap migrant labor. Like everything with her mother, it was something of a front. She had no problem with the interior being messy once they didn't have guests coming over. Also, she didn't trust outside labor enough to give them a key, so she did most of the interior cleaning herself.

One of the garage doors rolled open, and a light automatically turned on. The SUV drove in, and the door rolled closed behind it. Olivia and her mother got out and entered the house by an interior door.

On days her mother went to meet with the committee, her father cooked dinner. Her mother sometimes experimented with something fancy like Beef in Dark Ale and royally messed it up. Her father always kept it simple. You were probably getting chicken pitas, as it was one of only two dishes he knew how to cook.

There was a flurry of activity as Olivia's father laid out the dinner on the dining table, and they all sat down. A meal of chicken pitas was laid out before them, her father predictable as a clock.

Next to Olivia was her younger brother, Jamie. He was fourteen years old with a mop of messy hair, a little darker brown than Olivia's. He'd had to move school a year before because he was being bullied. His mother wouldn't admit it, as if it was a sign of weakness. She told people the new school had a better system for high-performing students.

Jamie wore baggy jeans and a T-shirt with a videogame logo on it called *Battle to Survive*, Olivia found bleak humor in the T-shirt given her current circumstances, then she questioned why she was even there. She should have been upstairs preparing.

Keep up appearances till after dinner, then plan.

Olivia's father, Alan, sat across the table. He was fifty-two but still in good shape, tall and broad, with a head of gray hair flecked with some remaining black. He wouldn't have looked out of place on the cover of a boring magazine about entrepreneurs. Olivia often wondered about the age gap between her parents.

She once overheard one of the other mothers remark that her mom *married well* and was a social climber. Olivia didn't know if it was true or not. They seemed happy enough together. Olivia couldn't imagine marrying someone because it was a good financial decision, but she couldn't imagine marrying at all. It seemed such a foreign concept at her age. The family all locked arms around the table and closed their eyes, as her mother prepared to lead the prayer.

"Lord, your body burned so we might have life. You sacrificed yourself so we might see the golden path," her mother spoke solemnly.

Olivia opened her eyes for a sneaky peek. The rest of the family all had theirs shut. She looked to the prominent effigy on the wall of a man burning alive on a pyre. It seemed to judge her for opening her eyes, so she shut them again.

"Please, bless this food so it might sustain us on the journey to your kingdom. So be it," Marina concluded. The family opened their eyes and unlocked their arms.

They tucked into the meal. Olivia only took a single pita and a small amount of filling, her appetite nonexistent.

"How was school?" Alan asked the table in general.

"Fine," Jamie answered.

Alan nodded his head like he was accustomed to single-syllable answers from his son, given at the boy's age.

"And you, Olivia?" he asked, clearly hoping for something a little more in-depth.

"Same old, same old," Olivia answered. A part of her wondered what mayhem would ensue over the next hours if she told them the truth.

"Not so," Marina said before cupping her hands in a poor attempt to stop Jamie from hearing. "They had an active shooter drill."

Jamie heard but seemed completely unperturbed. He was too busy stuffing his face.

"Oh, I see. Terrible tragedy what happened," her father said.

"Not terrible enough that they'll do something about it," Olivia said.

Her mother arched her eyebrow upward to Olivia, annoyed at her pessimistic response.

"Steps are being taken at a national and local level, Olivia. The parents' committee is drafting an action plan," her mother said, breaking into what seemed to be a prepared sermon.

Alan raised his eyebrows at the mention of the word *committee* as if to say, 'Here we go again.' Olivia noticed and gave him a little smile. He winked back at her, Marina was oblivious and continued with her sermon.

"We are going to propose that any student making vampire sympathetic comments should be automatically suspended…" her mother continued. Olivia gritted her teeth and had to purse her lips shut so she wouldn't look like a snarling dog.

"A second offense would mean expulsion from school."

"Yeah, ostracizing kids from school, I'm sure that will make them less angry," Olivia said.

"Does seem a bit extreme," Alan remarked, but he didn't push it. He wanted an easy life, too.

Face red with anger, her mother's anger seemed to fume, like a kettle slowing coming to a boil. Marina was used to her daughter questioning her every action, but she clearly didn't like being undermined by her husband when it came to political issues. The tone of conversation at the dinner table soured. Olivia didn't care. She was in a fighting mood.

"The *Book of Truths* is very clear on vampi—" Marina attempted to start an angry lecture but was cut off.

"The *Book of Truths* doesn't even mention vampires because they didn't exist back then," Olivia told her mother, whose anger only built further.

"It mentions ungodly creatures on many occasions, young lady."

Olivia knew she was riling her mother up because she just broke out the *young lady*. That was always a sign she was flipping her shit, but Olivia was in a mood to keep poking the bear.

"Yeah, but I'm pretty sure it's just referring to goats," Olivia said.

True enough, *The Book of Truths* specifically stated goats were ungodly. It was something to do with their unusual eyes being windows for evil to see into the world. Olivia had only seen goats in nature videos. They had them in Simonia and plenty of other countries, and she thought they looked kinda cute.

"It is referring to all ungodly creatures, including vampires and those who aid them, and I will not have this kind of talk at my dinner table," her mother barked at her. This was how most of their arguments ended recently. It didn't seem to matter the topic.

"Fine, I'll eat in my room then," Olivia said.

It was a good excuse to break away from dinner early. She needed the time to plan her next move and couldn't stomach looking at her mother for much longer anyway. Taking her plate, she stood. Her mother threw her napkin onto the table as Olivia walked toward the door.

"Sometimes, I don't know why I bother," Marina said, shaking her head.

Alan clearly wasn't going to point out he was the one who made dinner that night. He didn't have a death wish. There was an awkward silence for a few seconds.

"The food was really good," Jamie said, trying to lighten the mood. No one responded, and he kept on eating.

Olivia walked up the large wooden staircase to the second floor. They had moved into the house when she was four years old. It was her home, and she knew every inch of it. Knew which of the steps creaked when you needed to sneak into the house late. Knew that at the bottom of the stairs, if you looked close enough at the wall, you could still see where it had been re-plastered after Jamie dove head-first into it wearing a sports helmet.

The first room just past the top of the stairs was hers. When she was younger, edgy posters were pinned to it. Older now, supposedly more mature, it was blank. She opened the door, went inside, and turned on the light. A typical teenager's bedroom, messy with a slight smell, a floordrobe of clothes sat in a pile near the bed. Stuck to a mirror were old ticket stubs to concerts she'd been to, mostly inoffensive pop and soft rock bands.

Although she had some degree of freedom on the music front, her mother took a grim view of what she called *anti-social music*. That was code for punk and rap. In the corner of the room sat a wooden study desk with an old fat laptop covered in stickers.

Olivia locked the door behind and put the plate of food on the desk, then sat on the edge of the bed. And that's where she remained for some time, like a statue, no emotions, no expressions, her tall thin frame still as the night. It was the first time she was alone with her thoughts somewhere private since the diagnosis.

Her brain didn't know quite what to do, so it just went into a sort of shutdown mode for a while. Eventually, she picked up a pillow from the bed, buried her face into it, and screamed in horror. When she was done, she sat there, face contorted, babbling.

"I am so fucked, I am so fucked, I am so fucked," more a chant than actual speaking.

Eventually, she went silent again. One way or another, her life as it had been, was over. Images of her surrendering herself to the authorities formed in her mind. Could she walk to the slaughterhouse so willingly? No, some deeper survival instinct would rebel somehow, desperate to stay alive even if the conscious mind was unwilling.

The alternative was equally grim. She'd turn into something else, someone else, something wholly different, inhuman. Maybe that was as good as dead anyway. It really didn't matter. If she didn't make it to the border, they'd come for her, put her down like a rabid dog. If she wanted to live, she had to run, there was no other way.

Earlier in the day, looking at the map at school, the journey seemed possible. Now, sitting alone in her room, the weight of the task became all too real. She'd have to traverse almost the entire length of the country.

OK, focus. Information, you need information. She got up and went over to the desk with the laptop, swung it opened, and pressed the power button. The old hard drive took an age to boot.

"Come on, you useless piece of crap," she insulted the computer as it went about its business.

Eventually, the welcome screen appeared. She logged in and opened a search browser. Her hands shook, hovering over the keyboard for a few seconds before she typed:

VAMPIRE DIAGNOSIS INFORMATION

As her hand was about to instinctively hit the enter key, she retracted it. Fear entered her mind. Did the government track these things? Would a record be kept at the ISP even if she cleared the history? She panicked and hit backspace, deleting the text from the search box and closed the browser window.

A creaking sound came from the stairs below, light-footed. It was her brother. The steps drew closer, and then went down the hall to his room. Olivia sat and listened, thinking. A video game could be heard launching, and then the sound was muted by headphones. Olivia sprung up from her desk and unlocked the door. She went down the hall to Jamie's room. The door had a videogame poster on it that read: Do Not Enter - Battler's Domain. She knocked.

"It's unlocked," came Jamie's voice from the other side.

Olivia opened the door and entered. Jamie's room was neater than hers but smelled vaguely of sweat and energy drinks. It was jam-packed with so much stuff it was a wonder he managed to amass it all in his short life. Games, movies, shelves filled with action figures, and foam dart guns. His schoolbooks and notes were neatly ordered on a dedicated study desk in the corner.

Their parents didn't know, but a section of the desk had been sanded and repainted. Jamie had tried an ill-advised cellphone repair, ruptured the lithium battery, and nearly burned the house down. It was one of the few times she had to cover for him rather than vice-versa, but she always held it over him.

Jamie sat at his gaming desk in the corner with a headset on. He played a sedate-looking game, building a house in a forest clearing with some others online.

She sat down on the end of the bed near him.

"What's up?" he asked.

"Not much. Just came to say hello."

He turned around to speak to her, ignoring his game for a while.

"You only come into my room when you want something from me, or you need me to lie to Mom. So, which is it?" he asked.

"What do you know about VPNs?" she didn't beat around the bush.

Jamie pulled the headset out of the audio jack on the speaker, turned down the volume, and stopped playing. He took a long hard look at his sister before speaking. "Nothing, why?" he was a poor liar, at least when it came to Olivia.

"Liar. I know you subscribe to one."

"What do you need with a VPN anyway?" he asked her.

"That's my business," she responded.

"Well, you can take your business elsewhere then," he replied and turned back to his game.

"You know what's a really cool website?" Olivia paused for effect. "Sexy-milf-teachers.nsc."

Jamie turned to her again, face red, embarrassment and anger, dagger eyes trained on Olivia. He got up from the desk, stormed over to the door, looked outside to check that the coast was clear, and then rounded on Olivia.

"I accidentally visited that site one time, one time, and you still hold it over me," Jamie angrily whispered at her.

"Oh, yeah. I'm sure people *accidentally* visit sexy-milf-teachers.nsc all the time," she said. "It's such as short website address, it's bound to happen."

"Shhh. Keep your damn voice down." Jamie raised a finger to his lips.

"Such an oddly specific website as well."

"Alright, alright, you made your point," Jamie gave in.

"Tell me about the VPN. I know how they work, just not how you paid for it. You steal Mom’s credit card or something?"

"No, I don't have a death wish. She checks her statements. I use gift cards," he told her.

"Gift cards?"

"You can buy them with cash, and then use that to pay for the VPN."

"Kinda like shitty money laundering. You have any of these gift cards spare?" she asked.

"I have a ten-dollar card, enough for a couple of months subscription," he said.

Olivia took a beaten-up-looking wallet from her jeans pocket. "How much?" she asked.

"For you. Twenty bucks," he responded. Olivia cut him a look that said, 'Really?'

"It's a sellers’ market," he informed her, relishing how the tables had turned.

"Ten, and I forget all about sexy-milf-teachers.nsc forever. I swear it."

"And the desk incident?"

"Fine, and you almost burning down the house, too. Deal?"

A rare earnest look in Olivia's eyes told Jamie his sister was serious. She may have been many things, a shitty sister included but, generally, if she promised something, she tried to keep it in as good faith as possible.

"Deal," he agreed. Snatching the money, he shook her hand.

Jamie walked over to his computer desk, fished inside the drawer, and produced the gift card. He handed it to Olivia, who stuffed it in her hoodie pocket, then he sat down next to her on the bed.

"You in some kind of trouble?" he asked.

"No."

"OK."

The boy looked unconvinced by his sister's response. Olivia's face took on a somber look, her brain processing the information that this would probably be the last time she'd ever speak to her brother. She searched for something meaningful to say but spoke before fully thinking through where she was going.

"You know I'm only busting your balls about that website, right?"

"Yeah, I know," he answered.

"When I go away to college next year, take care of yourself. Don't do anything stupid, OK?"

"I won't. It's gonna be weird with you not around."

"And don't believe all the religious crap they teach you in school."

Shocked by her blunt statement, Jamie looked up at her. As a general rule, Olivia and her brother toed the party and family line when it came to religion. Yes, there might be some dissent from time to time about some issues from Olivia but calling religion crap seemed to be a little too much for Jamie, who didn't know how to respond.

"Oh, well, I …"

"And if you get a girlfriend, don't bring her to meet Mom."

"That would involve me actually talking to girls first, but I guess that gets a lot easier as you get older."

"It doesn't. Everybody's terrified. It never really goes away."

"Oh."

Olivia didn't know where she was going with the conversation, trying to give him some kind of half-assed talk about growing up but failing badly. She worried about him, always felt he was far too innocent for his age and that's why he got bullied at school. At the time she told him, 'Just try to fit in more, go to parties, have fun,' as if fundamentally changing who you were was all so easy.

He seemed to have found a group of friends at his new school who were as nerdy as he was, and their parents seemed happy with that, but there was always a niggle in the back of Olivia's head that her brother was a bit of a loser. It shouldn't have bothered her but, somehow, it did. At least until today, everything she once thought important didn't seem to matter anymore.

She embraced her brother, who was visibly shocked by the sudden transition from awkward heart-to-heart talk to bear-hug. He opened his eyes wide in surprise, clearly unsure of how to respond, unaccustomed to this kind of genuine emotion from his sister. Olivia couldn't see it. She had her eyes tightly shut, tears forming, head rested on his shoulder. He could clearly sense the sentiment was genuine, so he hugged her back tightly. Olivia broke the embrace as quickly and unexpectedly as it had started. She stood up from the bed and wiped her eyes dry.

"You sure you're not in some kind of trouble?" Jamie asked her again.

"I'm fine. Thanks for the help."

"No problem."

Olivia gave him a well-practiced fake smile. He looked unconvinced. She walked out of the room, closing the door behind her.

Back in her room now, at her computer, she'd made some attempt to eat the chicken pita bread but only managed to get about half down before nausea got the better of her. It was lesser in the past few days but still clawing. She glanced over to the door as if it might have magically unlocked itself.

A year or so ago, she'd caught her mother snooping through the keyhole after she'd been reprimanded at school. Since then, it was her habit to hang a hoodie on the door handle to block the keyhole whenever she wanted to be certain of complete privacy. Next to the plate of half-eaten food was the gift card, the foil scratched off to reveal a code beneath.

The desktop of Olivia's computer was a cluttered mess, audio and video file icons, and word processor documents plastered across the screen in no particular order. It was a mirror of her mind, chaotic and disorganized. A small window near the tray icons in the bottom right of the screen read:

VIPER VPN - TUNNEL ESTABLISHED

The cursor hovered over an icon of the world. She double-clicked the mouse button, and the laptop chugged to life, its cooling fans kicking in at the struggle of even this simple task. Eventually, a landing page with a search bar awaiting a query appeared. She hesitated for a moment, glancing toward the door before quickly typing:

VAMPIRE DIAGNOSIS INFORMATION

She hit the enter key hard as soon as it was typed, like ripping off a Band-Aid. She didn't want to give herself a chance to chicken out. The results loaded on the screen. The first was an advert that read:

5 WAYS TO SPOT A VAMPIRE - NO.3 WILL SHOCK YOU!

Olivia's eyes glazed over it like it wasn't there. She knew better than to fall for clickbait. The first organic result lay below the advert. It read:

VAMPIRE DIAGNOSIS PROCEDURE INFORMATION

The text seemed innocuous enough, but below the URL read:

WWW.V1.GOV/VAMPIRE-DIAGNOSIS

It was an official government resource website. All government websites had the same domain. Scrolling past it, she decided there would be nothing useful on it that Nurse Ramirez hadn't already told her. She also feared a government website might track visitors somehow. Exactly how she was unsure, but she didn't have total faith in the VPN.

DEALING WITH A DIFFICULT DIAGNOSIS - CHAT WITH US - FREE IMPARTIAL ADVICE

Eyes scanned the text. It was ambiguous, unwanted pregnancy, drug addiction, who knew. Maybe it was a catch-all for a general advice organization. The URL below was little help:

WWW.DIFFICULT-DIAGNOSIS.NSC

She moved the mouse cursor over the link, ready to click it, deciding it might be worth investigating. As the cursor hovered over the link, a small context-sensitive box appeared from the VPN software. It read:

URL OWNED BY CENTER OF FRIENDS

Olivia had heard of the organization before briefly. It was one of the groups along with PAVS that had recently been given extra funding and minor oversight powers. She knew little else about them but decided if they were like PAVS, they weren't to be trusted. Her finger continued to roll the mouse wheel. More results displayed on the screen. One looked promising, catching her attention:

THE FIRST THREE DAYS - MAKING IT TO THE BORDER ALIVE

Below the link the URL was displayed:

WWW.PEACEBRIDGE.NSC/3DAYS

Peacebridge came up on the news a lot. Tom Clarkson on the *Insight Hour* was always harping on about how they were a borderline terrorist organization. That should be outlawed because they give support to our enemies and spread anti-social information. The mouse hovered over the link. The VPN's context-sensitive box appeared and informed her:

URL OWNED BY PEACEBRIDGE NON-PROFIT ORGANIZATION

"Best ten bucks I ever spent," she said to herself.

The text was reassuring, and Jim Clarkson's anti-endorsement of the group sealed the deal. She decided the site might have some useful information, so she took a deep breath and clicked on the link. A simple website loaded. It had no flashy animations or stylistic flair. It was to convey information, nothing more. The text was black on an off-white background. A heading at the top read:

MAKING IT TO THE BORDER

Below was a short message reading:

WE ADVISE YOU ACCESS THIS SITE USING A VPN IF POSSIBLE.

"Way ahead of ya," Olivia said.

An icon in the top-right corner of the screen redirected to a Ruhmic version of the site, the language they spoke in Simonia, presumably with different advice based on the laws there. A sidebar with several menu links was located on the left-hand side of the page:

DOS AND DON'TS

WHAT TO PACK

MAPS/ROUTES

PURIFICATION SQUADS

PHYSICAL CHANGES

DONATE ANONYMOUSLY - HOW YOU CAN HELP

Olivia surveyed the site. It seemed to be straightforward enough. The low-budget simplistic design reassured her it was probably legitimate and not a front for something more sinister. The only thing that made her heart pump a little faster was the link about purification squads. She had heard the term before, but only when the government was denying they existed.

She didn't know what their alleged role was claimed to be. Dos and don'ts seemed like a good place to start. She clicked the link, and a page loaded with a list of bullet points, each with a little description detailed below.

DON'T GET HELP FROM FRIENDS OR FAMILY

Giving anything other than advice to a person intending to cross into the Vampire Union is a criminal offense with significant penalties. A friend or family member might feel obligated to help you if you reveal your diagnosis to them, putting them in jeopardy. If at all possible, make your way to the border under your own steam.

DON'T TELL ANYONE NO MATTER HOW TRUSTED

As above, aside from the legal jeopardy your loved ones might face, there is a significant risk to you if you divulge your diagnosis to anyone. You might trust a family member or close friend, but if they tell even one other person, your diagnosis is no longer a secret, putting your life at serious risk. (See PURIFICATION SQUAD link for more detailed information.)

DON'T TALK TO LAW ENFORCEMENT

Legally, law enforcement cannot prevent you from traveling to and across the border but, in recent years, some law enforcement agencies have begun holding people on suspicion of trivial offenses if they know the person has a V1 diagnosis. This can delay the person by twenty-four or even forty-eight hours. This has been a death sentence for many. Although minors only make up a tiny fraction of people with V1 diagnosis, they are particularly vulnerable to this type of abuse, if they are reported missing, authorities are legally bound to intervene. If you are arrested, ask to see a civil rights lawyer immediately.

DON'T KEEP A MAP OF YOUR ROUTE

Plan a route but don't keep a physical map or use a GPS. Try to memorize the major points along your route and nothing more. Be prepared to change it if you run into trouble. As above, never reveal your route to anyone.

DON'T CARRY ANYTHING THAT COULD REVEAL YOUR DIAGNOSIS

Don't carry any information pamphlets, printouts, or handwritten notes identifying your diagnosis on your person. Also, do not carry a goodbye letter to family or friends. In the past, these have been used as evidence to convict family members.

DON'T GET TRICKED INTO ENTERING A VEHICLE

Do not get lured, tricked, or forced into entering a private vehicle. An offer of a free ride toward your goal from a friend or kind stranger can be tempting, but many who disappear on their way to the border were last seen entering an unknown vehicle. If you do not have access to a private vehicle of your own, stick to public transport. (See PURIFICATION SQUAD link for more detailed information.)

It was a wall of information. Olivia tried to digest it all. She slowly realized the perilous nature of her situation. Her heart thudded harder in her chest. If she was an adult and owned a car, she could just pack up some things and drive away, not stop till the border. Being a minor complicated everything.

She knew most people who got the V1 diagnosis were young, but few were as young as her. Their names appeared on a list on a special page in the national newspapers each week. Some weeks, there were only a handful of names. Other weeks, there might be a dozen. The lists were available online, but it was one of the few things people still bought print newspapers for; morbid curiosity, like reading the obituaries.

Unlike the obituaries, there were no stories attached to the names, just a photo, age, and occupation, as if their stories had been wiped clean, their lives boiled down to a number and a job: Alice Nowak, 22, Nurse; Anik Bhatt, 20, Mechanic; Sofia Moretti, 28, Housewife; Simon McAvoy, 17, Student. There was no mention in the newspapers of whether the person made it to the border or not, not even in the odd event that someone surrendered themselves voluntarily. No statistics were published. It was considered a state secret.

The diagnosis was very rare, but Olivia was unsure how rare exactly. When Simon McAvoy's diagnosis was revealed, it was said the school hadn't had a current or former student diagnosed in its twenty-year history. It was good news for her. People would be less likely to think lighting had struck twice when she went missing.

Simon McAvoy, how had he made it, if he made it. It couldn't be that hard. Keep your head down, don't talk to the cops, get a few buses and trains, and that was it. He was smart enough if she remembered right and looked a little older than his age. Maybe it was a cakewalk for him. A young man traveling alone raised a lot fewer questions than a young woman.

Maybe it would be easy for her, too. In a few days, she'd be laughing about why she was so worried. Laughing from where, though? The streets in some desolate country, feeding on dogs or…people? How did it work? What kind of abomination would she become? She punched herself hard in the side of the head.

Focus on the next three days, don't think about anything else. Turning her attention back to the screen, she read the DOS section:

DO LEAVE AS SOON AS POSSIBLE

Time is your enemy. Be gone as soon as it is feasible, and after you have packed some necessities. Even if you are near the border, give yourself as much time extra time as possible. No one ever died from getting to the border early. Try to account for changes in weather, especially during winter as this can block roads and delay public transport.

DO TRAVEL LIGHT

Don't try to carry your entire life with you. It will draw too much attention, and you won't be able to cross the border with most of your possessions anyway. Pack light and bring appropriate clothes for the season. (See preparation page for details.)

DO BE CAUTIOUS WITH YOUR PHONE

During your three-day window, the police should not know of your diagnosis and won't be legally allowed to track your phone location even if they do. (Unless you are suspected of some other serious crime.) However, you should still use your phone with an abundance of caution as it, too, can be a record of your diagnosis, and messages could be used to incriminate others whether you make it to the border or not.

DO TAKE AN UNEXPECTED ROUTE

Try to take an unusual or unexpected route. This will make you harder to track if someone notices your absence. Use all means of public transport at your disposal. Only use a private vehicle you own and are driving yourself. If the car isn't yours, it can be reported stolen.

DO STAY IN PUBLIC PLACES WITH CROWDS

If you need to stop on your journey, try to remain in public areas with crowds. They provide cover for your movements.

DO BRING AS MUCH CASH AS POSSIBLE

Cash is king. It can't be traced like ATM or credit card transactions. Take as much money from your account as you can at the start of your trip. Try not to make card-based transactions after that point, especially on joint accounts as this reveals your location to others.

Money, as much as possible. She had a little herself but needed more, though she knew where to get some but just hoped there'd be enough. Pupils as small as pinholes in the bright light from the laptop screen, her eyes darted about, focusing on different links on the screen, finally resting on PHYSICAL CHANGES.

A lump formed in her throat. She swallowed it and moved the mouse over to click it. In truth, she didn't want to know the details, not yet anyway. She didn't feel ready, but her hand took over and clicked anyway. Her heart thumped steadily against its chest wall, and the air hung in her lungs as the page loaded. Eventually, a page with a few lines of text was displayed:

PHYSICAL CHANGES

Under the Corvin Act, we can no longer give information about the physical changes you will undergo as a result of your diagnosis. (Help Repeal the Corvin Act - Contact your Representative.)

Blue-balled, she exhaled slowly, the tension released somewhat. Ignorance was bliss. It was better that way. Better not to know till later, to keep focused on the now. Her attention returned to the other links and clicked on the next link.

WHAT TO PACK

Travel light. Dress in layers of clothing you can double up in cold weather or take off in hot. The following items are useful:

Backpack, winter clothes, walking sneakers or boots, a lighter, bottles of water, prepackaged foods, as much cash as possible, mobile phone charger, burner/disposable phone, pen, and paper.

Eyes rapidly scanning the page, she made a mental note of all the items. Some were close at hand in the room, some she could get downstairs later. So far, the website had been reassuring. There was nothing she thought she couldn't handle, the advice clear and concise.

You can do this, you can do this.

Footsteps came up the stairs, a little heavier than her little brother but not heavy enough to be her father. The footsteps stopped outside the door.

"Night, Olivia," came her mother's voice from the other side.

Voice conciliatory, like she was apologizing for earlier. Olivia, engrossed in research couldn't think of any meaningful final words to say to her mother.

"Night, Mom," she replied.

The footsteps shuffled away down the hall to her parents' bedroom. Was that really the last conversation she'd ever have with her mother. Olivia felt cold like it meant nothing, or maybe her mind just couldn't deal with it at that moment, so she stored it up for later. Like a person bereaved person who feels nothing at first, then breaks down in the grocery store two years later. She's never had anyone close to her die or any other great tragedy in her life, but she knew enough to know people didn't always react the way they did on TV.

Research paused for a while, Olivia slumped back in the chair and swiveled around. Her mother could be heard preparing for bed down the hall, but there was no longer any noise from Jamie's room. She looked over at the alarm clock near the bed. The digits read 22:35. She'd been reading for longer than she'd thought and lost track of time.

Condensation covered the window near the desk. She wiped it off and looked outside. A still night, the branches of the oak tree that stood in the back garden barely swaying in the wind. A half-moon glowed bright in the sky, bathing the land a pale blue. In the windowsill sat an old, framed photo of her and her friends. It was two and a half years old, a lifetime ago to a teenager.

Summer, they were all smiling, wearing shorts and T-shirts, standing arm-in-arm in front of Lake Clearview, a popular day-trip destination. Sara was on the left, linked to Jasmine, who was next to Amber, and then Olivia on the right, just in frame, left arm cut off. The photo, like so many other things in her county, was a lie, but the photo was a lie she'd constructed. She picked up the frame turned it around and undid the latches on the back. The rear section pulled away, and she removed the photo. It had once been fitted in a bigger frame but was now folded to fit in the smaller one.

The photo was unfolded to reveal a hidden portion. Linked to Olivia's left arm was Angie McAvoy, who smiled down at Olivia rather than looking at the camera. She was the only one brave enough to wear a bikini top that day. They'd all agreed to do it despite their mothers forbidding it, but Angie was the only one who didn't chicken out. Olivia wished she had the balls Angie McAvoy had. She put the photo face down on the windowsill, unable to bear looking at it any longer.

The chair swiveled back around to face the computer. The harsh light of the LCD screen made Olivia's face glow. There were only two links left unclicked, PURIFICATION SQUADS and MAPS/ROUTES. She clicked the link for the squads. Other than the name sounding sinister, she knew nothing about the term. A page loaded with a large message in bold red lettering across the top:

THIS PAGE COULD SAVE YOUR LIFE

It consisted of several embedded video files with small paragraphs of text underneath each one. Olivia opened the desk drawer and pulled out a set of over-ear headphones. She put them on and plugged the connector into the jack on the side of the laptop. Once connected, they gave a small hum, and all other sound in the house was silenced. Turning the volume up to fifty percent, she pressed play on the first video.

The headphones were useless for the video as it had no audio track. Footage captured from some kind of security camera, the picture was good quality, but the watermark with the time and date indicating when the video had been recorded was blurred out. It depicted a deserted corner of an outdoor parking lot at night, the only source of light a solitary flickering lamppost. A worried-looking young black man about twenty-two years old stood near a dirty-looking white van, the engine still running, steam coming off it in plumes in the cold night.

The man gesticulated and held his hands to his face, visibly nervous, twitchy. He talked to another young man about the same age but a little taller. Maybe a friend, who knew. The footage gave no indication. The second man seemed to be trying to calm the first. Eventually, he removed what looked like a wad of cash from his pocket and held it out to the nervous man, then put his hand on the man's shoulder in reassurance.

The first man seemed relieved and appeared to almost break down in tears. He reached out and embraced the second man. The second man held his embrace tightly, too tightly, and the nervous man tried to break free. Two figures wearing ski masks emerged from the shadows near the van. They grabbed the nervous man from behind and quickly put a sack hood over his head.

He kicked and fought light crazy but was overwhelmed. They cable-tied his hands, opened the side door of the van, and bundled him inside, then climbed in after him. The other man who'd embraced him got into the front of the van and it drove away. Its silent diorama played out the video ended.

Olivia stared at the screen, unnerved. The video could have been anything, a simple kidnapping, a drug deal gone bad. She turned her attention to the paragraph beneath:

JAMAL WILLIAMS

Jamal Williams was a care assistant for the elderly before he got his V1 diagnosis. He didn't make it to the border. His body was never recovered. His van was found burned-out on waste ground near where this footage was captured. He trusted his cousin, and his cousin betrayed him. Despite the clear evidence from a newly installed security camera, no one has ever been charged with his disappearance or murder.

She swallowed hard, heart beating harder now, but she kept her nerve. It was just a video, and there was no audio. You could write any narrative you wanted underneath it, it didn't necessarily make it true. Maybe it was just propaganda. She clicked on the next video before reading the description.

Footage from a handheld video camera or a cellphone, shaky but clear. Someone held it. They were in a forest, a clear morning. The camera rose. A young woman, not much older than Olivia, bound to a tree with rope in a forest. Her jeans and top were dirty like she'd fallen in the mud, cheek split open and bleeding below her right eye, she'd taken a punch or two.

The knuckles on her right hand were bloody and torn. She'd fought back, maybe got in a few decent blows on her attackers but now she looked defeated, head bowed, body held fast to the tree. A man in a black hood came into shot, and the cameraman focused on him. He held a copy of *The Book of Truths*, the flaming emblem of the lord burning on a pyre inset in gold leaf on the cover. Holding the tome aloft, he began a short sermon.

"*The Book of Truths* is our guiding light in this life and the next," he said.

He was a young man trying to sound older and more authoritative than his years. Like a youth preacher who hadn't quite perfected his craft. Still, he was filled with enough fire and brimstone to cover for his lack of oratorical skill.

"It teaches us about the creeping unholy evils of the world. How they first infect the body, and if left to fester, will corrupt the very soul of man with unnatural wants and desires. Once the soul is corrupted, there is no return, no redemption, no chance to follow the lord's golden path to salvation."

"Please…" the girl pleaded.

She barely had the strength to speak. The preacher continued undeterred, and the cameraman continued to film, a silent observer.

"We are here today for the salvation of this young woman, for although her body is corrupted, her soul can still be saved!" Sermon finished, he stepped out of shot.

"Do you have any final words?" he asked from somewhere behind the camera.

"Please…this isn't God's will, it's yours. You don't have to do this…please…"

The young woman pleaded with what little strength was left in her, then her head dropped again, and she sobbed uncontrollably. Another hooded man came into shot carrying a jerry-can and doused her in gasoline.

"Not like this, please, not like this. I'm begging you!"

Finding some final reserve of inner strength, the young woman roared at the men like a cornered animal. The man with the jerry-can showed no pity or hesitation of any kind. He ignited the gasoline with a cigarette lighter. Her clothes were quickly engulfed in flames, her long hair catching fire, skin starting to burn. She let loose a bloodcurdling scream in the empty forest.

The video stopped suddenly, not because it was over but because the stop button had been pressed. Olivia couldn't watch anymore. Tears poured down her face. Hands covered her mouth, a near-silent scream echoed into them. The first video was ambiguous, could have been anything, and she could delude herself about its context, but not this one.

She couldn't lie to herself it was just some found footage movie, it was too real. There were no actors that good. The video was what it was, a girl not much older than herself being burned alive. Olivia pulled the headphones off and sobbed uncontrollably.

"I don't wanna die, I don't wanna die, I don't wanna die," she whispered to herself over and over again through tears.

Before watching the video, the danger had seemed distant, not fully real somehow, like some minor trouble she had gotten into that her father could pressure someone to make go away. But things were clear as day now, and the weight of it was crushing. Fanatics wanted to murder her, and the government didn't care. They'd even lend a hand by turning a blind eye to it.

If the fanatics didn't get the job done in three days, it wouldn't matter. The government would come to do the job themselves, all nice and legal. The tears had made tracks down Olivia's cheeks, face contorted by fear, eyes wide with terror. She looked back to the screen. She couldn't finish the video, but she needed to know how the girl came to be in the woods, how they'd caught her. The passage below read:

AMY SANDHERST

Amy Sandherst was at university studying accountancy when she got her diagnosis. With no one to turn to for advice, she sought help from a non-profit group that claimed to help people in her situation. The group illegally passed her information to a religious purification squad. She was kidnapped and burned alive. She was a few days past her 19th birthday.

Olivia's gut instinct not to trust the advice groups was on the money, but she hadn't realized how dangerous it could be. She couldn't trust anyone, friends, family, it didn't matter. It only took one set of loose lips to end up tied to a tree like the girl in the video. She wasn't going to let that happen, no way. She'd jump off a bridge if she had to, but she wasn't gonna get burned alive tied to a fucking tree. Face hardened, she steadied herself.

Scrolling further down the page, there were more videos, but she didn't want to watch them. At the bottom of the page was another section in bold red lettering, it dominated the page:

CARRYING A WEAPON IN PUBLIC SUCH AS A KNIFE OR FIREARM IS ILLEGAL IN THE NSC, SO WE CANNOT *LEGALLY* RECOMMEND THAT YOU CARRY A WEAPON CONCEALED ON YOUR PERSON.

She was smart enough to read between the lines, didn't need to be told twice. Wiping the tears clear with her sleeve, she got out of the chair with a purpose. Her face was sharp with conviction, twitchy, nodding quickly.

“Right, right.”

She reached under her bed and fished out a backpack a little larger than a schoolbag. It was old, gray, and a bit beaten-up. It didn't look like the kind of bag a kid would have.

Frantically surveying the floordrobe of clothes near the bed, she pulled two T-shirts from the pile and examined them quickly. One was plain gray. She stuffed it in the bag. The other had the logo of a band she liked, The Axel Kings.

Do twenty year olds like The Axel Kings? No, she barely liked 'The Axel Kings' anymore. She threw the T-shirt back in the pile and choose a blander one that just had the digits 97 in red letters emblazoned on a blue background. It had a few tiny holes in it and looked like the kind of T-shirt a person would wear to work. She stuffed it in the bag, then grabbed a spare pair of jeans and threw them in as well, not caring if they were clean or dirty.

Picking up a pair of underwear from the floor, she gave them a quick smell test from a safe distance, then decided she had some hygiene standards and threw them back on the ground. Quickly moving to a small bedside locker, she pulled out the middle drawer and tipped the contents onto the floor. Only two pairs of clean underwear left, one regular pair and one more sensible period underwear, she stuffed them both in the bag along with a few pairs of balled-up socks.

The underwear reminded her that her period would probably hit in four or five days. *Do vampires even fucking menstruate?* Pulling open the top drawer, she grabbed a few tampons and a sanitary pad and put them in a small side pocket of the backpack, deciding it was better to have them and not need them than need them and not have them.

Moving back to the clothes pile, she grabbed a plain zip-up hoodie and stuffed it into the bag with the rest of the clothes. *Jacket, jacket.* She moved over to the main wardrobe and swung it open. It never got bitterly cold in Greenfields so she had no real need for a heavy winter jacket. The only jacket in the wardrobe remotely suitable was a light parka. She took it down from the hanger. It had very little weight to it, more showy than practical, but it was the best available, so she tossed it over beside the backpack.

The meager supplies looked pathetic. Was this really all the clothes she was going to take to start a new life? No, it was just to get through the next three days. '*Pack light,*' that's what the website said. Moving with the bag over to the computer desk, she pulled out the bottom drawer completely. Hidden underneath was a metal cookie box.

She took it out and pulled the lid open. A hidden stash of contraband. A small wad of cash, a fake ID, and an open pack of cigarettes with a lighter stuffed inside. It was all she dared keep in the house. If anything more serious like condoms were found, her mother would probably have had her shipped off to a religious boarding school the next day. None of that mattered now. *Nothing* really mattered anymore, only survival.

She put the pack of cigarettes into the side pocket with the tampons and zipped it up, then she examined the fake ID. The name read Anna Jankowski, the date of birth indicting she was twenty years old. When Olivia got it a year and a half ago, it claimed she was eighteen, just old enough to drink. The ID hadn't been used in a while. Amber's older brother usually bought them booze.

Would anyone really buy her as a twenty-year-old? Doubtful, she took her legitimate ID from her wallet and compared the two side-by-side. The fake was decent quality, the two indistinguishable to her eyes, but would she bet her life on it? The real ID could get her sent back home as a minor if her parents reported her missing. The fake ID could get her held in a jail cell for a day or so. Both were death sentences.

Hedging her bets, she decided to take both. She hid the real ID in the back of her wallet and put the fake front and center. She'd just have to sell the fact she was twenty as best possible. *You're Anna Jankowski now, dickhead. Don't forget it.*

Grabbing the money, she flicked through the bills, counting carefully. The faces of different religious and political figures of the NSC flicked past, silently judging her. Ninety-seven dollars. Not enough, not even close. She closed the tin, put it back in its hiding place, and replaced the drawer, then she stood up and walked toward the door. Glancing at the alarm clock, the time read: 23:22

Late enough everyone would be in bed, probably already asleep. She took off her sneakers, unlocked the door, and slid silently out into the hall. Making her way down the stairs, she avoided the creaking steps. Once on the ground floor, she made her way down the long hallway. Passing the living room, there was a glow from the TV inside. Her father must have forgotten to turn it off. At the end of the hall, she entered her father's home office.

He worked from home some days, and some evenings as well. The office was simple, a chair, a desk with a computer, some filing cabinets. Olivia knew exactly what she was looking for, having done this heist on a much smaller scale before. She opened the top drawer of the desk as quietly as possible and pulled out a small red lockbox. The keys were in the lock, her father too trusting.

It was a personal petty cash box for the minor expenses of her father's business. He was an accountant. If he bought an ice cream on his lunch break, the receipt went into the box without fail. She opened the lid and removed a thick layer of receipts to reveal her true quarry, but there was much less than expected, only ninety-two dollars by her count. Normally, there were three or four hundred in small bills.

Maybe he wasn't so trusting after all. Maybe he noticed some missing recently and put less inside to test if some went missing. Twenty dollars taken from ninety-two was a lot more obvious. She grabbed the money and stuffed it into her wallet, cursing herself for her previous thefts. As she did, something caught her eye at the bottom of the lockbox. A credit card:

Alan Thompson

Thompson Accountancy Consulting LTD

First Settlers Bank

4551 4887 2536 7062

A hundred and eighty-nine dollars might not be enough, if you run out, you're dead.' She knew the pin code. It was her own birthday reversed. She'd seen her father input it once when they went for lunch together during the summer. He'd only paid for his own food with the card of course. Olivia told him he was far too honest for his own good.

She stood staring at the card like it was bar of solid gold bullion. Taking it might implicate her father, but she desperately needed a plan B. She snatched it from the box and put it in her wallet in one quick motion. It was just in case of an emergency if she was desperate. She'd leave a note saying she stole the card. Besides, she was about to steal something much more serious. 'In for a dime, in for a dollar,' as Sara would say before doing something reckless. The lockbox was put back where it was found.

Olivia tapped her foot in a few different spots on the carpeted floor, searching for something. Each time her foot registered cold concrete underneath, but she knew it was there somewhere. Eventually, she tapped in the corner, and there was a hollower sound, subtle, but she'd found what she was looking for. Kneeling, she examined the carpet floor tiles and pulled the corner one up to reveal a small safe. 'Secure Armaments 3000,' read the logo. There was a small digital keypad and an LCD display.

Unfortunately, Olivia didn't know this pin. She was only aware of the safe's existence because her mother produced the pistol from the office one night when there was a strange man wandering around in the garden, much to the shock of her and her brother. It turned out to be the grandfather of the Donnelly's who lived down the road. He had advanced Alzheimer's and wandered out into the night buck naked.

My birthday backwards. Olivia pressed the buttons, and the LCD display lit up. 'Incorrect Code - Attempt 1,' read the display.

Jamie's birthday backwards. She punched the numbers into the keypad, the display duly responded "Incorrect Code - Attempt 2.'

Mine and Jamie's combined. The buttons were perfectly silent. They gave no confirmation clicks or beeps as they were pressed. On the third attempt, the result was a little different. Text scrolled across the LCD panel: 'Incorrect Code - Attempt 3 - Warning ***Further incorrect attempts will alert Secure Armaments action center***'

Fuck, Fuck, Fuck! I needed that gun. Slumping down on the floor beside the safe a quiet rage flowed through Olivia. She'd never fired a gun, hell, never even held one. She'd only know how to operate one from what she'd seen in the movies. Could she even shoot someone if she needed to? It didn't matter. A gun was scary, and just having it would make people back off, even if you weren't going to use it.

She sat there for a few seconds in silence before getting up with an idea. Putting everything carefully back the way it had been, she turned off the light and slipped out of the room.

Olivia padded her way to the very end of the corridor and unlocked the interior door to the garage. She stepped inside and flicked only a single light switch. A corner of the garage was illuminated by a small incandescent light. Eyes scanned like a hawk and quickly locked onto her father's fishing rods, then tracked down to the red tackle box on the floor.

The plastic tackle box squeaked open. She couldn't remember the last time her father went fishing, not since his friend Sigurd got cancer anyway, and that was a couple of years ago. The lure trays were filled with bizarre-looking imitation plastic and metal fish. Olivia always wondered how these unusual contraptions fooled the other fish. They barely looked real, but she supposed they only needed to fool the fish for a split-second until it was too late. She extended the lure tray to access the main compartment. The prize lay below. She reached in and pulled it out.

A folding buck knife, about five inches long, with a brown wooden handle. She used her thumb to fold out the blade. It was a little stiff, but it extended and clicked into place. It still looked sharp, glinting in the light under examination. If Olivia was unsure if she could shoot someone, she was even less sure she could stab them.

A knife wasn't as useful as a gun. You could warn someone away with a gun, but you had to commit with a knife. Could she? What if she was being dragged into the woods like the girl in the video? She tried to imagine herself driving the blade into someone’s chest but couldn't visualize it. It didn't matter for now. It was the best weapon available, so she folded up the blade and put it in her hoodie pocket.

Passing the living room door, the flicker of the TV set caught her attention again. She heard something faint, barely audible, breathing maybe. Pushing the door, she silently padded inside. The TV was on mute, broadcasting twenty-four-hour financial news, stock markets opening halfway around the world. The breathing was coming from the reclining sofa chair facing the TV. She moved around slowly until she could see it was her father.

He was in a deep slumber, breathing shallow, barely making a sound. It was odd that she managed to hear him at all. He sometimes did this, usually after a very long day at work, or less frequently after a big argument with her mother. Maybe they argued about Olivia's behavior, or his response to it. Her mother was always chastising him for undermining her when she disciplined Olivia. The phrase 'Instilling faith-based values' often came up. It was a phrase parroted from the minister at church.

She looked down at her father in the chair and smiled. He looked peaceful, calm, and that calm radiated to her a little bit. It always did. From Olivia's perspective, her father was almost infallible. He could always talk to someone, who knew someone, who could have a word with someone else. When Jamie had had enough of his school, her father had gotten him into a better one, even though they weren't taking on new students and it was mid-term.

Olivia felt safe when he was around, like no one in the world could hurt her. The house was sleeping. She could wake him up right now, tell him everything. He'd reassure her, give her more money, maybe contact someone he trusted who would drive her to the border. She wouldn't need to worry about anything. Her hand reached out almost instinctively, ready to gently shake him awake, but then it froze.

But who could her father trust completely? Almost all their family's friends were involved with the church or local government in some way. It was good for her father's business to know the right people. Local representatives for the ruling CFU party (Conservative Faith Union), ministers, cops, all pillars of the community.

Even if her father did know someone else, someone with a more dubious background, willing to take that risk, it only took one careless word for her to end up like the girl in the video. Even if he managed to help her somehow, would he end up in prison, for how long? Five years? Ten? She retracted her hand retracted slowly.

No, not this time, he can't fix this. There's no fixing this.

"Goodnight, Daddy," she whispered to him like she was ten years old again, her voice breaking.

Walking away in total silence, she sipped out of the room. Like a wraith haunting her own home, she floated down the hallway toward the kitchen and opened the refrigerator. Olivia was illuminated in its glow. There wasn't much worth taking. She grabbed a couple of bottles of water and a few yogurt tube snacks, but nothing else was particularly portable. She'd get food on the way as needed.

The fridge shut, the kitchen consumed by darkness again. Her eyes adjusted, but she could see perfectly despite the dark. Maybe it was the moonlight giving everything a soft glow. There was an erasable notepad on the front of the refrigerator door used to leave messages. Olivia wiped it clean and wrote:

'Getting the early bus to school tomorrow. Need to finish an assignment. Staying at Sara's after. - Olivia'

She drew a small smiley face to help sell the story. It only needed to get her through the morning so she could leave town. After lunch, the school might call her mother and start asking questions, after that all bets were off. People would start looking.

Mounting the stairs, Olivia padded her way back to her room. Once inside, she locked the door and threw the supplies into the backpack. She hid the buck knife in a pair of socks and put it near the bottom of the bag. That was it. That was all she was taking, almost nothing. That was good. Travel light. It wouldn't look like she was leaving the country, just a young woman on her way to work or university.

Returning to the computer, it had automatically locked itself, so she entered the password. The screen still displayed the website from before. She clicked the MAPS/ROUTES link on the side of the screen. A new page loaded with a large interactive map of the NSC, Simonia, and the Vampire Union, along with several new icons ran down the side of the page.

If they'd cheaped out on the rest of the website, this is where they spent the money. Every border crossing from the NSC and Simonia into the Vampire Union was marked, minor and major. Only the NSC crossings were useful to Olivia. There were two major crossings, one at Freeport City in the far northeast, and the other at Sasatorin.

The crossings used to be vital trade routes, back when the NSC still traded with the Vampire Union. Now, they were more like border fortifications. The only thing crossing was people like Olivia, and that was a rare occurrence.

Freeport city was a possible route, but it meant going through lots of minor industrial cities, which meant lots of train and bus transfers, something she wanted to avoid. If she messed up or missed a connection, it could be fatal. It also meant buying and checking more tickets, more chance to get questioned or caught.

The crossing at Sasatorin was the largest. They always showed footage of it on the news. Massive, intimidating, the sight of it alone used to scare Olivia when she saw it on the news as a kid. It was out of the question. It was a direct route but would add at least a day to the journey, a day she really didn't have. She would have had to have left as soon as she got the diagnosis.

There were about fourteen minor crossings at small towns and cities dotted along the border's two-thousand-mile span. Being generous, only about six were reachable given her truncated timeframe and how far south she was. Under perfect conditions, you could white-knuckle drive for about sixteen hours and reach any of the six, but she had public transport to contend with.

She still had two full days. If things went smoothly, she'd make it in a day and a half, a day if she was really lucky. 'A public transport system the envy of the free world,' they always said. Olivia prayed it was true.

She sat hunched over the laptop for a time, trying out different route combinations. Each route gave a time estimate. They were higher than expected as they seemed to contain significant safety buffers. At least four of the six possible crossings seemed too risky, so she focused on the remaining two. One crossed at White Falls into a town on the Vampire Union side called Silent Lake. The other crossed from Overton to Vampire's Rest, the town she'd seen on the map at school. One destination looked as valid as the other.

Like an amateur at a horse track, she chose Vampire's Rest simply because she liked the name. She'd need to get a local bus to Greenfield's bus station, then get a coach north to a major city, Edmunsburg or Ashtown. From there, she could get a high-speed train all the way to the border at Overton. Edmunsburg was closer, but she knew Ashtown, spent a weekend there on a field trip. She and her friends had snuck out to go drinking.

It wasn't much, but she reasoned it was better to go somewhere at least somewhat familiar. Another advantage Ashtown had was the Taber River. It had commuter river ferries that went north, only a short distance, but maybe enough to get her past Ashtown if the train wasn't running or she ran into trouble.

Greenfields, Ashtown, Overton, Vampire's rest, that could be the path. She clicked the route. It took a second to calculate:

sixteen hours and ten minutes via public transport. The journey could be made with a day to spare. She stared at the map. She could do this. It wasn't so bad.

A local bus from Home to Greenfields, a coach from there to Ashtown, then the high-speed train all the way to Overton, and a hop, skip, and a jump over the border. Easy...as long as nothing goes wrong. She didn't need to write it down. It was easy to remember, only three stops. Two if she didn't count Greenfields.

The clock in the corner of the laptop screen read: 01:14. Late, she couldn't research or prepare anymore. She had to get a decent night's sleep. It might be the last she got for a few days. Closing the website tab, she cleared the history, then disabled the VPN, and shut down the laptop. Finally, she took a piece of paper and quickly scrawled a note:

I'M SORRY - HAD TO GO - STOLE DAD'S CREDIT CARD - OLIVIA

It was all written in block capitals, except the signature. Was it important she signed it? Maybe, if the note was questioned by the cops or in court it might make all the difference. She folded up the note and put it in the top drawer. It would be easy to find when they came looking. And they would come looking, she knew that with certainty, her parents first, then others. Standing, she walked over to the backpack and double-checked everything. She didn't feel ready. She never would, not until she took that first step.

Sitting on the edge of the bed, she set her old alarm clock for 06:30. For safety, she set three more alarms on her phone for

06:35, 06:40, and 06:45, not taking any chances. Taking off her clothes, she set them down near the bed, ready for the morning. She sat for a moment in her T-shirt and underwear on the edge of the bed. Her reflection sat across from her in the full-length mirror near the door. She regarded herself with a harsh eye: S*crawny, weak, tired, ugly, no tits.*

These weren't new insults. She insulted herself like this on an almost daily basis but, today, some of the insults mattered. Tired and weak. Could the girl in the mirror make the journey, could she pass for an adult, lie to the police convincingly if needed, survive in some new country without the support of her family, change into whatever it was she was going to change into?

Staring into the mirror, a sudden thought occurred to her. In the movies, vampires never had reflections. It was probably just a myth. She still looked solid enough for the moment anyway. It might not have been the worst thing if it was true. At the very least, she'd be able to stop judging herself in the mirror. Also, the scrawny look was probably more popular in the Vampire Union. She'd never seen a fat vampire in the movies. She laughed to herself quietly. Humor was a better coping mechanism than crying.

Switching off the light, she climbed into bed, two tiny oceans of blue the only color in the room. She shut her eyes, and there was only darkness. Lying flat on her back, body heavy, the day had taken a lot from her, maybe everything. Mind too exhausted to think anymore, it gave up, numb. She lay there like that for a time, in the still silence of the night. Eventually, the exhaustion overtook her, and she fell into a deep slumber. She didn't dream that night.

Wake Up

A high-pitched buzzing sound rang in Olivia's ears. Instinctively, she reached out and hammered the snooze button on the alarm clock. Somewhere between sleep and consciousness, her mind was calm and relaxed for a brief few seconds, then the crushing weight of her situation flooded back into her mind.

Her eyes sprung open as if they were on wires, and she stared at the ceiling for a few seconds in abject horror, until some force of willpower propelled her out of the bed like a rocket. She threw on her clothes as quickly as possible. The alarm clock went off again as she was putting on her jeans. She pulled the power cable out in a fury to silence it.

Once dressed, she canceled the extra alarms on her phone, wanting to avoid anyone else waking up if possible. After throwing on her jacket and zipping up her bag, she paused for a moment. *Is this it?* No, she decided as she unplugged her phone charger from the wall and stuffed it in the bag.

Pee, gotta pee.

She slipped out of her room into the bathroom and took the fastest piss of her life. While there, she grabbed her toothbrush and a half-empty tube of toothpaste, then made her way back to the bedroom. Was that it, anything else? Unsure, she double-checked everything in the backpack and her wallet, especially the knife. Everything was all present and accounted for.

She stood for a short moment, unsure what to do next. *You have to go now.* She swung the backpack onto her back and walked out of the room. As she crept down the stairs, she avoided the creaky ones and made her way to the front door. Just beside the front door, she came to a halt, stopped in her tracks by the entire family looking down at her from a photo on the wall. It was a professional one with the whole family posed in awkward sincerity.

Olivia hated the photo. Every family she knew had a similar one hanging in their house for guests to see. Another front. The families always looked so creepily perfect you'd swear they'd never had to piss or shit or function like a human being. She looked at herself in the photo, smiling, like butter wouldn't melt.

"Fuck are you lookin' at?" she quietly asked the perfect Olivia in the photo, then she opened the front door and walked out.

Walk

For a winter's morning, it wasn't too cold, but the grass was still frosted with ice, and a mist hung on the roads. They were virtually deserted. Only the odd car broke through the mist and sped past. Olivia speed-walked to the local roadside bus stop. She suddenly stopped dead in her tracks and violently vomited into the ditch at the roadside. Whatever adrenaline had driven her out of the house and powering down the road had run out. She took out a bottle of water, rinsed out her mouth, and quickly started walking again, not daring to stop for long.

After about half a mile, she reached the roadside bus stop. It had a plastic bench and a simple canopy for shelter. Checking her phone, it read 06:57. There with three minutes to spare. If the rest of her journey went like that, everything would work out just fine.

She sat on the plastic bench and waited but couldn't relax, not until she was out of Greenfields at the very least. Her foot shook up and down, and she constantly took out her phone to check the time. 7:00 AM came and went, and the bus didn't arrive. She looked at the screen of her phone in a panic 07:02. *Come on, where the hell are you?* As if a bus had never been two minutes late in her life.

A minute or so later, a low rumbling could be heard, and the bus slowly chugged out of the mist. She waved her hand. It slowed to a stop and pulled up beside her.

North

The doors swung open. Olivia boarded and paid the fare. Wallet two dollars lighter, she made her way down the aisle and took a seat on one of the uncomfortable, molded plastic chairs. Luckily, there were only had a handful of other passengers on the bus. She didn't recognize any of them.

The bus cut its way slowly through the fog, probably why it was running late. Then after a short time, it slowed and stopped at another small stop where a young girl boarded. Olivia recognized her, and her Olivia. It was the girl from Olivia's year at school. Francesca Bianchi, short and thin with a bob haircut and glasses.

It was safe. She was a nobody in Olivia's book, kept herself to herself. She definitely wouldn't try to spark up a conversation and ask unwanted questions. The two didn't acknowledge each other like neither existed in the world of the other.

The bus continued its journey, snaking along country roads until it hit the town of Greenfields. As it neared the stop for Olivia's school, Francesca rang the bell to get off. The bus slowed, and Francesca made her way to the front to get off. Finally, the bus halted, and the doors opened. Just as Francesca was about to get off the bus, she looked behind at Olivia, as if she was confused as to why she wasn't also getting off the bus as well. It was only a glance, a second of time at best, then she got off.

The doors closed, and the bus took off, Francesca glanced up at Olivia again from outside the bus as it pulled away. *Nosy bitch.* It didn't matter, Francesca wouldn't be gossiping to anyone anyway. She didn't have any friends Olivia knew of.

Continuing its journey, the bus cut around the edge of town. Eventually, it arrived at the Greenfields bus terminal. Olivia and the remaining passengers got off.

Brighter now, the sun's rays, although not yet visible on the horizon, still managed to light the land in a pale glow. The bus terminal was small but clean and well-maintained. There were no addicts or alcoholics who might ordinarily call a bus station home. Greeenfields didn't suffer from the drug problems plaguing many of the larger towns in the NSC. It helped that it was affluent. People like that were moved along pretty quickly.

Olivia queued with a few others for a ticket at the kiosk. It didn't take long. The station was manned by a friendly-looking woman in her mid-twenties, with a narrow face and glasses. Olivia was relieved she didn't recognize the woman.

"How can I help you today?" the woman asked.

"I need a ticket to Ashtown?"

"One way or return?"

Olivia paused for a moment. It was a small town. It'd look odd if she bought a one-way ticket to Ashtown and might arouse unwanted suspicions.

"Oh, a return please."

"Student?"

"No."

"ID?" the woman asked.

"What?"

"Driver's License, passport?" the woman asked in a soft friendly voice. "Sorry, gotta ask. It's one of the new emergency laws."

"Oh, yeah, of course."

Fumbling in her wallet, Olivia produced the fake driver's license and put it in the sliding metal drawer. It was pulled to the other side of the glass by the teller. The woman examined the fake ID, flipping it over several times like she was looking for something but wasn't fully sure what. Olivia's heart rate increased rapidly as the woman typed something into the computer. Was she alerting the police, checking some serial number on the ID. Was it too late to run, try a different plan, talk to her father, beg him to…

"That's fifteen-fifty," the teller finally declared with a smile and pushed the drawer back toward a dumbfounded Olivia.

Olivia put two crumpled ten-dollar bills in the metal tray, and it continued its merry to and fro journey between her and the teller. The woman tapped away at the computer, the cash drawer slid open, and a ticket printed from a machine beside it. The teller tore it off and put it into the metal drawer, along with the change, and slid it back to her. Olivia took the ticket and change and gave the teller a nice warm smile.

"Have a nice day," said the teller.

"Yeah, you too."

Walking away, Olivia breathed slowly and deliberately, trying to calm herself, nerves on a knife's edge. *Nobody knows. They're all oblivious, so don't freak out every time somebody asks you for some basic shit.* An intimidating-looking security guard with broad shoulders patrolled the terminal. He glanced at Olivia as she walked by. *He doesn't know shit either, just keep calm.*

She sat down on a plastic bench and waited, eyes darting around the terminal at the tired morning commuters, hoping she didn't know anyone. Greenfields was small enough that you'd recognized a lot of peoples' faces but big enough you didn't know their names or business. She recognized several of the people in the bus terminal but none by name, just local faces.

In a few days, Olivia's name would show up in the papers. They'd say they saw that girl leaving town. 'She looked sick, panicked', 'They say her family was well to do', 'Her mother claims she never even had a daughter.'

An electronic board showed the time for the incoming buses. The one for Ashtown already showed it four minutes late when it pulled into the bay. Olivia got up and joined the queue. Most of the people looked half-asleep, commuters going to the bigger towns for work. They shuffled out into the cold air to board.

A blast of warm air hit Olivia as she climbed the steps. It was a modern coach, built for long distances. It would be comfortable at the very least and might have a bathroom if she was lucky. Ticket punched, she made her way down the aisle to near the back of the coach and sat in one of the ugly-patterned maroon fabric seats.

To dissuade anyone from sitting next to her, she took the window seat and put her backpack on the aisle seat. It wasn't foolproof, but it usually worked if the bus wasn't full. Olivia looked out the window nervously, unable to relax until the coach was in motion and on its way out of Greenfields. The last passengers filed onto the coach.

It was barely a quarter full when the driver pulled the lever to close the doors. Running behind time already, he pulled the vehicle away from the terminal without any further delay. Some of the tension in Olivia's body eased as the coach maneuvered away from the terminal. A tiny respite. She hoped the journey would be uneventful.

The coach had barely moved twenty feet when it slammed to a halt. Someone banged on the doors. The driver pushed a button in frustration and, with a hiss, they swung open. The broad-shouldered security guard boarded the coach and spoke to the driver, who gestured down the bus with his thumb.

Oh, fuck.

He must have been six-four and a hundred and ninety pounds, the intimidating size of the man more apparent in the confines of the coach. Instinctively, he hunched his head down slightly as men of his height tended to do in cramped conditions. It made him look more menacing. He made his way toward Olivia.

There was no escaping. It was more like a wall than a person blocking the aisle. She was paralyzed with fear as the colossus approached her seat.

This is it. This is how it ends.

"Anna?" his voice came out softer than Olivia expected.

It took a couple of revolutions of the hamster running in the wheel in Olivia's brain before she could process what was happening and respond.

"Yes, Anna Jankowski, that's me," she replied.

"You left this at the ticket kiosk."

Held in his shovel-like hand was Olivia’s fake ID. He handed it out to her. She took it with a smile while her insides coursed with adrenaline and her stomach churned.

"Thanks. I'm such a ditz."

"Don't worry, it happens at least three times a day since the new rules came in."

He turned and lumbered away down the aisle, looking more like a friendly forest bear now than the human brick wall that approached seconds earlier. After he exited, the doors swung closed behind him, and the coach moved again. This time, it kept moving. It pulled out of the terminal and onto a narrow road.

Olivia kept her body and mind tense, no relaxing, not until she was far away from Greenfields. Surveying her surroundings, she noticed there was an emergency exit at the back of the bus, and in the corner of the window next to her was an emergency hammer to break the glass. Both were viable escape routes she could have used if things had gone differently.

Gotta start noticing these things.

Slumped in the seat, Olivia hoped she wouldn't be spotted by anyone in town. Her eyes could just about see out the window. Buildings flicked past, the pharmacy, the grocery store, a bowling alley she and her friends used to hang out at. Then the movie theater where she had her awkward first kiss, the cafe where she'd meet her dad for lunch during the summer.

It was as if the town mocked her. None of these things mattered anymore. Her life hadn't mattered. She'd be forgotten, just like all the other people on the special page of the newspapers. Whether she made it to the border alive or not, one thing was certain, this would be the last time she'd ever see her hometown. No crying or sobbing. Instead, she hardened herself.

Well, you always talked about getting out of this shithole. You're just doing it a little earlier than expected. It's just a town, bricks and mortar, nothing more. The coach agreed. It picked up speed as it hit a larger road. Eventually, the town vanished over the horizon. Olivia didn't look back, either because she couldn't bear to or she didn't care, she wasn't entirely sure.

Rapid heartbeats slowed, breathing steadied, she sat up in the seat. The coach moved at pace. It wouldn't be stopped now. She'd passed the first hurdle and made it out of town. From here on out, she'd be anonymous, no need to worry about local busybodies.

She afforded herself a little smile. Maybe she could make the journey after all.

A digital information board hung from the ceiling. It gave time estimates to each of the stops:

Dukebury - 40 Mins

Bashinghill - 1 Hr 15 Mins

Ailton - 2 Hrs 10 Mins

Carrion City - 3 Hrs 30 Mins

Carrion City University Campus (CCU) - 3 Hrs 50 Mins

Ashtown - 4 Hrs 30 Mins

Solhvor - 5 Hrs 10 Mins

Through bloodshot eyes, Olivia read the times on the board. She hadn't got enough sleep the night before. She'd been sleeping less and less every night recently. Maybe it was part of whatever changes she was going through. No way to know for certain, there was no one to tell her.

Not ready for sleep yet, she took the time to recheck everything in her wallet and backpack. It all seemed to be still there, save for one object she couldn't find. Where was the buck knife, had she forgotten it, had it fallen out? Her mind conjured up the image of the girl in the video again, like a specter haunting her. Panicked fingers probed every corner of the bag before they finally settled on a hard object in one of the pairs of socks. Fishing her hand inside the sock, her skin touched the cold steel of her father's buck knife. It was reassuring.

Like some kind of magical talisman, just touching it temporarily banished the girl in the video from her mind. Retracting her hand, she zipped up the backpack and put it back on the seat next to her. Using her foot, she flicked the footrest down from the seat in front and put her feet up. It would be a long ride.

Rolling green hills flicked past the coach window. Morning had broken. Shafts of winter sun managed to cut through the oncoming storm clouds and light the cattle fields as they whipped past the window. It was hypnotic. Slumped in her chair, the tiredness from the lack of sleep the night before overcame her, and she drifted off.

Light feet bound through the forest, twigs snap, branches whip. Breathless, heart pounding, running on empty, turn to see who's pursuing, find nothing. *Keep running, don't stop.* Running again, lungs ready to explode. *Can't stop. Can't stop.* A clearing ahead, legs weak, failing. *Have to make it.* Running again, full pelt, a hand reaches out and grabs…

A loud hiss of brakes releasing woke Olivia from her nightmare with a start. Her heart thumped hard in her chest. A hand shook her. Instinctively, she grabbed the wrist belonging to it in a vice-like grip. Eyes adjusted to the waking world, the wrist was attached to a young man, maybe nineteen or twenty years old. He looked friendly enough and just seemed to want to sit down. Olivia released his wrist.

"Sorry, didn't mean to startle you. Could you move your bag? There are no free seats," he said.

Olivia popped her head up to survey the coach. It had almost entirely filled up while she slept. The only other free seat aside from the one her bag sat on was across the aisle. It was occupied by a haggard-looking bum sleeping in a trench coat and hat, a bottle of unknown booze in a brown paper bag cradled in his arm like a baby.

"There's a seat over there," Olivia replied, gesturing to the empty seat next to the sleeping bum.

"He smells of piss," the young man whispered.

Olivia cracked a smile at his frankness. She took her bag from the seat and put it on the ground at her feet.

"Thanks," he said with a smile.

As he maneuvered into the seat, she took a good look at him. His mop of wavy black hair was a little out of fashion. Most guys Olivia's age had side cuts. It didn't matter. The guy was damn good-looking no matter what hairstyle he sported. Sharp-jawed, good skin, dark brown eyes, a casting director’s dream.

He looked like the kind of clean-cut wholesome guy a girl in a romantic comedy would spurn in the first act but have fallen madly in love with by the end of the third. Aware she stared, Olivia turned and looked forward at nothing.

"Long Journey?" he broke the silence after a few minutes.

"Long enough, I guess."

"It's just you were fast asleep."

"Yeah, my mother lives in Basinghill. I was down visiting for a few days. It's a bit of a trek."

Olivia lied on the fly, something she generally only did with her parents or teachers. She tried to make her voice sound serious, more adult, a little deeper.

"Oh, so where do you live?" he inquired.

"Ashtown."

"Ouch. You're right, that is a trek."

"You?" Olivia asked, trying to change the focus of the conversation to him.

"Mercifully, my journey's short. I go to college at CCU. It's just down the road. You go to Ashtown Tech? Maybe I've seen you at some of the games?"

"Unlikely. I don't go to college. I work in a club."

"Oh, that's cool. Me and my friends always go up to Ashtown for the winter festival. What club do you work in?"

Olivia squirmed inside at the probing questions. For him, it was just idle chit-chat but, for her, it was dangerous. The more lies she had to tell, the more her bullshit might catch up with her. Someone might overhear, get suspicious at the inconsistencies.

"You ask an awful lot of questions," Olivia said in a sharp, cutting tone.

"Sorry, I'm a talker. My friends sometimes have to tell me to shut up 'cause I ramble a little."

The guy looked genuinely hurt at Olivia's sudden change of tone. His deep brown eyes looked sad, and he diverted them to stare at the back of the seat in front of him. Olivia felt like she'd just kicked an adorable but annoying puppy.

"Sorry, I'm just groggy, and I'm pissed I have to work tonight. I didn't mean to snap at you," she said.

"Hey, I understand. I didn't mean to make you feel uncomfortable asking so many questions."

He gave Olivia a disarming smile, and she returned it in kind.

"If you really wanna know, it's a club called the Sandman. It's pretty popular."

Olivia was a decent enough liar, she generally built her lies around some grain of truth or at least something she knew enough to bluff about. She'd been to 'The Sandman' before, she and her friends had snuck out to go drinking there when they were on a school field trip in Ashtown. The place was huge and a popular tourist trap, so they had a lot of staff.

"Oh, I know it. It's the one with a bridge that goes over one of the dance floors."

"That's the place," she said.

"Must be exciting working at a club like that."

"Not when you're sober and you can smell the stale beer and puke in the carpet it's not."

He broke out into a little laugh, and so did Olivia. Lying was becoming more natural. His deep brown eyes were warm and stared into hers for a brief moment.

"CCU campus, all passengers for CCU campus," came the coach driver's voice over the speaker.

A lot of the other passengers got their bags ready, some making their way to the front of the coach, but the young man didn't stir.

"Isn't this your stop?" Olivia asked him.

"Oh, shoot. My head's all over the place."

Grabbing his bag, he stood up and got out into the aisle, then turned to Olivia.

"My name's David, by the way."

"Anna," Olivia responded after a split-second's hesitation. "Nice to meet you."

The two shook hands.

"Next time I'm in Ashtown, I'll have to drop into the Sandman to say hello," he said as he walked down the aisle.

"Yeah, I'll fix you a drink."

David winked at Olivia, put his bag on his shoulder, and filtered off the coach with the rest of the passengers. The doors closed. The coach moved on. She sat there with a little smile on her face. The chat with David had made her forget her problems, for a little while, at least. Being Anna was easier than being Olivia.

A light flurry of snowflakes fell, big flakes swirling gently in the wind like they danced to some unseen tune. As the coach picked up speed and entered open countryside, the snow intensified and built up in little clumps in the corner of all the windows.

The bus had shed more than half its passengers when it stopped at the university. The drunk in the seat opposite was still present, though. If not totally in mind, then at least in body, a body which reeked of fruit schnapps of some description. He muttered to himself in the fashion bums are wont to do. Olivia did her best to ignore him, staring blankly at the seat in front of her so as not to draw his attention.

"Little shit…you stink of piss…" he muttered to no one in particular.

Don't look over at the crazy man. Don't look over at the crazy man. Involuntarily, she glanced over at him and instantly regretted it. Her eyes locked with his for a fraction of a second, just long enough to give him an opening.

"Hey, can you help out a war veteran with five bucks, young lady?" he began. "I can tell you a good story in exchange."

Dressed in a dark brown trench coat and wide-brimmed hat, he looked like a drifter from an old western. Face like weathered leather, full of creases and folds, like he'd spent more than a few nights at the mercy of the elements in his time. Slumped in the seat, his frame didn't seem particularly tall or imposing, but something suggested he could handle himself even in his drunken state.

The smell of schnapps was more potent when he spoke. His blood-alcohol level might have killed a lesser human, but he didn't slur a single word. When he'd finished speaking, he tipped his hat with a prosthetic claw hand.

"Sorry, I can't help you." Olivia pulled her backpack in close and stared at the seat in front.

"OK, that's no problem, ma'am. Thank you for your time. But I gotta tell ya, this could have been the most important story of your life."

He slumped back in his chair and took a swig from his bottle. Olivia sat there contemplating the bum's grandiose claim. *Fuck would his story be important to anyone?* It niggled at her. Was it just a ploy he used on everyone to get money?

"This story of yours, what's it about?" she asked.

"It's about people I see and things I hear while I'm riding this bus."

"That's it? How would that be the most important story of my life?"

"Well, maybe the things I hear would be important to someone like you."

What does he mean like you*?* Olivia was concerned now. Something in his voice sounded like a warning. Not wanting him to see how much money she had in her wallet, she turned into the corner of her seat for privacy before producing a crumpled five-dollar bill. The bum's eyes gleamed like he looked at the pearl of the world. He reached out to take the note, but it was quickly retracted by Olivia.

"This story of yours, it's gonna be worth it, right? 'Cause I can't afford to waste this money."

"Trust me, it'll be worth it."

Holding out the note, the bum plucked it from her hand, then slumped back into his seat.

"So?" she asked.

"Your pretty new friend."

"David?"

"Yeah, the kid who said I stank of piss, which I don't."

"True, you don't, but you do smell of schnapps."

"That's fair."

"David, what about him? You know him or something?"

"So, I get this bus almost every day," the bum said.

"Why?"

"It's warm and comfortable. Keeps me out of the snow during winter. For some of the day, at least."

"How the hell can you afford it?"

"Wounded veterans pass. I travel free everywhere. 'Bout the only good thing our piece-of-shit government ever did for us after the war."

Olivia was a little taken aback by someone openly calling the government pieces-of-shit. It just wasn't done in her world, certainly not since the CFU were in power.

"You fight in the Final War or something?"

He laughed a sad little laugh. Olivia observed him, trying to figure him out.

"Yeah, I fought. You know the vampires called it The Third Vampireo-Human War. I guess they have longer memories than us."

The drunk's mood turned somber for a moment, and he stared into space as if he was remembering something.

"So, David?" Olivia asked, trying to steer him back on track, conscious she'd paid five bucks for the conversation.

"Oh, yeah," he began. "So, I see that same kid on this route pretty often. He seems to spark up a conversation with someone every time I see him."

"So? He goes to college on this route. Makes sense you'd see him, and he seems to a bit of a talker."

"Yeah maybe. Except I remember distinctly seeing him about six ago, he sat down next to another young guy, much less pretty than him, and they sparked up a conversation. Except he had a completely different story than the one he just told you."

Olivia's face turned deadly serious at the new information. Her mind raced. David had seemed so genuine, friendly, disarming.

"What'd he say to this other guy?"

"Claimed he tended bar in the Coal Bunker. You know where the Coal Bunker is?" he asked Olivia.

"No."

"You should. It's down an alleyway beside the Sandman. The place you claimed you work at," he quietly informed her with a wink.

Her face lost all color. She quickly popped her head up and glanced around the bus, hoping none of the other passengers further up the aisle heard what he'd said.

"Relax, I ain't shoutin'," he reassured her.

"You sure it was the same guy talking to me just now? You might've made a mistake. You do like a drink."

"I was designated marksman for my platoon, I didn't mistake shit. It was him."

The bum looked genuinely hurt at the accusation that he might have made a mistake while under the influence. Clearly, he still had some pride, and Olivia had just offended it.

"OK, so it was him. He was talkin' to this other guy. Did he say anything else?"

"I could only hear fragments of the conversation. I was a couple of rows back, but I picked up the general tone of most of it."

"Tone?" Olivia asked.

"He was sweet talkin' him, same as he was with you just now."

"Bullshit."

"His voice was a little lighter, his mannerism a little more effeminate, but it was him, no mistake."

"And this Coal Bunker?"

"It's a fag bar."

"You're sure?"

"Yeah, used to go there myself when I was a younger man, before the war. It didn't have a sign back then, you had to knock to get in. You could take a beatin' just for being seen walking out of a place like that back then."

"So, David, you think he's…"

"…whatever he needs to be on any given day," the bum finished Olivia's sentence for her.

Anger and fear rose in her. The emotions flowed from her brain to her heart, and it beat steadily faster. She'd been played, she could see it now. She'd tripped at the first hurdle. How bad was the damage, how much danger had she put herself in just to appease a pretty face?

"So what? I've got nothing to hide," Olivia tried to act nonchalant about the whole thing, but her face betrayed her. It burned with a quiet rage.

"If you say so. But if I had to guess, I'd say he knew you were lying to him at the very least. But people lie for a lot of reasons, maybe you're just runnin' away from home."

"I didn't lie."

"He knows."

"He doesn't know shit, and neither do you," Olivia responded, angry now.

"You hesitated."

"I hesitated?"

"Yeah, you hesitated, just for a split-second when you told him your name was Anna. Long enough that I picked up on it, so he probably did, too. If you're gonna use a fake name, you gotta drill it into your mind till you forget your real one," the bum schooled her.

"And that hesitation, that'd be enough to raise suspicion?"

"Enough to put you on his radar, yeah. But as I said, people lie for a lot of reasons. He might not know why in your case."

"How do I know you're not in cahoots with him, this isn't some kinda shitty double-act?"

"Guess you don't," the bum answered, shrugging without letting go of his schnapps bottle.

Lying to the bum wasn't the same as lying to her parents, it was the big leagues. He probably lied every day to survive. She couldn't pull the wool over his eyes, so she stopped trying.

"You coulda warned me he was a problem before I started talking to him."

"Look," he began, "nobody's gonna bat an eyelid if some old drunk washes up dead on a riverbank 'cause he stuck his nose where it wasn't wanted. But I did warn you. After the fact, when it was safer, true, but I'm still taking that risk to some degree."

The bum's face sank with shame, he seemed to be wrestling with his conscience, trying to justify the decision to Olivia and himself. Maybe as a younger man, he might have openly stood up to people like David, but not anymore. Nobody wanted to challenge the religious powers anymore. People were afraid. She looked into his eyes. They looked sad and tired, just an old man trying to survive.

"You did warn me. I guess that counts for something…even if it did cost me five dollars," said Olivia.

"A man's gotta eat, and that last kid I told you about, he haggled. He only paid two-fifty."

"Great, I got ripped off, too."

"They might have a bead on you now, so I'll give you the same advice I gave that other kid. Change up your appearance the first chance you get, make it dramatic so you look unrecognizable. Try to avoid lying. Bribing people is easier. They ask fewer questions. If you do have to lie, commit to it, don't hesitate, believe the bullshit yourself."

Olivia had a look of deep concentration on her face as she listened to the drunk's 101 class in street survival. It might have been the most important lecture of her life.

"Do I get anything extra for the other two-fifty?" Olivia asked.

The drunk paused for a moment, his eyes glazed over, and he looked out the window as he fished in his semi-inebriated brain for something useful to tell her. Eventually, his face hardened, and he looked at her with deep lines etched in his face.

"If you're cornered and you have to stab someone, aim for the chest or neck and make sure you twist the blade before you pull it out. After that, you won't need to worry about that person ever again. Long as they're human, that is."

His tone of voice became colder as he spoke like a memory had sobered him up for a few seconds. Olivia was enraptured with his advice but was confused at his comment, 'As long as they're human.'

"Weren't you just fighting Vampires during the Final War?" she asked.

"War's complicated, gray, hard to tell who the good guys are, or if you're even one of them. I guess they don't teach you about that kinda stuff in school."

Afraid to probe into the veteran's oblique answer, she accepted it for what it sounded like. There may have been some infighting or power struggle on the human side during the war.

How much of what she was told in school were lies, how much of it was bullshit papering over the unpalatable cracks in history?

"You don't hate…you know, because of the war?" Olivia asked.

"Vampires? No, gave up my hate of your kind a long time ago. Now, I just need to stop hating myself."

Olivia sprung her head up like some desert rodent looking for birds of prey, terrified someone had heard him. No one was within earshot to care about their conversation.

"They're not my kind. I don't know what the hell you're talking about," she scolded him in a hushed voice.

"Sure, whatever you say."

They sat in awkward silence for a while. Olivia was annoyed at how the old veteran could see straight through her lies but didn't seem to care. For his part, the bum seemed a little repentant he had come straight out and called her a vampire.

"If you never miss a thing, how'd you lose the arm?" Olivia asked in an awkward attempt to break the silence.

"This?" the bum raised his prosthetic claw arm. "Good old-fashioned frostbite. Neither side won that war, winter beat us both. Our bodies froze, and so did their tanks. You should've brought more warm weather clothes if you're going far north. It gets colder than you can imagine up there."

"I'm not going far north," Olivia replied confidently.

"That's good. You're starting to sound like you believe it yourself."

The bum smiled to himself, happy Olivia was already putting his advice to good use.

"You have a name?"

"Guys in my unit used to call me Barrow. It's not my real name, but I've been using it so long it might as well be."

"Well, I'm Anna. Nice to meet you, Barrow."

"Nice you meet you, too, Anna, but I'm guessing that no matter what happens, this will be our first and last meeting."

"Never say never, as my dad likes to say."

The bum chuckled at the comment as he slumped into his chair again, preparing for sleep, seemingly content he had imparted at least some advice that might keep her alive.

"You want me to wake you when we get to Ashtown?" she asked.

"Naw, I'm gonna ride to the end of the line. It's cold out, and I can't rub my hands together to keep warm."

One-handed, homeless, and still laughing at the world. Would she still have a sense of humor after all this was over? Barrow slumped in his seat and slipped into some state between sleep and alcohol-induced stupor. Olivia turned her attention back to the window. Snow slowly built outside, swirling in tiny whirlwinds. Mercifully, the roads were still clear. The gritters must have been out that morning.

Barely visible through the snow, she could see black plumes pouring from smokestacks, the first sign of the city of Ashtown on the horizon. She felt reassured even after the run-in with David. It was a big city. Even if people were looking for her, she could blend in. She'd heed Barrow's advice, change how she looked, plan an alternate route.

Unable to sleep, she stared out the window as tall industrial buildings grew on the horizon. *My name's Anna Jankowski, I'm twenty, I'm from Basinghill. I'm Sarah Walshe. I'm eighteen. I just moved here from Deep Valley. I'm looking for work. Name's Kara De Jong. I'm nineteen, I study at CCU, Accountancy and Business Administration.* She tried a dozen different names and lies to go with them, rolled them over in her head, and repeated them over and over until they sounded convincing, then she asked herself mock questions. *Where'd you go to school? I was homeschooled. Where are you going? Eisenberg. A cousin has a job lined up for me at a manufacturing plant. Where are your parents? Ha, I must be doing something right if I still look that young.*

As Olivia practiced her lies, the coach slowly cut its way into the city. Monstrous constructions of redbrick stained with two hundred years of soot and ash towered over the coach. The cities name was well-earned. Ashtown was founded near the coal mines in the surrounding hills.

Factories sprung up, and the city grew, sucking in all the rural settlers with the promise of jobs and a better life. The last coal mines stopped being viable about twenty years ago, and the city suffered. It hemorrhaged jobs and was now a shadow of its former glory.

Few industries survived in the city, but it was still a hotspot for tourists and people who wanted to party, its nightlife notorious. The governing CFU was trying to crack down on its bars and clubs, said the city was a den of sin. They wanted to sanitize the place, cut away its seedier underbelly and leave only the tourist sites. So far, the city had managed to maintain its independent spirit.

"Ashtown," called the bus driver over the loudspeaker.

The coach pulled into a bay at an enormous bus terminal. Tired passengers wrestled with their possessions. Only a few seemed to stay onboard to the final stop. Olivia got up, slung her bag over her shoulder, and pulled up the hood on her hoodie. Barrow lay slumbering. She nodded at him in thanks before filing off the bus with the others.

The City

Snow fell in large flakes, two inches or so covering the ground. Olivia's sneakers were close to useless, so she tried to stay on the parts of the sidewalk that had been cleared. It was the middle of the day, but the streets of the old town area were still busy, locals going about their business mixed with a smattering of tourists.

You could spot the tourists a mile away. Like Olivia, they weren't dressed properly for the biting cold. The last time she was in Ashtown, it was summer. She knew it would be cold this time, but nothing prepared her for the biting wind cutting at her face. The light parka in her backpack would help, but she didn't want to be seen putting it on. She had a plan for it.

Paranoid, she glanced behind her every few seconds. Was someone following her? She didn't know. Every face covered and uncovered could have been watching. A young man in a beanie with a scar on his face, an older man smoking a cigarette. What about girls? Did she need to look out for them, too?

Don't panic and do something stupid to give yourself away. It won't happen here. They want you alone, somewhere secluded. She had to be unpredictable, couldn't just go straight to the train station. People might be waiting.

A large signpost at the end of the street showed points of interest for pedestrians. Pointing east was a sign for the central train station, north for the river ferry terminal and Martyrs' Bridge, a famous tourist attraction. To the west, the sign read 'Mayhew

Street,' but underneath in parentheses was written 'The Street of Thirst.' Olivia went west at the crosswalk, heading toward The Street of Thirst.

About sixty years ago, a satirist who thought he was far funnier than he actually was gave Mayhew Street its nickname, The Street of Thirst, on account of it having so many drinking establishments. Maybe it was funnier at the time, or maybe it was always a shit joke, but the name stuck either way. It was a mile-long pedestrian street packed with tall redbrick buildings like most of the rest of the old town.

Bar after bar, nightclub after nightclub, only broken up by the odd fast-food joint or convenience store. If it was summer, the bars would already be busy with tourists, sitting out front drinking in the sun. That's how Olivia remembered the place looking, not grim and depressing like it was now.

Olivia's feet hurt from the cold. She'd been walking for a while, but she was getting close. Eventually, she arrived at an impressive-looking five-story building that loomed over the others. It had an elaborate façade of almost jet-black brick, the claim being they hadn't cleaned the soot off the bricks since the building was constructed two hundred years ago.

Currently unlit, a massive neon sign depicting a man holding an umbrella with the words 'The Sandman' under it took up at least a quarter of the façade. The place was a landmark for the city, and people came from all over to see it. A smattering of tourists took photos of the sign, and then wandered inside. There were no bouncers on duty on account of it being off-season. Olivia walked in without any hesitation like she worked there.

The plan wasn't particularly complex, but it was threefold. First, she had told David she worked at the Sandman. If someone was following her, and the first place she went was the Sandman, it might be enough to throw them off the scent if they were already on the fence about her story. Second, she could use the bathrooms to put on her parka to change her appearance, at least a little. Third, the place was big enough that it had multiple entrances, so she could slip out a different one than she came in.

Inside, the place was huge, furnished in dark wood, with multiple bars and dance floors spread across its five floors. It wasn't too busy but, luckily, there were just enough tourists in the place to give Olivia cover to move. She made her way up a flight of wooden stairs to the first floor. From there, she could see down from a balcony area to the floor below. Her eyes scanned the patrons, none seemed to be paying her any attention at all.

Maybe you're just being paranoid. Maybe Barrow was full of shit. Maybe David was just a nice wholesome guy who thought you were cute. Or maybe whoever's following you is good at it and doesn't get spotted easily. Maybe they're biding their time, and since when do you attract nice wholesome guys anyway. Why didn't you keep your dumb mouth shut?

A sign nearby indicated the bathrooms, so she made her way toward them but took one last look at the floor below, an attempt to see if anyone had moved toward the stairs when she turned her back. Nothing, just dumb-ass tourists touristing.

An automatic fluorescent light flickered on as Olivia entered the bathroom. For such a popular establishment, the toilets were badly maintained, many of the tiles were broken and one of the cubicle doors kicked in. Maybe that was supposed to be part of the rustic charm of places like the Sandman, hovering over the toilet bowl while you took a dump.

Of the two cubicles with intact doors, the one on the left looked cleanest. *I'll take door number one, please.* She awkwardly squeezed into the cubicle with her backpack and slid the latch to the locked position. Still shivering from the cold, she moved as quickly as the tight space would allow. Putting the toilet lid down, she sat on it, opened her backpack, took out the parka, and put it on. Moving onto her numb feet, she took off her sneakers. Her socks were soaking wet, so she took them off as well and put them in a side pocket of her bag.

Taking care not to touch her feet on the grimy floor, she took two fresh pairs of socks from the backpack. One of the socks contained the buck knife, she took it out and put it in her pocket. She put both pairs of socks on her feet, hoping the extra layer would keep her feet a little warmer, at least until she could get on the train.

As she was about to put her sneakers back on, she heard the door to the bathroom open. Someone walked inside. Correction, two someones. One set of footsteps was heavier than the other. Olivia froze. It was probably nothing, just people looking to use the bathroom. She gripped the knife in her pocket silently deliberating whether to put on her sneakers or not.

Making her choice, she left the sneakers on the ground and quietly pulled her feet up to her body to hide them. The footsteps walked toward the cubicles. One of them was a man, the steps too heavy for a woman. She panicked. What the hell was a man doing in the women's bathrooms? The lighter of the two people bent down, just enough to see under the gap at the bottom of the cubicle door. They were checking for feet. All they'd see was Olivia's empty sneakers, but it might be enough. *It's them. Oh, fuck, it's them.* She sat like a statue, the buck knife held in a death-grip in her pocket. No movement, no breathing, just waiting for the kick at the door, but it didn't come, not yet.

"There's an empty pair of sneakers," came the faintest whisper of a woman's voice on the other side of the door.

The woman was clearly talking to the man. Somehow, in her hyper-focused state, Olivia could make out the whisper perfectly.

"Probably left behind by some junkie," the man whispered back.

"They look too clean to be a junkie's, and the door's locked. I think someone's actually in there," the woman replied.

Olivia's eyes burned wild. They had her cornered, there was no escape. The only chance would be to fight her way out now.

"Anyone in there?" the man spoke clearly now, addressing Olivia's cubicle door. She didn't respond.

"Nothing, so are we doing this or not?" the man addressed the woman, not bothering to whisper anymore.

"OK," the woman responded.

Olivia took the buck knife out of her pocket and extended the blade, but not enough so that it made a sound locking into position. She wanted to keep silent until the last second. For all they knew, they were kicking in the door of an empty cubicle with some discarded sneakers. Olivia waited for the kick like a cornered rat. It would come any second now.

She'd have to do the unthinkable now, go for the neck on the guy. The woman seemed unsure of herself. She might lose her nerve once she saw her partner get stabbed. *Don't think about it, just do it!* Movement. The footsteps moved, but they didn't kick Olivia's door in. Instead, the two fumbled into the adjoining cubicle and locked the door behind them.

Olivia used the noise as cover to lock the blade into position. What the hell were they up to? Were they gonna come over the top of the cubicle? She could almost feel their hearts beating, the only thing separating them being the thin partition wall. She held the blade above her head, ready to stab at any face foolish enough to peer over the top. Rustling, the sound of a small plastic bag, then tapping, then a low snorting sound, then more snorting.

The expression of abject terror on Olivia's face melted away, replaced with disbelief. *Assholes! Who the hell takes cocaine at 2 PM on a fuckin' weekday?*

"Fuck, that's good," said the woman on the other side of the cubicle.

The couple clearly occupied, Olivia folded the blade into its handle and put it back into her bag. She sat there and waited in silence, not wanting to let them know she was there all along. The couple's hearts seemed to be beating much faster now, the cocaine in their systems. Could she really hear them at this distance or was it just her mind playing tricks.

Maybe it was possible. She knew nothing about the physical changes her body was going through. Maybe it was some hunting instinct vampires had. As Olivia considered the magnitude of the physical changes her body might be undergoing, her thought process was interrupted by an unzipping sound from the other cubicle.

You gotta be kidding me.

Jeans were being pulled down, then a small delay, and a slurping sound began. Olivia had stayed silent through everything, but she'd be damned if she was gonna sit there and listen to a messy coked-up blowjob in a dirty toilet cubicle. Making as much noise as possible, she put on her sneakers, zipped up her bag, and unlocked the door. The couple in the other cubicle went deathly silent.

Seconds earlier, Olivia had been working up the courage to stab someone. Now, she could only laugh at the situation as she walked out of the bathroom. Maybe the couple would find it funny later on but, for now, they stayed perfectly silent.

Not wanting to have an awkward run-in with the couple if they emerged from the bathroom, she decided to leave the area as quickly as possible. Olivia made her way down to the ground floor via a different set of stairs. She opened a set of heavy doors and emerged into an interior courtyard smoking area. Overhead were dark wooden beams strung with the type of old-fashioned incandescent bulbs that adorned every hipster bar, restaurant, and nightclub in the country.

Above the beams was a small aperture in the ceiling, maybe five feet wide that legally speaking made it an outdoor smoking area. A couple of people sat smoking on a dilapidated sofa near a tall gas heater that resembled a metal tree. Consumed in their conversation, they paid no attention to Olivia. At a tiny bar in the corner, a brunette in her mid-thirties flirted with the bartender who was at least fifteen years her junior, alcohol bridging the age gap.

Another gas heater burned away unloved near an empty pair of torn chesterfield style armchairs. Her Face still freezing cold, the heater called to Olivia the same way it might call to a confused moth. She wandered over almost instinctively and slumped into one of the comfy chairs. *Just five minutes to warm up. Have a smoke, you'll look less suspicious.*

Rummaging in a side pocket of her bag, she produced the pack of cigarettes. Butler's Lights, the favored brand of teenagers and social smokers who weren't quite sure of themselves. Olivia took out a smoke and put it in her mouth but didn't light it. Instead, she just let it sit on her lips while she basked in the warm glow of the heater like a lizard.

Eventually, she took out her cheap plastic lighter, lit it, and brought the flame up to the cigarette. As she drew the smoke into her lungs, the sensation triggered a memory. She'd been to the

Sandman before, obviously, but only now did she remember this very room.

As Olivia's memory blended with reality, the cheap plastic lighter in front of her changed to a storm lighter with a perfect spike of a blue flame igniting her cigarette. It was being held by Angie McAvoy, who had a smile on her face. The place was packed with people. It was early in the summer and hot as hell. Everyone was drenched in sweat, but nobody cared. Amber and Jasmine were over at the bar harassing the inexperienced bartender. Olivia and Sara were hanging out with two guys who looked underage, too, but neither group wanted to admit it.

Sara was vigorously making out with one of the guys she'd set her sights on earlier that night. She'd convinced Olivia to keep talking to his friend even though she had no interest in him. Angie acted as something of a third wheel. Olivia had asked her to stick around so she wouldn't have to talk to the guy alone. As the night progressed and her unwanted partner got drunker, he tried to put the moves on Olivia. She was having none of it and gave him the dreaded side-face when he went in for a poorly attempted kiss. Firmly rejected, her suitor leaned back against the wall, annoyed.

"Slut," he said under his breath.

"Fuck you call me?" Olivia spat back at him.

"The fuck you say to her?" Angie seconded the thought.

Sara and her date were still mauling each other like a pair of wild animals, unaware of the brewing storm two feet away. The drunk guy lurched forward to go to another part of the bar.

"You've been wasting my time all night, you and your ginger dyke friend," he said as he barged past Olivia.

What happened next took only a heartbeat. Sensing what was coming, the guy raised his hands in a defensive posture, but he was too late. Angie hit him in the face with a clean right hook. His body fell like it was made of jelly, a nearby chair breaking his fall and protecting his head.

Olivia had never seen someone knocked out like that. Sure, she'd seen people faint, but this was different. He was out cold. Angie looked at Olivia like, 'I didn't mean to hit him that hard.' An agonizing few seconds passed, other people in the bar started to notice, gasping. Sara and the guy's friend broke their embrace.

"What the hell happened? Charlie, are you OK?" his friend asked as he barged over to check on him.

To both Angie and Olivia's relief, the unconscious guy started to come around and was talking to his friend.

"Did you just pass out?" his friend asked him, confused at the situation.

The commotion had raised attention. Olivia spotted two colossal bouncers entering the room. They barged their way through the crowd of people like they were ragdolls. Olivia grabbed Angie and Sara by the arms and dragged them toward Amber and Jasmine at the bar.

"He's fine, he's fine, but we need to leave, right fucking now!" Olivia told Sara.

"What the fuck did you morons do?" Sara asked.

"Nothing he didn't deserve," Olivia told her.

Grabbing amber and Jasmine, they pushed their way toward a side exit. People pointed at them as they barged through. One of the bouncers broke off from helping the guy who'd been knocked unconscious and fought his way through the crowd to get to the girls.

Reaching the side door, the girls burst out into the humid night and sprinted up The Street of Thirst. The bouncer emerged at the door, but seeing them running away, decided not to give chase. Somewhere along The Street of Thirst, the girls ran out of steam, half-drunk, half-exhausted. Confident no one was following them, they slowed to a walk.

"You mind telling us what all that was about?" Jasmine asked.

"Angie knocked a guy out," Olivia told Jasmine and Amber.

"What the fuck, Angie!" said Sara.

"He called me a slut and Angie a dyke," Olivia informed the group.

"It doesn't matter. You can't just knock people the fuck out because they call you names," Sara responded.

"I dunno, it seemed like a punchable offense to me," said Olivia.

"Well, it's not, and she ruined everyone's night," Sara spoke for the rest of the group, who remained silent.

"Come on, Sara. You're just annoyed because you're not getting fingered by his friend right now," said Olivia, half-drunk.

Amber and Jasmine burst out laughing. Sara boiled with rage. Even Angie looked surprised Olivia had decided to challenge Sara so openly.

"You know what," Sara began, "that guy was right. She's probably a dyke. Why do you think she's always hanging around you like a bad smell and not off looking for a guy herself? How can you not see it?"

"Fuck you?" Angie swore at Sara.

"You wish," Sara responded.

It was the final straw. Angie lunged for Sara. Olivia got in the way and tried to hold Angie back as best she could, barely capable, but she sensed Angie wasn't using her full strength. Sara laughed at Angie, mocking her. Amber and Jasmine, sensing the danger, pulled Sara away up the street, splitting the group. Olivia and Angie waited a while, giving the others time to walk far ahead, time for heads to cool.

The pair marched in silence through the summer crowds of revelers. Neither wanted to break the silence between them. Was what Sara said true? Did it matter if it was? Here in Ashtown, none of that stuff seemed to matter. You could be who you wanted to be, but at home in Greenfields, it was important. People judged you. If you hung around with certain people, you were guilty by association.

But Angie had always been there for Olivia, through thick and thin, Sara was fine, but she wasn't dependable. She'd abandon you for some guy at the drop of a hat. Maybe it was the booze, or the fact she was outside of the bubble of her hometown, but Olivia decided she didn't give a damn what Angie was or wasn't. She was her friend, one willing to throw a punch for her, and that's all that mattered.

"Hey, thanks for sticking up for me. The guy was asking for it," said Olivia.

Both the girls laughed out loud.

"Yeah, I guess he was," Angie replied.

"Don't worry about Sara. She'll calm down once she moves onto the next guy."

"Yeah, I don't know about that."

The next morning, as they tried to hide hangovers from their teachers, apologies were made. Sara claimed to have been so drunk she couldn't even remember what she'd said. No one in the group truly believed it but, silently, they all accepted the selective drunken amnesia excuse as if nothing had really happened. But something *had* happened.

The group was never the same after that trip. Angie was never the same, and neither was Olivia. Even before Angie’s brother went missing, the other girls were subtly pushing Angie and

Olivia out of the group. Backhanded complements given, party invites forgotten.

But Olivia stuck through it with Angie. They were friends, would always be friends. Until Angie's brother went missing, that is. It was different. It wasn't just some catty girls at school ostracizing Angie. It was Olivia's mother forbidding her from seeing Angie. It was Angie's family not coming to church anymore. It was the whole town ostracizing Angie and her family.

Olivia wished she'd had the strength to ignore all of them. Wished she kept hanging out with Angie despite everything. Wished she'd called her to see if she was OK after her brother went missing. Most of all, Olivia wished she was a better person, but she wasn't.

A loud cackle of laughter snapped Olivia out of her now toxic memories, the brunette leaning on the bar was still being entertained by the bartender. Standing up, Olivia took one last long draw of her cigarette. *Time to face the cold.* With that, she put her bag on her back and walked over to a wall-mounted ashtray. As she stubbed out her cigarette, something caught her eye.

Set on a side table filled with ashtrays and cleaning products was a bartender's apron with the logo of the Sandman on it. The nametag was still attached and reflected in the light like it was some precious gemstone. It called to Olivia. If she was caught and had to lie the apron would corroborate her story at least at a surface level. Even if it only bought her a little time, it might make all the difference.

Take it.

The bartender still absorbed with the brunette wasn't paying much attention. Olivia took out her cellphone and pretended to be taking tourist snaps of the ornate wooden beams with their hipster lights. As she snapped photos, she backed toward the apron, finally snatching it with her right hand and awkwardly stuffing it into the pocket of her parka. Glancing around, no one seemed to have noticed her crime. Her heart raced as she pushed open the side door and walked out into the cold.

It was still steadily snowing, but the deserted side street was somewhat sheltered. In front of her was a small alleyway. At its end, there was a wooden signpost depicting a caricature of a bare-chested coal miner above what looked like a basement club. The sign read, 'The Coal Bunker.' Last time she'd exited the Sandman, she was in something of a hurry and didn't notice much, but she noticed now. Now, the detail in almost everything was important, especially if those details kept her alive.

At the very least, some of Barrow's story checked out. She wondered if David could really be a member of a purification squad. He seemed so genuine and disarming. It didn't matter. Either way, she had to have eyes in the back of her head and assume people were looking for her.

She took the stolen apron out of her pocket and took a quick look before stuffing it into her bag. The nametag read, 'Mary.' A woman's name. A fifty-fifty coin flip had gone her way. Maybe it was fate. Smiling, she pulled up the hood on her parka and zipped it all the way to the top so it covered most of her face. Warmer, safer, just another set of eyes in the snow, faceless, anonymous.

To be sure, she took a different route back to the train station. She got a little lost along the way, but nothing too time-consuming. Just breaking through the clouds, the sun hung low in the sky. As she rounded a corner, the enormous wrought iron and glass roof of the terminal came into view. Goal in sight, Olivia powered her way forward and eventually made her way into the terminal.

Most of the roof was covered in snow, but some stubborn shafts of light still managed to project through the iron and glass roof, illuminating the atrium with the last of the day's winter sun. As Olivia entered, a security guard gestured to her and pointed at a sign, it had a pictogram of a covered face with and large X through it. *So much for anonymity.* She pulled down the hood on her parka and unzipped it so her face was visible.

The station was thronged with people crisscrossing in every direction. In the center of the atrium lay the main information desk, a large crowd gathered near it. They gesticulated at two security guards, who tried to placate them. Olivia made a beeline for the main ticket kiosks at the far-left-hand side of the hall.

There were plenty of kiosks, so the queues weren't so bad. Olivia joined one and shuffled her way forward with the rest of the travelers. Eventually, she got to the kiosk. Behind the grimy plexiglass was a plump, somber-looking woman wearing big round glasses with vibrant red frames.

"How can I help you today?" she asked flatly through the mic.

"I need an express ticket to Overton, please. How long does the journey usually take?" Olivia asked in as adult a voice as she could manage.

"Ten hours and twenty minutes, but you're not leaving today."

"What?"

"The service to Overton is canceled till tomorrow at the earliest."

"Why?"

"I'm not sure. We just got word ourselves about ten minutes ago, but no reason was given. You'll need to talk to the Northern Star representative near the information desk. He'll have more information for you." The woman pointed over toward the large group of people Olivia had seen milling around the information desk.

Internally, Olivia was having a meltdown. *How the hell is the train not running? What kind of tinpot, shithole country is this? And fuck you, fatso, and your stupid fucking glasses.* Outwardly, she kept her composure perfectly.

"Is there an alternate route? My mom is sick, I need to get to Overton in a hurry, that's why I'm taking the express."

"I'm sorry, I really am, but you'll need to talk to the representative. Do you still want the ticket? You can exchange it tomorrow if necessary. If the train runs, at least you'll be guaranteed a seat."

Olivia paused for a moment. If she bought the ticket and the train still didn't run tomorrow, she was in serious trouble, but an alternate route was just as risky, if not more so. In the end, she decided it was better to have a place booked than not.

"Yeah, I do. How much is a return?"

"One hundred and seventy dollars."

The price stung. She couldn't keep up the façade of a return journey, not at that price.

"On second thought, gimme a one-way. Depending on my mom's condition, I might need to stay a while," Olivia lied through her teeth. She was getting better at it.

"I understand. One-way is ninety-two dollars."

The woman pushed the two-way slot tray over to Olivia. Its flap opened automatically like the gaping maw of some metallic beast, hungry for her money. Fishing in her wallet, she removed the bills and fed them to the tray.

"And your ID."

Olivia took out the fake ID, put it in the tray, and gave the woman a butter-wouldn't-melt smile.

The tray was pulled back to the other side, and the woman took the money and ID. She eyed the plastic card suspiciously through her large glasses. After a few seconds, the woman showed the ID to her colleague manning the next window over. They were talking, but Olivia couldn't hear them. *Keep calm, you're the customer, you're in charge. Act like it.*

"Is there something wrong?" Olivia asked in the same tone of voice her mother used in situations like this.

"Oh." The woman returned to the mic. "Technically, this older style of ID isn't valid anymore. You need to exchange it for the one with the chip in it."

"What? When was this implemented?"

"About a week ago. We haven't been given proper guidelines on what to do yet, and a lot of people are still turning up with older types of IDs."

"Well, I don't think I should be restricted in my movement because of poor guidelines. Look, while I'm in Overton, I'll get it exchanged at the city council offices for the new type so I won't have any issue on the way back," Olivia was telling her, not asking.

"OK. It's fine for now, but get it swapped out in Overton. Soon, this type won't be accepted anywhere."

The woman rang up the purchase, the thermal printer made almost no sound as the ticket slid out of the slot. When it finished printing, she put it in the drawer, along with Olivia's ID and change and slid it back over.

"Have a nice day, ma'am."

"You too," replied Olivia.

She took the items with a smile. *Damn fake ID's gonna get me killed.* Walking away, she examined the ticket. It was blue, printed on thermal paper with a laminate back, and it read, 'Northern Star Railways - Anna Jankowski - One Way - Overton – Express,' along with the date.

Maybe seventy people strong now, the crowd at the information desk looked agitated. The security guards from earlier had been replaced by an armed soldier. A young representative stood on a plastic crate addressing the crowd. He looked out of his depth, intimidated.

"I understand your frustration, but the north line to Overton will not be running until tomorrow at 8 AM," the rep informed them.

The crowd let out a sigh of frustration and anger. Everyone had somewhere to be, but Olivia's journey was life and death. 8 AM tomorrow still gave her enough time to make it to the border, but it was a big risk. What if the train still didn't run the next day? Did she need to think about an alternate route? Bribe someone to drive her. Maybe the river ferries. Stuck at the back of the crowd, Olivia stood on her tippy toes trying to get a better look.

"Why? What the hell is going on?" asked a tall black man in a business suit.

"A section of the line between Brownville and Jukestown has been sabotaged," the rep informed the crowd.

"By who?" asked a fat woman near the front, incredulous at the excuse.

"Most likely a vampire sympathizer group," the rep told them.

An almost synchronized groan of disapproval emerged from the crowd like they'd heard this kind of excuse before. They were getting more frustrated, some were swearing. They didn't seem to be buying the rep's story.

"Bullshit! They'd never damage the lines going north, their people need them," another woman shouted from the center where Olivia couldn't see.

"They're just covering for poor maintenance. It's always the same excuses," came the angry voice of a young man in the center of the crowd. He threw a balled-up piece of receipt paper at the representative.

The crowd was becoming more hostile, angry at the thought they might all be stuck in Ashtown for the night. Not wanting things to get out of hand, the soldier stepped forward. He didn't even need to speak, he just held up his hand, and the crowd got the message to cool it.

"What are our options?" asked a woman somewhere near the front.

"If you absolutely must leave today, then you can take a train to Osfort and get a replacement bus service to Dukesville, where you'll be able to continue your journey north," he informed them with a straight face.

Olivia couldn't have pointed out Osfort on a map, but she knew for certain it was far west of Ashtown, comically far west for an alternate route. Everyone in the crowd seemed to come to the same conclusion. Their mood turned even sourer.

"Are you out of your damn mind? That'll take twice as long than if we just stayed here," the man in the suit shouted at the rep. He echoed the sentiments of the entire crowd.

"I understand your frustration—" began the rep.

"I'm about to frustrate my foot up your ass," the fat woman at the front shouted.

The crowd was getting rowdy again, unproductive. Olivia wanted answers, and no one was asking the right questions.

"Will the service definitely run tomorrow? The weather's getting bad," Olivia shouted from the back of the crowd.

"I've been assured by head office that our crews are doing everything in their power to have the 8 AM service run tomorrow. There's a storm front coming in, but the train should leave well ahead of it."

"What about hotels, can we get vouchers? We're all stuck in Ashtown for the night," asked Olivia, aware of her precarious financial situation.

"The company cannot provide vouchers, but if you keep receipts, we will refund forty percent of the cost of your hotel stay, once it's below an eighty dollars threshold," he responded.

The paltry refund and bizarre bureaucracy were the final straw for the crowd. They started cursing and throwing objects at the representative, who now looked genuinely frightened. A baying crowd could be a dangerous thing, and the soldier knew it. It clearly wasn't his first rodeo.

Stepping between the crowd and the representative, he pulled the charging handle on his rifle. The mechanical racking sound of a live round being chambered ended the conversation. It ended most conversations in the NSC recently, vested interests protected, dissent less tolerated, the people less heard.

"Envy of the free world, my ass," Olivia muttered.

"You said it," replied one of the men from the crowd who'd overheard her.

Cowed as they were, the crowd filtered away, resigned to looking for alternate arrangements for the night. The soldier escorted the rep across the atrium. Olivia stayed standing there with a sad look on her face as the crowd dissipated, her plans in tatters, life in danger. After a few seconds, she started walking, but she wasn't sure where.

The Night

It was dark. All cities change personality when the sun goes down, but Ashtown had a reputation. You didn't wanna be on the streets any longer than necessary, especially if you strayed from the well-worn tourist paths. The mercury had dropped substantially, and the wind was picking up. Clouds of frozen breath emitted from Olivia's parka.

She stood outside a dive of a hotel, the fourth place she'd tried. They were all booked up. The trains north not running must have stranded at least a few thousand people in Ashtown for the night, all desperate for a last-minute hotel room. Not having the luxury of being able to book online with a credit card, she had to march through the cold to each hotel checking for vacancies.

Her father's credit card still sat in her wallet, tempting, but she held her resolve. Walking down the street, she stopped in an alcove for shelter and took out her phone. Frozen hands hurt as she tapped away at the screen, widening the search area for hotels away from the train station. As she scrolled through a series of cheap hotels, the screen changed, it read, 'Incoming call - Mom.'

"Shit!"

A flash of sudden realization. It was after 5:00 PM. People were starting to notice she was missing. Really missing, not just a cut class missing. Hadn't been at school and wasn't at Sara's, they'd start to worry. Dismissing the call, she quickly wrote a text message.

'Staying the night at Sara's tonight, remember? I left a note on the refrigerator :).'

Hitting send, she hopped the ruse would hold till morning. She returned to looking at hotels, but the phone rang again. Once again, it was dismissed, and the hotel search continued. A text message came through.

'Answer the phone! The school called. You didn't show up today!!!'

Olivia bit her lip. She's hoped to be further along her journey by the time the inevitable arrived. Taking a deep breath, she hit the block number icon next to her mother's name. After a second's pause, she opened the phone-book app and did the same for her father's number. She looked up into the night sky in quiet desperation. *Keep it together, get a hotel room, get off the streets.*

The hotel hunt continued. They were listed by distance from the train station. The further she scrolled down the page, the farther away they were but also more likely to have rooms still available. She settled on a picture of a narrow quaint looking hotel with a two-star rating. More importantly, the rooms started at forty dollars, and some showed as still available.

There was no phone number for the hotel shown, and no guarantee the rooms would still be empty when she got there, but she was running out of options, and her legs were starting to go numb from the cold. *1.4 miles. You better still be available when I get there.* Paranoid, she searched for four or five more hotels on the outskirts of the city. It was unlikely she'd been officially reported missing yet and, even then, she didn't think the cops could instantly gain access to phone location data for a missing minor without some kind of judicial warrant. Olivia decided to take the risk and keep the phone turned on for the time being. Sara might text her with information about people freaking out back home.

Beginning her trek, she stopped almost immediately and did a double-take, then backed up a few steps. Across the street was a convenience store. In the window was an advert for an off-brand hair dye. It had a picture of a woman with a shock of jet-black hair, finger resting on her lip suggestively. 'Who says blondes have more fun?' read the laziest advertising slogan in history.

Barrow's advice about changing the way she looked rang in Olivia's head. Mindlessly sprinting across the road, she was almost hit by oncoming traffic. A bell rang as she entered the store. Five minutes later, she emerged with some supplies, wallet eleven dollars lighter.

Marching through the snow, every muscle and bone in her body seemed to stab with pain, except for feet, which had gone completely numb. She'd never experienced cold like that before, let alone been stuck out in it. It would be worth the pain. The hotel would be perfect, warm, and they'd have a fire roaring in the lobby and some complimentary hot chocolate. The lies made the journey more bearable.

The farther she walked away from the old town, the more the city showed its true colors. Buildings became more rundown, and strange characters hung out in doorways. Olivia passed two women wearing thick fur coats, leaning into a car window. She knew enough not to hang around and picked up the pace despite the pain. Eventually, she arrived at the hotel. The street wasn't as bad as a couple she'd walked through to get there, but it still looked like it had seen better days.

Taking out her phone, she held up the pleasant-looking photo of the hotel on the screen to the real-world version, unsure if she was even at the right building. *You can never trust a profile picture*. Tall and narrow, the building must have been a hundred and fifty years old at least, built in the great expansion style. It had an ornate façade with lots of unnecessary adornments and extravagances, most of which were now cracked or crumbling.

It desperately needed a paint job, covered in an ugly shade of burgundy that was badly faded and flaking all over. Above the front entrance, the name of the hotel was displayed in large black wooden letters, 'The Carfax Hotel.' To the right of the hotel, the fire escapes seemed to exit out into a dark, narrow alleyway. Olivia took note of it as she crossed the street and walked in the main doors.

The lobby, like the hotel's exterior, had seen better days. The brass fittings were all tarnished, the furniture looked thirty years out of date, and the burgundy striped wallpaper peeled in several places. The place wasn't grubby so much as it was just trapped in the past, a ruptured time capsule of a bygone era, slowly decaying. Having walked in the biting cold for well over an hour, any misgivings Olivia had about the state of the hotel dissipated when a blast of warm air hit her from an overhead vent.

Five stars, best hotel ever.

She stood under the vent for at least a minute, eyes closed, just absorbing the heat like a lizard until a cough interrupted her.

"Can I help you, ma'am?" asked a voice.

The concierge, like the rest of the hotel, was oddly stuck in time. He was maybe fifty years old, with slick hair, a perfectly groomed mustache. He spoke with a posh accent that didn't seem to come from any region of the NSC in particular.

"I need a room for one for the night. Do you have one still available?" she told him, pulling down her hood.

"We have a small number of rooms still available. Single rooms are fifty dollars for the standard or fifty-five for a room with a view."

"Fifty? The hotel booking site said forty."

The concierge looked frustrated like he'd had this conversation with a thousand different guests over the course of a decade.

"The booking websites often give discounts for booking through them. You are more than welcome to book online if you wish."

"Forget it, I'll pay cash."

"Excellent. Would you like to upgrade to a room with a view?"

"What's the view?" Olivia asked him, confused at what would be worth looking at.

"The historic James Street, of course."

"That's the street I just came in by?"

"It is."

"And the standard rooms, they look into the alleyway?"

"They do."

"I'll take the standard room," Olivia told him with a smile.

Removing the fifty dollars from her wallet, she handed the bills to the concierge, who entered details into an old desktop computer.

"Thank you and, finally, can I see some identification?"

Olivia didn't want to risk using the ID. Every time she'd pulled the damn thing out, it had almost got her caught.

"Is that strictly necessary? I left my ID at home."

"I'm afraid so. With these new anti-terrorism laws, we are obliged to demand it from our guests. Personally, I believe it's an unnecessary intrusion into a guest's privacy. After all, the hotel trade was built on a certain…discretion."

"Isn't there some way we could just…overlook it then?"

The concierge curled his lip and shrugged a little. Olivia had always assumed people stayed in dumps like the Carfax because they were cheap, but she was learning they clearly had some other fringe benefits. Her wallet was almost dry, a ten-dollar bill, a couple of singles, and some loose change.

She took out the ten-dollar bill and gingerly slid it across the counter. The concierge raised an eyebrow as if to say, 'Do better.' It was all she had, though. Her phone was worth quite a bit, but she couldn't part with it. Desperately, she padded every pocket she had. Eventually, she reached into the pocket on the back of her jeans and found something.

Pulling it out, she looked at it in utter confusion. A crumpled ten-dollar bill. It took her mind a while to process how it got there. *Jamie*. Her brother had slipped it back in her pocket, knew she was in some trouble, might need it. Flattening out the bill, she added it to the other ten-dollar bill on the counter and slid it over to the concierge. Price met, the eyebrow dropped. He took the cash with a smile.

"The name's Karen Smith," Olivia told him.

"Of course, Miss Smith," he responded, taking a key from a pigeonhole. "Room 508, fifth floor. The elevator is through the lounge area, checkout is 10 AM."

"Thanks," said Olivia as she took the set of keys.

As she walked away from the lobby, she stopped dead in her tracks, mind spinning like a clockwork machine. *A man who can be bought for twenty dollars might sell you out for two hundred.* She turned back to face him.

"Oh, I forgot, do you know what time the river-ferry leaves for Redhorn in the morning?" she asked.

"Every hour, on the hour, starting at 7 AM, ma'am."

"Can I get a wake-up call at 9 AM then? I'll try to catch the ferry at ten."

"Of course, ma'am. Have a pleasant night."

"Thanks," Olivia replied as she walked away.

Next to the check-in desk was the main staircase. Olivia's legs were like jelly from the long walk, she didn't intend to climb five floors worth of steps. Walking through the open double doors that adjoined the reception took her into the lounge area. Just a handful of tables and chairs surrounding a fireplace that wasn't lit. The elevator was at the end of the room.

Once inside, Olivia pulled the old scissor-gate closed and pressed the five button. She'd only seen elevators like this one in movies. It shook as it pulled itself upward. It didn't seem very reliable. In the morning she'd use the stairs, not wanting to tempt fate.

Surveying the corridor, she was pleased to see there were no security cameras, another benefit of that discretion the concierge was so proud of. She made her way along a well-worn path in the old carpet. *502...504...506...508*. The room was right at the end of the hall. Next to the door was a window covered by thick purple drapes. Parting the drapes, the window led out onto the fire escape. *Good, good.*

She opened the door to room 508 and quickly slipped inside. Turning on the light, she turned to secure the door. It was a solid-looking hardwood fire door, she double-locked it and put on the heavy chain-bolt for good measure.

Olivia surveyed the room. A single bed, a desk with a kettle, and some cups for coffee, a small TV, bathroom on the right, window on the left. The place was spartan for sure, but Olivia didn't care. It was warm and seemed safe enough. It might as well have been a palace after the day she'd had. Dropping the backpack, she took off her parka and hoodie and collapsed onto the bed.

"Still alive, I guess," she said to herself.

Her body was a rock, the weight of itself pinning her to the bed. Had she ever been this tired before? She couldn't remember. Lying there, her mind swam with scenarios. What if the train didn't run the next day? What if someone was waiting at the station? What if the concierge ratted her out? She didn't trust him, hoped he'd bought the bullshit story about the river ferry terminal.

The ferry was most likely useless to her now anyway. It probably wouldn't take her far enough north to bypass the break in the tracks. But if the train didn't run, she'd still needed an alternative, and she was out of money. Her dad's credit card was still untouched. He probably hadn't even noticed it missing yet.

There'd be no option but to use it, take out as much cash as possible, get a cab to drive her north to Dukesville, past the break in the lines, then get on the train to Overton. It might even be faster than getting the train straight from Ashtown. It wasn't a great plan, but she couldn't think of a better one at that moment. Her brain was fried. Body and mind exhausted, she could have slept right there and then. *Don't even think about falling asleep. Not yet.*

Olivia reluctantly pulled her aching body into an upright position. She took off her soaking wet sneakers, socks, and jeans, then got up and laid them on the old oil radiator to dry. Using the remote, she turned on the TV, rapidly flicking through channel after channel of trash. Eventually, she stopped at a local news channel for East Plains Province, Ashtown was at its heart.

The channel was an affiliate of a national news channel, but not the one watched at home in Greenfields. This was what her mother would refer to as left-wing liberal propaganda. In truth, it leaned center-right and still had a government stamp of approval, for now.

"...public service unions say that new laws concerning when a person must present ID are unclear and poorly written. This leaves their members struggling to implement ambiguous guidelines with no additional training, compounded by continued confusion over which ID types are still valid..." the formal voice of a reporter spoke over stock footage of airport terminals and train stations.

Attention focused on the news report, Olivia sat back down on the edge of the bed. The information was useful. If she got asked for ID, she might be able to weasel out of it if she pushed hard enough.

"The government, for their part, say unions are simply using the new laws as leverage to demand the reinstatement of pay increments frozen due to the poor economic conditions. Union leaders reject the accusation. Back to you in the studio, Pam," the reporter signed off, now visible standing in the freezing cold outside a bus station somewhere.

"Thanks, Adam. Now, we're gonna take you straight over to Russel Jacobs with an update on the big storm coming our way," the bottle blonde anchor said, making the quick transition.

A tall, black meteorologist with a friendly smile stood in front of an interactive map of East Plains. A large circular vortex on the east side of the map could be seen approaching.

"Thanks, Pam," the meteorologist said. "As most of you are already aware, we have this massive cold vortex that's coming in from the east. That's gonna drop temperatures way below freezing and dump up to three feet of snow in some areas, with drifts of up to five feet. Right now, the vortex is situated here over Redhook, Johnson, and Cook counties. But as we progress through the night and into tomorrow, it will keep sweeping west, hitting major population centers, with Ashtown expected to feel the full force of the storm by 11 AM tomorrow."

Vision laser-focused on the TV, Olivia absently scratched her chest like a gorilla. The weather report was good. If the tracks were fixed, the train to Overton would most likely run. If it left at 8 AM, it'd be well away from Ashtown before the storm hit. The train going northwest, it would probably stay ahead of the weather if she was lucky. *Gotta make that damn train.*

"Authorities have issued a status red travel advisory. This means the public should avoid unnecessary journeys, and if you must travel, plan to do so well before the storm hits your area."

"Yeah, well, I'd say my journey's pretty damn necessary," Olivia spoke aloud to the TV.

"For those not planning journeys, the advice is simple. Check on vulnerable neighbors, bring in pets, and then hunker down indoors with the heat on. Back to you, Pam," the meteorologist said, handing it back to the blonde news anchor.

"Well," she began, "I know I'll be taking that advice and staying indoors with a nice cup of cocoa tomorrow. I've been Pam Foster, and this has been your evening update."

"Well, fuck you, too, Pam," Olivia said to the TV as she muted it and changed the channel.

You have work to do.

Olivia made her way over to the window and parted the drapes. The window led out onto the fire escape. She pulled it up firmly. It was a little stiff, but it opened. *Good, Good.* Next, she turned her attention to the backpack, fished inside for the buck knife, pulled it out, and put it under the bed pillow. Finally, the contents of the convenience store plastic bag were emptied onto the bed: a few individually wrapped crème-filled sponge cakes, ramen noodles, a can of energy drink, scissors, and a box of black hair dye.

She surveyed the items for a moment, then opened one of the sponge cakes and ate it. It was hard work, wincing as it was forced down. Picking up the box of hair dye, she examined it, 'Dubh Hair Dye', a picture of a model with jet-black hair adorned the box. 'Remember: Always do a patch test,' warned the box.

Patch tests are for pussies.

She picked up the scissors and walked to the bathroom.

Flickering to life, the harsh florescent light over the mirror revealed a compact bathroom. The bath, toilet, tiles, and sink were all a dirty shade of olive green. Only the bath curtain and towels were spared the style onslaught. Like everything in the hotel, it looked like it was a few decades out of date, and whatever decade it was from didn't have any taste to start with.

Olivia looked at her face in the mirror, tired, pale, gaunt. The day had taken its toll. Matted and knotted from the cold, she ran her fingers through her sandy brown hair. A hairbrush hadn't been high on her priority list when she was packing for her life. She stared at herself in the mirror for a few seconds, then took a deep breath and cut.

The scissors were poor quality, more suited to cutting paper, so she had to really hack away to make any progress. It looked disastrous, but she couldn't stop once she'd started. *You don't need to look good, just different.* After a while, it started to take shape. Large wads of hair fell into the sink as she worked.

When she'd finished, her hair somewhat resembled a short crop cut, messy as hell, but it would have to do. There was no pause to admire her handiwork. Tearing open the box of hair dye she spilled its contents into the sink. Dye bottle, applicator brush, gloves.

She pulled on the gloves with a snap, like a surgeon in a bad medical TV show, then squirted the dye onto the applicator brush and awkwardly painted it into her hair. The dye wasn't like the more expensive ones she was used to. They were creamy and smelled of cocoa butter. This one was a foul viscous black, like treacle, and smelled like a chemical factory.

Hair now covered in black goo, she had time to kill before washing it out. She scooped up all the loose hair and dye paraphernalia, put it in the plastic bag, and put the bag in the sink, then she sat down against the tile wall and waited.

People knew she was missing now. Who knew, though. Just her family… No, the school knew, too. At least they knew she didn't come in that day. Still, vampirism was rare as hell. People didn't always jump to that conclusion. They'd just assume she got into trouble.

Sara and her Mom probably knew, too. Olivia's mother would have rung Sara's house first thing. Sara might be the only one who had guessed the truth by now. Olivia was desperate for information, but she knew she couldn't reach out herself. *No instant messages yet, at least. Maybe that's a good sign. It means none of the other girls know yet...or they all know, and they're already cutting all ties.*

For about twenty minutes, she sat torturing herself about who knew, and who didn't, and what they knew, and when, and what they'd do about it, or who they'd tell. Eventually, she sprung up in frustration. *Fuck it, that's thirty minutes.*

Kneeling over the green bathtub, she used the showerhead to wash out the hair dye and patted it dry with a towel, then stood up and looked in the mirror. It didn't look great, but it didn't look terrible, either. She fluffed it about to give it a messy look. The jet-black color suited the short hairstyle more than her natural brown.

Most importantly, it looked different, very different. She'd be unrecognizable to anyone who didn't know her well. They'd have a harder time spotting her now. A cheeky grin came across a face she barely recognized in the mirror. She might survive this yet. A notion took her, and she opened her mouth wide and ran her finger along her teeth, inspecting them. She found nothing and closed her mouth again.

"Not a vampire yet, I guess…just the world's worst goth." She winked at herself in the mirror and exited the bathroom.

Back in the bedroom, Olivia sat on the bed and planned alternate routes going north by train, ferry, and road. Still paranoid of being tracked, she must have search twenty routes, most of them red herrings. Most importantly, the 8:00 AM to Overton showed as running, for now. That could change, but that was tomorrow's problem.

She stared at a live weather map for over an hour, looking at the projected path of the oncoming storm. It didn't matter what her route north was, she needed to be gone before that storm hit Ashtown. She could only obsess about it for so long. Eventually, she locked the phone and threw it on the bed in frustration.

A while later, Olivia sat perched in the open windowsill, an unlit cigarette hanging from her mouth. Hair now fully dry, she'd put her hoodie back on and wore a fresh pair of jeans. The shorter haircut made her look a little older, certainly enough to pass for the twenty years indicated by her fake ID. A half-eaten cup of noodles sat on the floor near the window, and the TV was on.

Afraid she might set off a smoke alarm, she didn't immediately light the cigarette, but looking up at the ceiling revealed tobacco stains and an old-fashioned alarm with the battery removed. It took a couple of attempts and some shaking but, eventually, the lighter ignited. It was running out of gas. She took a long drag on the cigarette and blew the smoke out the window into the pitch-black night.

The hotel didn't have any premium channels, so she put on a classic movie channel, the kind that only played movies nobody had ever heard of. The kind her dad might watch on a lazy Sunday. It was comforting somehow. A decades-old horror film was playing. It looked like it had originally been in black and white, and then had the color added later.

A frightened-looking group of villagers carrying torches was being addressed by a priest or minister of some kind in a town square. He was dressed in a long brown leather coat and had a wide-brimmed hat to match, an effigy of the lord burning on a pyre hung around his neck.

"How many more of our sons and daughters will be taken before we rouse from our slumber and strike back at the corruption in our land?" the minister asked the crowd, his lines delivered in an old fashion theatrical style.

The villagers looked skittish, fearful like they might disband. A few at the back were already walking away.

"But what can we do against such evil?" asked a young man at the front of the crowd. "We're butchers, carpenters, smiths…not soldiers."

"The lord of hate and darkness cares not if you are a carpenter, a baker, or a smith," the minster gesticulated as he spoke. "To him, you are no more than cattle, there to provide him with your children, the strong of which he will add to his army of the undead. The weak he will feed upon to sustain his unholy existence for generation after generation…unless we stand this night and stop him."

The crowd looked angry, like he'd hit a nerve with them. The ones at the back rejoined.

"But we don't have any real weapons or good steel to make them, only the crude pikes the smith fashioned for us!" called another man.

"This is madness. We should wait! I heard a rumor the duke of Sardovia is sending a knight and thirty men-at-arms," said another. The crowd seemed less than convinced by the man's suggestion.

"You could wait a lifetime and those soldiers won't arrive, brother. We are alone," a man beside him said.

The crowd realized their dire situation. No one was coming to save them. The minister saw his opening and pounced.

"No, brother, we are not alone. The lord is here with us," he said. "And to him, you are not cattle. To him, each and every one of you is a soldier in his army, glistening in holy armor." The crowd gained courage and nodded in agreement.

"But we still need weapons!" said the first young man.

"Brother, don't you see? The lord has already provided all the weapons you need!" he pointed to different men as he spoke. "Has the butcher not a cleaver to cut down the servants of hate? Has the carpenter not fashioned stakes for you? And has the smith not hammers to drive them through the dark lord's black heart. But we must strike tonight. There can be no delay."

The speech had its desired effect. The crowd roared. Incensed, their eyes burned with a zealous rage like they could almost see themselves wearing the shining holy armor the minister described. They grabbed anything that could act as a weapon, pitchforks and axes, scythes and sickles, then they marched out of the town.

Olivia lit another cigarette, eyes now transfixed on the screen. She knew where the film was going, knew who the bad guy was, and how it was going to end. These types of films always ended the same way. It was just a movie, but she looked at it now with different eyes than she might have two days ago.

Lit only by torchlight, the chain of human vengeance snaked into the night. The mob made its way up a winding path, a matte painting of an imposing castle under a full moon their destination. Eventually, they arrived at the castle gates. The vampire's craven servants, shrouded in hoods, lay waiting. An orgy of violence ensued. Men were impaled on pitchforks, set alight, bludgeoned with hammers. Both sides took heavy losses, but the villagers prevailed. They hammered at the gates, using a cart filled with stones as an impromptu battering ram. They would soon storm the castle proper.

The scene cut to the castle's main dining room. Little did the villagers know, but a hero was already inside the castle fighting the vampire lord in single combat. Hideous, snarling, fangs bared like an animal, the vampire sprung at the hero. At the last second, the hero fired a crossbow. It missed the vampire's heart and lodged in the lower right of his torso. The vampire lord snarled in pain…

Olivia's phone suddenly rang, and she almost fell out of the windowsill with fright.

'Lil Bro,' read the name on the screen, with a goofy picture of Jamie. Rejecting the call, she paused for a moment, then deliberately banged the back of her head against the window frame. *Do it*. She tried to block her brother's number but was too slow. A message arrived.

'Don't block me, it's serious.'

They knew now, but only that she was missing.

'What's happening?' Olivia messaged back.

'Mom and Dad are freaking out. They know you didn't show up to school today, and they know you're not at any of your friends.'

She closed her eyes in quiet frustration for a moment, then typed feverishly. 'Look, I got into some trouble, but I've straightened it out now. I'll be home tomorrow morning. Can you cover for me?'

Message sent, she took a long drag of her cigarette and nervously tipped the ash out the window. The response took time, the wait agonizing. She stared at the message thread. Maybe her brother could buy her some time, even if just till the morning, but she didn't want to put him in jeopardy. The phone hummed, and a message arrived.

'Sis, I've heard all your lies at least a dozen times. I found the photo in your room, the one you took out of the frame, saw who was in it. You're not coming back, are you?'

Fear seeped into every pore of Olivia's body. She'd left evidence behind, the photo with Angie. Nothing incriminating to a casual observer, but her brother was smart as a whip. With the talk from the night before, he'd put it together. It wasn't hard. On borrowed time now, how long before her parents and everyone else figured out why she was missing?

But she still couldn't admit the truth to Jamie, even though he already knew it. The cops might eventually trawl through his messages. She threw the last of the cigarette out and shut the window, then typed, 'Lol, it's not what you think, dumbass. Just tell Mon and Dad to stop freaking out, I'll be home in the morning :)'

The message was hollow, childish, but it would give him some deniability. They usually went easier on younger teenagers…usually, but only from a legal standpoint.

The response took time. Something was badly wrong. She knew it. Phone held in a death grip, she stared at the screen, waiting.

"Come on," she said to herself.

Eventually, the phone hummed to life again.

'I can't, not this time, not even if I wanted to. Mom and Dad are talking about reporting you missing, the cops are already on their way to the house to take a formal statement. I told Mom you'd blocked my number, so do it now. Otherwise, I'm a dead man.'

The message was like a bolt-gun to the head, everything suddenly too real. If they reported her missing and she was found, she could be picked up, dragged back to Greenfields; with her clock counting down it would be a death sentence. Hand trembling, she made a fist with her right hand and sank her teeth into it, almost breaking the skin. Her scream was silenced, and the pain steadied her nerves.

Prepare. Prepare and you can survive.

Taking the fist from her mouth, a ring or teeth-marks lined the knuckles. Trembling, she typed a final message to her brother.

'Thanks, lil bro, for everything. Love you. I mean that. Goodbye.'

A shaking index finger hovered over the send button, then it moved to the backspace button and pressed down. Character by character, the message was wiped clean. In its place a new message was quickly typed.

'I'll be home in the morning. Thanks for nothing, dickhead!'

The send button was pressed, and the message floated off into the ether to her brother. She hoped he'd understand. She blocked his number and bowed her head in despair. She wanted to cry but couldn't afford to. Olivia realized the phone was a liability now. There could be no more contacts from home. Maybe she could use the phone in an emergency, but even that would be a major risk. She opened the settings to set the phone to airline mode. As she did, a new message appeared.

'UNKNOWN CONTACT'

Olivia paused for a moment before opening the message,eyebrows furrowed, a look of apprehension on her face.

'If you're dumb enough to still have your phone, get rid of it now.'

What the fuck?

Her brother calling from a burner phone maybe, but unlikely. It could only be one of a very small group of people. Sara had to have worked out what was wrong by now. She'd half-guessed it already the other day at school. *It has to be her*. Olivia needed to know for sure but didn't want to get her into serious trouble. Fingers typed frantically.

'This is Kelly. New phone. Who dis?'

The reply only took a matter of seconds to arrive.

'Just destroy the phone if you want to stay alive, idiot.'

Olivia read the message several times over, hoping to somehow divine the sender from the wording. *Amber's far too dumb to block her number even if she somehow knew. Jasmine wouldn't stick her neck out for me, we're not that close. It has to be Sara. There's no one else.*

She smiled at the thought that at least someone seemed to be looking out for her, then the smile faded. Her life was on the line, and the sum total of support she got was a call from her brother and a couple of texts, maybe from Sara. Utterly alone in the world now, even people who wanted to help her couldn't.

This was how they wanted you, isolated, fearful, running out of options. They let you run for the sake of holding up their side of the peace treaty, but they'd do everything in their power to stop you from making it. Could she even trust the message she'd just received?

She needed the phone for maps and any emergencies that might come up, but the mystery messenger had spooked her. If she was formally reported missing, the cops might be able to pinpoint her location from the phone somehow, even if it was turned off. She'd seen it mentioned on the news in murder trials, but that was way after the fact. They needed to trawl through cell tower records.

She was more concerned about purification squads. Could they be given more detailed information like browsing history by someone on the inside at a phone company. Deciding to hedge her bets, she didn't destroy the phone but turned it off and put it back in her jeans pocket. The stakes had become all too real all too suddenly.

There'll be no more calls from Greenfields. You've never been there. Olivia Thompson is dead now, forget her name. You're Anna or Karen or Mary or whoever the fuck you need to be to survive.

Olivia took her wallet from her pocket, then bounded over to the bathroom. Rooting in the back of the wallet, she pulled out her real ID hidden in the back. She took one last look at it, the fresh-faced Olivia in the photo with long sandy hair looked nothing like the girl in the mirror. She tossed the ID into the bag of cut hair in the sink and tied it up. She'd dump it in a public trashcan in the morning.

The hour was late now. Earlier Olivia had gulped the sickly-sweet energy drink in one go and spent the rest of the night making sure everything was ready for the morning. The still wet sneakers were put next to the bed, but all her other dried clothes were put back into the backpack.

Dim red digits glowed on the bedside clock. The time read 11:15 PM. There was nothing more that could be done for the night. The energy drink that had kept her functioning for the past couple of hours wore off. The piper had to be paid, and she was exhausted, eyes stinging from the heating. She took off her jeans, socks, and hoodie and placed them next to the bed, ready for the morning, then she set the small bedside alarm clock for 6:40 AM.

Slipping into bed, she turned off the light with a switch on the wall near her head, then lay flat on her back in the darkness.

Electric blue eyes burned in the darkness, like two tiny gas flames. Almost no light made it into the room through the blackout drapes, but her vision quickly adjusted to the darkness. She could see just fine, like every object in the room had a faint blue halo glow around them. Disconcerted, she projected her hand in front of her as far as possible. The effect was more exaggerated with her hand, the halo stronger, a slightly deeper blue.

Was it just exhaustion, stress, or was this how it began, whatever change she was going through? When she was a kid, she always imagined the transformation to be sudden, like in the movies. You were human one minute and transformed into some horrific creature the next. To some extent, that idea still stuck with her, even though it made no sense.

Logically, she knew it must have been a longer process, it had to be. Otherwise, the three-day rule wouldn't exist. Nurse Ramirez told her it would take weeks. How long had these effects been creeping up on her, becoming more pronounced while she wasn't paying attention? *Close your eyes, sleep, worry about these problems when you make it to the border.*

Shutting her eyes, darkness brought little comfort. Sleep was still elusive for a time, haunted by images of her brother in an interrogation cell, shackled, being questioned by detectives, covered in bruises, bleeding. 'Confess, make it easy on yourself,' they told him. Then her mother, giving a speech at church, fire and brimstone, decrying Olivia, calling her an abomination.

Shaking the thoughts from her head, she imagined the route to the border instead, the train journey, the last short walk to the border and, finally, presenting herself to make the crossing. *Tomorrow will be different, tomorrow will be better. Tomorrow will be different, tomorrow will be better....*

Eventually, sleep took hold as the mantra was repeated over and over.

Awake

Eyelids sprung open like an animal, alert, pupils expanded to let in what little light was in the room, jet-black discs in a sea of blue. Footsteps, heavy, somewhere up the corridor, whispered voices, distant, faint, but she could just make them out.

"To the right 501 to 508," a man's voice spoke lowly.

"Keep your damn voice down," a second man scolded him in barely a whisper.

"Relax, she's early stage, she won't notice us coming till it's too late," the first man responded, but quieter this time.

"Yeah, well I don't wanna roll that dice. I don't want a repeat of Blakeville. Make sure you have the syringe ready," the first man told him.

Terror and adrenaline pumped through Olivia's veins, but her body remained frozen in place. The footsteps moved up the corridor, louder now. There were at least three men out there, she knew. This wasn't a trial run like at the bathroom at the Sandman. There was no doubt these men were here to take her.

Move, do something!

Her hand reached under the pillow, grabbed the buck knife, and extended the blade. She slid out of the bed onto the floor and leaned against it. The footsteps were at the door. There was no more talking from the men. They'd gone silent, but she could hear their breathing outside, loud, as if they were horses.

The window was the only option. She could try to make a quick escape, but how far would she get with no clothes or wallet? She'd die of hypothermia before the night was through. The sound of a key jangling. There was no time left. She would need to buy time for her escape.

Some unknown force propelled her forward. Moving in her bare feet, silent like a cat, she quickly padded her way across the room to the doorway. Tall and skinny, half-naked, lurking in the darkness with a sharpened blade, she resembled some horrific wraith in that moment but, in her mind, she was just a terrified girl trying to survive. Her heart thudded steadily, ready for what was coming. There was no other option now. She had to be the monster they feared. It was the only way she'd survive.

Metal on metal, the key slid gently into the lock, a spare from the reception desk. They'd still need to get past the chain-bolt, that's when she'd strike. The key turned. It made little sound in the well-oiled lock, and the door slowly inched open. Very little light spilled in. They must have turned off the bulb in the corridor near the door. They were well-prepared and had done this before to others.

The door stopped as it hit the heavy chain-bolt. Olivia raised the buck knife silently, breathing shallow, not even a whisper. A large man's fingers slowly reached through the crack and tried to loop some fishing line around the chain-lock to pull it open.

Do it now.

The task was difficult in darkness, the man's fingers barely fitting through the crack in the door, and he fumbled with the fishing wire.

Do it! do it!

The knife in Olivia's hand still hung in the air, waiting for some unknown moment. The man, clearly frustrated, squeezed his entire hand in through the door crack in a final attempt to get the line in place.

DO IT!

Olivia's face contorted, a vein pulsing on the side of her head. A massive adrenaline rush washed through her, and the knife was brought down with unmerciful force. The blade struck its target perfectly, digging in deep between the knuckles of the massive hand. A scream of immense pain came from the other side. The man tried to retract his hand, but Olivia slammed all her weight against the door, trapping it in place.

Her eyes burned in a frenzy, as she brought the blade down again and again, fingers, palm, and wrist sliced open. She hit the bone and kept stabbing regardless. Blood sprayed from the hand like a fountain. Her eyes widened at the sight of the blood and her breathing deepened like some hungry animal. The whole series of events could only have lasted five seconds or less, but the damage to the man's hand was stomach-churning.

The assault was only interrupted when a second man shoulder charged the door, knocking Olivia off her feet. The chain lock held, but the butchered hand was retracted. Olivia quickly kicked the door closed and snapped out of her frenzy.

"Oh, shit, my fucking hand! Fuck!" the man's voice dripped with fear.

"What should we do?" came a second man's voice, clearly rattled.

"Kick the damn door down," it was a third voice, one Olivia hadn't heard before, calm, collected.

"Man, look at my fucking hand."

"We'll deal with your damn hand later. Kick the door."

Olivia didn't wait for them to start. Eyes adjusted to the dark she could she sprinted over to her clothes and threw them on as quickly as possible. A heavy kick hit the door and shook the entire room, but the door held. They didn't want to even risk using the key again for fear a blade might emerge. She threw on her parka and pulled up the hood, slung her backpack on, and made for the window but stopped dead in her tracks. The bag in the sink with the hair and ID, it had to be taken or destroyed, and she needed a distraction.

Another kick struck the door, harder this time. There was a cracking sound. The door was giving way. Bounding over to the bathroom, she threw the chair from the desk over to the door, another obstacle to slow her pursuers.

The bag of hair sat tied up in the sink. Pulling out the lighter, she frantically cranked the wheel. Sparks emerged from the flint, but the lighter wasn't playing ball. More cranking, only sparks. Another massive kick at the door, a sickening *crack*, wood splitting. The door had given way, but the chain bolt held.

Olivia panicked. She only had seconds at best. A sudden idea struck her. She took her phone and threw it in the sink with the bag, then she stabbed at the cellphone with the buck knife. The phone was sturdy. It survived the initial assault with only a tiny hole pierced in the aluminum housing.

Come on!

She brought the blade down with more force on the second attempt, and it pierced through the screen and into the body of the phone. She quickly pulled the blade out. Almost instantly, she knew it had worked. The smell of burning silicon, the battery had been punctured. A jet of bright green flame emerged from the hole. In a heartbeat, the entire phone combusted in a bright chemical fire and set the bag of hair alight. Acrid black smoke quickly filled the tiny bathroom. Picking up the flaming bag, she tossed it into the bedroom and ran out after it.

"Fuck is that smell?" asked one of the men to the other outside the door.

"Crazy cunt is setting the damn place on fire!" the calm voice sounded less calm.

"Man, we need to get the fuck out of here." The wounded man sounded weak, maybe in shock.

"Keep kicking!"

Bang, bang. They were taking turns now. The chain-bolt wouldn't hold much longer. Olivia quickly pulled open the window and climbed out into the freezing night. As she shut the window, a massive cracking sound was heard. The chain had given way.

Snow swirled around her as she quickly made her way down the fire escape to the floor below. The sound of a fire alarm, loud, from inside the hotel. The smoke from the room must have set off the working detectors in the corridor.

Good, more chaos, easier to escape.

Reaching the floor below and picking up the pace, she bounded down the next flight of stairs. But she was stopped dead in her tracks on the third floor. Olivia stared dumbfounded into the darkened abyss in disbelief. The entire fire escape below the third floor was missing. Some mangled metal was all that remained of the ladder that should have led to safety.

Piece of shit hotel!

Too far to jump, but she couldn't stop. The men might have realized their quarry wasn't hiding under the bed by now.

Turning her attention to the window, she tried to pull it open, but it wouldn't budge. She stuck the blade of the buck knife into the jamb of the window and used it as a lever to try to pry it open. It worked. The window gave way, but so did the buck knife. The blade snapped off at the hilt. She tossed the knife away, then pulled open the window to the third-floor corridor.

The fire alarm blared from inside. Before entering, she glanced up for a split-second. Silhouetted by moonlight, the head and shoulders of a man emerged from the window above. She dived in through the third-floor window.

In the narrow confines of the corridor, the fire alarm was ear-splittingly loud. Olivia emerged from behind the velour drapes. People ran toward her, two men. Confused in the cacophony of noise, and with no weapon to defend herself, she was about to turn tail and try jumping from the broken fire escape. Then her brain clicked into gear. One of the men wore pajamas, the other a tired-looking suit. *Just startled guests.* Others came out of their rooms in various states of undress. A mother with two frighten looking children emerged from a door beside Olivia.

Think fast.

"The fire escape's broken. We can't go this way. We need to go back down the main stairs!" she shouted at them over the din of the alarm.

"Is there really a fire?" the mother asked.

"Yeah, the entire top floor of the hotel is on fire. Don't wait, get out now!" Olivia addressed everyone who could hear her over the alarm.

Even those who couldn't hear got the message. She looked terrified. It wasn't a joke. People started moving, but slowly at first. The mother sprinted past everyone toward the main stairs, dragging her two children like ragdolls behind. It was an impressive and terrifying sight. Everyone followed her lead and picked up the pace. Olivia walked behind two tall men. By the time they reached the main staircase, the crowd was getting large. Guests even spilled down from the floors above, maybe just enough to cover her escape.

As Olivia was about to start her descent of the main staircase, she looked to the floor above. There on the landing, in the crowd of people, was a face she recognized. David, the boy from the bus. He looked to the floors above, not evacuating. Pulling the hood on her parka tighter, she pushed down the crowded staircase with the other guests.

"She's not here. Get down to the lobby," an instruction shouted to David from the floor above, barely audible over the alarm, but Olivia just heard it.

As they descended the floors, more guests joined the throng from above and below, some foolishly dragging their luggage. The crowd wasn't huge but still enough to jam the halls of the narrow old hotel. Olivia was thankful. She needed all the cover she could get. David was coming somewhere behind. Had he spotted her yet? Maybe.

The alarm shut off mid-beep. Either the fire was out, or someone had cut the alarm. Almost at the lobby now, she could taste the cold air blowing in, freedom within reach. The crowd spilled into the tiny lobby and pushed toward the main exit. The doors to the lounge were open. Olivia risked a glance as she passed, checking if her pursuers were coming from the elevator.

The concierge sat in on one of the chairs near the fireplace, lip and cheek split open. He looked frightened. A bald man with a serious expression stood watch over him. She turned her head away, not wanting to risk being seen by either man. Freedom was barely twenty feet away. Ice-cold wind hit the guests in their various states of undress. They were slower to brave the freezing night now that the alarm had been cut off.

"Hey, watch it asshole," the voice of a disgruntled guest from behind.

Instinctively, Olivia glanced behind for a split-second, just long enough to see David trying to barge his way through the crowd. He was a couple of feet behind. Had he spotted her? Maybe he was just powering his way to the front so he could see everyone who came out the front doors. Either way, she couldn't keep shuffling slowly with the crowd or he'd be on top of her in seconds. Nimble enough, Olivia managed to slip through the crowd and pushed her way forward quicker than David, until she tried to pass a heavy-set woman who was in no mood.

"Excuse me," the woman shouted at Olivia.

Olivia's movement had been noticed. There was a sudden push from the back. A hand reached out and grabbed her shoulder, trying to drag her backward.

"Tommy, get out here!" David shouted to the man in the lounge area.

Arm stretched, David reached past several guests, but like a hawk, still managed to keep a tight grip on his prey. In desperation, Olivia tripped the heavy-set woman, who stumbled, allowing Olivia to slip past. The distance now too great. She was able to pull free of David's clawing hand. Powering forward, she reached the doorway and burst out into the ice-cold night with about five other guests.

Not stopping for even a heartbeat, barging past the other guests, she sprinted across the street through thick swirls of snow. A car skidded violently to avoid hitting her. In seconds she was moving down an alleyway on the other side of the street in total darkness.

"Fuck!" a voice roared into the void of the night.

It was David. He'd lost sight of her. Olivia grinned a little at the sound of his frustration but kept moving as fast as possible. Sprinting out onto another street, she emerged near a twenty-four-hour liquor and convenience store. She was surprised to see people walking around despite the cold and the late hour. Shady people, true, but it didn't matter. Olivia's footprints in the snow blended with theirs, and she vanished into the night like a phantom.

Bridge

Olivia trudged across a deserted footbridge spanning a canal, body at the point of exhaustion, biting wind burning her face, feet frozen in damp sneakers. She hadn't stopped moving since fleeing the hotel and didn't have a clue where she was. She only knew one thing with certainty. If she didn't escape the cold, she'd be dead before morning.

Gotta get my bearings.

Midway over the bridge, a statue came into focus through the snow, the figure of a man carved out of stone illuminated by a flickering gas flame, a beacon in the darkness. Olivia marched toward it.

Surrounding the statue was a small semi-circle alcove with a wall higher than that of the rest of the bridge, shelter enough for a few minutes' mercy from the wind. Ducking into the alcove, Olivia found a few granite benches surrounding a public drinking water fountain. The fountain was kept from freezing over by a gas flame burning in an old-fashioned metal lantern bolted near the basin.

Hands frozen, she held them as close to the glass as possible without touching it, fearing her skin might stick. The flame burned furiously in its metal and glass prison. Not enough to warm her whole body, but enough to relieve the stabbing pains of cold in her hands. Looking up, Olivia surveyed the statue. Carved out of granite, it towered high above the alcove on a plinth. It was all sharp angles, a union leader. All the worker statues were in a similar style.

The current government had made a point of minimizing the history of the union leaders, saying the church was actually much more influential in the early formation of the state. Most of the union statues had been removed, but this one was still standing. She wiped a small covering of snow from a plaque at the base of the statue.

'The cause of labor is the cause of all. Let no prejudice stand in the way of unity between all workers - Gustav Lang.'

Not even the government would dare move this statue, not unless they wanted an entire city in revolt. Lang was a freed slave from one of the colonies. He'd formed the Skilled Workers Union. They'd built half of Ashtown, laid all the gas, water, and sewage pipes that helped the city grow into a global powerhouse in the Gas Age.

Lang's bridge. That makes this the Artery Canal.

The canal was well-known. Olivia learned about it in history class. It passed up near the train terminal for transporting freight in the old days. Looking to the other side of the bridge, she could see the building lights got brighter as they went up the canal. It had to lead back into the center of town near the station. All she had to do was follow it.

Hands still in pain, she returned to heating them by the gas flame. Illuminated by the fire, she could see her right hand was caked in dry blood. Some had wiped off on her parka sleeve. The man from the hotel. His hand had sprayed like a cut garden hose. She'd hit an artery or a vein, something major, she knew that much. Either way, a bloodstained hand was bound to draw attention.

Pressing the lever on the fountain, a small trickle of water flowed out of the spout. She stuck her mouth under. Despite her thirst, she could only stomach a tiny amount of the ice-cold water. Being further away from the heat source, the small basin below the spout was frozen over. Olivia struck the ice sheet with an elbow. It cracked apart, then she held the lever until fresh water filled up the basin.

Washing her hands in the icy water undid much of the reheating the lamp had done. As the dried blood turned liquid again, it tainted the basin water a light red. Olivia's breathing went to almost nothing, the blacks of her eyes growing till they swallowed almost all the blue. Saliva flooded her mouth. It had been the same at the hotel, but being thrown off her feet had snapped her out of the frenzy.

In less than a heartbeat, with only minimal input from her brain, she cupped her hands and gulped down the blood-tainted water. The cold of the water didn't matter now. She was ravenous, savage, not even stopping when the basin emptied. The hand was licked clean, too.

Only when it was done did her senses fully return and the weight of what she'd just done sink in. A more logical instinct then took hold of her, and she stuck her fingers down her throat. A small amount of liquid was vomited up. It splashed down into the snow, staining it red.

That's not all of it, keep going.

As she was about to induce a second bout of vomiting, she stopped. A light wave of euphoria washed through her. It was a mild buzz, nothing spectacular, like two beers drunk, but somehow sharper, more alert. She didn't feel so cold anymore. Deciding not to try to induce another round of vomiting, Olivia wiped her hand clean of the red spittle in the snow. She pulled up her hood and sat on one of the granite benches to think.

It was real now, there was no more doubt. Men were hunting her, and if they caught her, they'd burn her alive like the girl in the video. How had they tracked her? Did the phone give her away? At least she'd managed to destroy it. But if they already knew her name, destroying it may have been a waste of time. The fire was a good distraction either way. Without it, she wouldn't have escaped the hotel.

Light a fire, punch someone, flip some power breakers, create some chaos, it might give you a chance to escape.

The injured man, would he live? Probably, but he'd lost a lot of blood. Maybe they'd get some crooked doctor or vet to patch him up. There wouldn't be a police report. The fire was probably put out, and nobody would stick their nose too far into a stabbing at a sleazy hotel. They'd assume a drug deal gone bad. Would they give up now? No, they'd redouble their efforts, see her as more of a threat that needed to be wiped out, the mangled hand just further evidence she was the abomination they feared.

Where would they make their next attempt? The concierge had taken something of a beating before talking. Surprising, but maybe that discretion he'd harped on about meant something. Maybe others who paid a lot more for that discretion expected him to keep his mouth shut. *Everyone's got a code, I guess.*

Either way, twenty dollars only bought a few punches. He'd told them the room number and given them the spare key. But had he spilled the beans about the cock-and-bull story of going to the ferry terminal in the morning? Probably, but would they have believed it? Maybe, but she couldn't bet her life on a maybe.

If they were in any doubt, they might post a watch at the bus and train terminals. But they were down a man, might not want to spread themselves so thin if they didn't need to. If they were on the fence about whether she was going to the ferry terminal, she'd need to convince them. Rummaging in her jeans, Olivia pulled out her wallet and removed her father's credit card from the hidden back pouch. Colored gold, it glinted in the gaslight like some powerful relic, tempting her. She quickly returned the card to the wallet, as if to contain its power, then put the wallet back into her pocket.

A plan formed in her head. It wasn't a great plan, but it was something. Throwing up her hood, she pulled the strings to draw the hood in tight against the wind, then she stood and exited the alcove out into the freezing wind.

Walking away, Olivia looked up to the statue of Gustav Lang towering in the darkness. *Thanks for the help, Big Man.* Still riding a little warm buzz, she half-expected him to respond or wink.

She was left disappointed as the statue kept its silent vigil over the city. *Whatever man, later.* Olivia trudged away into the freezing night.

CANAL

The lights along the canal were brighter now, the buildings taller. Red brick replaced granite, but the street still looked shady. The old town must have still been a couple of miles away. It had stopped snowing, which was a small mercy, but the wind still cut like a razor. Whatever buzz of energy Olivia had received from the blood-tainted water was almost worn off, along with it, whatever beer-coat effect it had provided.

Shelter would be found soon, but she had a mission to complete before that despite the cold. *Gotta be one soon. They used to be fucking everywhere.* Looking east toward where the river should be, a massive blue sign shined into the night. The building towered above its neighbors and was at least fifteen stories.

The sign read: ROYSTON.

Royston was ubiquitous. They had a hotel in every city in the country, sometimes several. More importantly, they were expensive so they might still have rooms available. *You'll do.* Olivia powered onward, but not toward the hotel.

After some time searching and despairing of ever finding what she was looking for, Olivia took a detour down some side streets. Eventually, the goal of her quest came into focus, a small rectangle, glowing with a dim fluorescent light.

Very few public phonebooths remained. Even drug dealers had moved on to using burner phones, but here one stood, a relic from a bygone age, an age that had only gone by a decade ago.

Ashtown's phonebooths were different from in the rest of the country, larger, old-fashioned, they had elaborate wrought iron frames painted a dark green. Tourists often posed for pictures in them. Maybe that was the only reason they were still around.

Swinging open the door, a powerful stench of urine emerged. A few empty beer and vodka bottles sat in the corner. Olivia didn't have time to care about the smell. She stepped inside and stomached it. At least it was shelter from the wind, and there was a small heating element to stop the phone from freezing over.

Picking up the receiver, she was relieved to hear a dial-tone, but the phonebook had been stripped bare, probably for toilet paper. Only the spine remained. Rummaging in her pockets, a fistful of change and her wallet were produced. Olivia propped the receiver between her head and shoulder, then shoveled two bronze fifty-cent coins into the slot and punched some buttons.

"Directory inquiries, how may I help you this morning?" a friendly voice chimed on the other end.

"Yeah, I need the number for Royston hotel in Ashtown?"

"Of course, let me just pull that up for you." Rapid typing could be heard. "Ah, so we have three Royston's listed in Ashtown. Which one do you need?"

"Ah, I'm not sure. Do they have names or addresses listed?

"Yes, ma'am. So, there is the Ashtown Metro, Ashtown Riverfront—"

"Riverfront, riverfront," Olivia cut in.

"OK, ma'am. Would you like to be connected?"

"Yes, please."

"One moment."

Muzak played as the call was transferred. Olivia put in another fifty-cent coin to be sure she wasn't cut off. The glass of the phonebooth fogged over from Olivia's breath. She stamped her feet to keep warm. Ringing, ringing, then the phone on the other side finally picked up. Olivia prepared herself to put on her best formal voice despite the cold.

"Royston Riverfront, how may I help you this morning?" came the voice of the receptionist on the other end.

"Hello. I was wondering if you have any rooms available for tonight for one person?"

"Do you mean now, this morning? It's 3 AM or tonight?" The receptionist sounded a little confused. Olivia gave a fake laugh.

"I mean now, this morning. I got stuck in Ashtown with the train situation. I'm still in the office. I really only need the room for a few hours to freshen up. I'm catching the ferry to Redhorn at 8 AM tomorrow."

Olivia had to steady herself from the cold so her teeth didn't chatter on the call.

"Ah, I see. We've had a lot of last-minute bookings. Luckily, we do have a room available, however, it is a suite. It comes to six-hundred-forty-five dollars inclusive, but I would need to take payment up front for the room due to the late hour."

Olivia winced. It didn't matter whether it was a dollar or a thousand, the potential risk to her father was the same.

"That will do just fine. You are near the ferry terminal, correct?"

"Yes, ma'am. It's less than a half-mile straight down the street."

"Good, good. Would it be possible for you to book a car to the ferry terminal in the morning as well? I have a lot of luggage."

"Yes, ma'am? What time?"

"7:30 AM, and could you have the driver have a sign with my name on it. I really don't want to be delayed in the morning."

"Of course, ma'am. And the name?"

Olivia paused for a moment to think. She had to roll the dice and assume the men following her already knew her name and hope they'd take the bait. Either way, she couldn't book the room under a fake name with a credit card, assuming it hadn't been canceled already, in which case all this had been for naught.

"Olivia Thompson."

"And you are booking using a card in your own name?"

"My husband's, Alan Thompson. We work for the same firm."

Olivia rested her head against the body of the phone in shame.

"That's fine, Mrs. Thompson. Could you call out the long number on the front of the card?"

Olivia and the receptionist went through the to and fro of the booking. Finally, the receptionist completed her list of questions.

"OK great. I'll just pop you on hold. Sometimes the authorization takes a little time."

An age seemed to pass as more horrible Muzak played on the other end of the line. *They're declining the card. It's reported stolen. Hang up now. They might be able to trace it, you idiot.* Olivia made to hang up the phone when the Muzak stopped.

"That's just gone through now. We hope to see you soon, Mrs. Thompson."

"Thank you very much," Olivia answered, then hung up the phone.

The die had been cast. In desperation, the unthinkable done. She just hoped the authorities would accept the fact the card was stolen. The signed note left at home would help. It was a high-stakes gamble, and one with a completely uncertain payoff. The purification squad might not take the bait. Hell, they might not even know her real name, but anything was worth it if it gave even the slightest chance of an edge over her pursuers. Delaying them even half an hour might be the difference between life and death. *You're not gonna end up like the girl in the video. You're not—*

Chain of thought suddenly interrupted, Olivia froze. Someone was outside the phonebooth door. The sound of their footsteps had been silenced by the snow, but someone was there, she was certain. The windows of the booth were clouded by condensation from her body heat. She couldn't see who was out there but, in turn, they couldn't see in. It gave her an element of surprise. Reaching down, she silently picked up an empty beer bottle from the floor and put it in the pocket of her parka but kept her hand gripped on its neck.

With a swift kick to the phone booth door, it swung open with force. The person on the other side was knocked clean off their feet. Olivia pounced on them, ready to smash the beer bottle over their head.

"Aghhhhhh…"

Olivia straddled a homeless man wearing a half-dozen layers of clothing. Another second, and she might have clocked him over the head with the bottle.

"Oh, sorry. I just needed to make a phone call," she apologized, climbing off him.

"That's my phonebooth. I ain't got nothin' worth stealin'."

"Sorry, you just snuck up on me. I thought you were gonna try to rob me."

"I ain't never robbed no one."

The bum muttered incoherently as he helped himself to his feet with difficulty. He was loaded down with a backpack, a thick sleeping bag strapped to the back.

"Again, sorry. Hey, do you know of any homeless shelters around here?" Olivia asked.

"The hell would I help you? You were about to cave my damn head in."

"I'll give you a cigarette," Olivia offered.

"Ten bucks."

"A cigarette."

"Five bucks."

"A cigarette."

"OK," the bum relented, his negotiation leverage limited somewhat by Olivia still holding the bottle. "Go back to the canal and head north, only a few hundred feet. Lime Street. On the left, can't miss it. They might have a bed for ya."

"Thanks. Why don't you go there?" Olivia handed him the cigarette, and he stuck it behind his ear.

"I'm fine. Got a nice thick sleeping bag, and my phonebooth to keep me outta the wind."

"You could freeze to death."

"I've survived much worse nights than this, missy, let me tell ya."

"OK. Sorry again about the bottle."

The bum waived her off and entered his wrought-iron fortress, muttering. Olivia stuffed the beer bottle into her parka pocket. She was thankful, diversion arranged and a decent lead on a place to wait out the rest of the night.

You don't even need to sleep at the shelter, just rest for a few hours, get out of this cold.

Wind kicking up again, Olivia made her way back to the canal. The streets were almost deserted, save the odd shadowy figure trudging silently through the snow. Reaching a tiny footbridge over the canal, she looked west. Bolted to the corner building was the street name:

LIME ST.

About halfway down the street was a well-lit entranceway. One or two people seemed to be smoking outside the front door. *Sanctuary*. Cold seemed to penetrate every muscle in her body. It didn't matter, respite was in sight. Even if they didn't have a bed available, she'd ask to stay by the heat, just a couple of hours, on account of the weather.

The smokers nodded as she approached. The doors were wood with metal studs, sturdy with a small hatch to talk to people who wanted to enter. The building must have been two hundred years old. Above the door, the name of the facility was etched into a wooden plaque:

UNION HOUSE 08 - LIME STREET

Old poor houses built by the unions, now homeless shelters run by non-profits. Olivia pulled the large metal ring knocker and clanged it twice against the door, the dull thuds echoed in the night. Expecting the security hatch to open Olivia was surprised when the right-hand door opened a crack. A plume of hot air emerged along with a hand, attached to the hand was the friendly face of a young woman beckoning her in from the cold. She stepped tentatively through the threshold and the door was closed behind.

Olivia was stood in a stone room with a low ceiling and a small reception desk with a phone. To the left, through more modern-looking double doors, was a multipurpose hall filled with cots. The lights were dimmed. It looked warm, inviting. The young woman was about Olivia's height, hair in a ponytail, with a soft round face and big eyes. The exact kind of friendly face you pictured working in a homeless shelter, just as warm and inviting as the hall beyond the doors.

"Hey, I'm really stuck. Do you have any beds? If not, if I could just warm myself by the fire. My landlord…" Olivia began.

"Relax, we have a bed available. You don't need to tell us why you need it."

Olivia smiled, and the woman smiled back at her.

"The only thing we ask for is a name."

Olivia hesitated for a moment, suddenly concerned. What did they need a name for? It wasn't a damn hotel.

"Just a first name." The woman then cupped her hand and whispered, "It doesn't need to be your real name. We get a lot of domestic abuse cases here. We understand."

"Jane. My name's Jane," Olivia answered.

"Nice to meet you, Jane. I'm Magdalene." The woman scribbled on her clipboard and smiled. "Let's get you inside. I'll show you where you can set up shop. You look freezing."

"I am."

The young woman's wide eyes radiated a warm sympathy and she put a hand on Olivia's shoulder to comfort her. Olivia could have hugged her.

Despite the high ceiling, the hall wasn't cold, but it wasn't overly warm, either. The room held about thirty beds arranged in rows. About two-thirds were already occupied with sleeping residents. Another worker sat at a small desk and chair in the corner, probably in case of trouble during the night. A third worker seemed to be tending to a sick resident. All the cots near the radiators were taken. Magdalene walked Olivia silently over to a cot near the wall.

"This is you," Magdalene whispered.

"Thanks."

"You don't seem the type, but I have to say it anyway. Absolutely no drugs. You can smoke tobacco, but you have to go outside."

"I can live with that," Olivia answered with a smile. "Is it OK if I warm myself over by the radiators before I lie down?"

"Of course, and if you wanna talk at any point, I'm a pretty good listener." Magdalene smiled and walked away to a desk in the corner of the hall near the door.

The place seemed safe enough, but Olivia wasn't confident enough to leave her backpack by the bed. It wasn't heavy anyway, and she doubted they'd let someone else take the bed. Being careful not to wake anyone, Olivia made her way across the hall. The far wall had a bank of oil radiators with flaking white paint. They were going full blast to heat the massive room. A wall of warmth hit her as she approached.

Fingers flexed and unflexed as circulation returned to frozen hands. *Toasty*. All around her, the sounds of the sleeping residents rang out: snores, coughs, people turning in their sleep…light padding footsteps. Someone approached. Olivia was getting better at noticing. She turned to look. A very slight young woman in her socks came to warm herself by the radiators. The woman took up residence next to Olivia, holding out her hands to the heat.

"You new? I haven't seen you before," the woman asked.

"Yeah, I had some…domestic issues," Olivia responded.

"Tell me about it."

Olivia glanced at the woman's face. Her lip was split, and she had a black eye. Both were a few days old and healing. They shared a smile, then returned to staring at the radiator, hands outstretched like it was some life-giving deity.

"I'm Andrea, by the way. Well, that's what I call myself when I'm here. I don't want my ex calling around looking for me."

Although the woman seemed harmless enough, Olivia kept her guard up, nonetheless. The more questions someone asked, the more you could trip up, reveal something with a kernel of truth. Better to steer the conversation toward something mundane.

"I'm Jane. I'm stuck over near the wall. It's not so warm over there," Olivia said.

"Yeah. In winter, nobody wants those beds, and in summer, everyone wants 'em."

"Better than being out in the snow tonight. It's damn freezing out there. I was surprised they had any free beds at all."

"Before this week, I hadn't been here in at least a year," Andrea began. "But this place used to be packed. If you didn't show up before 8 PM, no bed."

"What changed?" Olivia asked.

"Got back with my ex again. Guess I didn't learn my lesson."

"No, I mean what changed here. The place is only two-thirds full with weather like this?"

Andrea seemed disappointed Olivia was more interested in the homeless shelter. She clearly just needed a friendly ear to listen.

"Oh, yeah. I think some folks are suspicious of the shelters with the new rule changes and all."

Ears suddenly pricked up. Rule changes, policy changes, new recommendations, government guidance. All those terms invariably meant trouble, but Olivia kept her cool.

"Rule changes?" Olivia asked.

"Is this your first time or something?"

"Yeah. I really don't wanna talk about it, if that's OK?"

"Nobody thinks they'll end up in a place like this till they do." Andrea put her tiny hand on Olivia's shoulder, who resisted the urge to pull away.

"Don't worry, the new rules aren't anything to worry about," Andrea said. "All these shelters used to be fully run by different charities. This one's run by the Shelter for All, but a while back, I think the government-mandated all shelters had to have a religious ethos or something."

"Oh, so what does that entail exactly?" Olivia asked.

"Not much. It just means that all the shelters are part-run by the Center of Friends now. Some of the older folks are overly suspicious of them, so they'd rather stay on the streets. In practice, all it means is, once in a while, you get an impromptu sermon from a wet behind the ears pastor."

Olivia's stomach dropped. *Fuck.* The Center of Friends was a conservative religious group with links to the government. They ran one of the shady websites Olivia had seen when she looked for advice about her diagnosis online. Suddenly gripped by paranoia, Olivia swept her gaze around the room as subtly as possible. The worker at the desk, was he a lookout? The man tending to the sick resident, what was he really checking? Looking to the entrance, she could see Magdalene, chatting away quietly on her cellphone.

You walked right into the lion's den, you fucking idiot.

"I think I can stomach a boring sermon if I don't have to stay out in the snow tonight," Olivia replied, laughing a little. Every nerve ending in her body was on edge.

"Yeah, I think it's just the older homeless. They're overly suspicious."

"Magdalene, was she here when you used to come here a year ago?" Olivia asked.

"No, I think she's new. She's really nice, though, and she's a great listener."

I bet she is. Olivia looked over at Magdalene across the hall, still on her cellphone.

"So, do you think you're gonna be staying a fe—"

"You smoke?" Olivia interrupted.

"Yeah, but I smoked my last one about an hour ago."

"I have smokes if you have a light. Wanna go out for one?" Olivia produced the pack from her pocket and handed one to Andrea.

"Sure, if you insist. Let me grab my shoes," Andrea answered with a smile.

"And that lighter," Olivia said after her in a hushed voice.

"And the lighter."

It'd look less suspicious if she left for a smoke with Andrea, more like she was gonna come back. As Andrea padded off to put on her shoes, Olivia gripped the neck of the beer bottle in her parka pocket. Magdalene was off the phone now and just sat there, smiling a broad, friendly smile far across the hall, like butter wouldn't melt. *Who the fuck were you talking to?*

Andrea quickly returned in her shoes and hoodie, cigarette already hanging from her mouth.

"Ready?" Andrea asked.

"Yup." Olivia took out a smoke and put it behind her ear to try to sell it as much as possible.

Both women walked silently toward the exit. Olivia kept one hand in her pocket gripped on the neck of the beer bottle. As they approached Magdalene's desk, she perked up.

"We're just gonna head out for a smoke," Andrea said in a hushed voice.

"OK, I'll let you guys out."

Hand like a claw gripping the bottle, Olivia smiled warmly at Magdalene. The three walked out together to the small stone room that led outside. Olivia was on a hair-trigger.

"Oh, Jane. You can leave your backpack in here. It's much safer," Magdalene told Olivia.

"Nah, I'd rather keep it with me. It's got all my stuff, and you know…"

"It's a rule we have when people go out to smoke." Magdalene started. "We want you to feel secure here. We have someone monitoring the hall to make sure there are no thefts."

"It's fine, Jane. No one’s gonna take it," Andrea told her.

"All the same, I'd like to keep it with me."

"It's just one of the rules, Jane," Magdalene insisted, smiling.

Three people, maybe all with assumed names having the friendliest life or death chat in the world. Olivia put her left hand on the bolt of the door to open it. Magdalene was about to reach out to stop her but froze when she noticed Olivia had something concealed in her pocket, then she spotted the blood on the parka sleeve. Olivia stared into Magdalene’s eyes in silence. Andrea seemed oblivious to the game of intimidation playing out right in front of her.

"It fine. It's not a hard and fast rule," Magdalene finally relented.

The bolt was slid over with a *clunk*, the door opened, and Olivia and Andrea stepped out into the snow. Magdalene didn't close it behind them. Instead, she hung by the door, waiting with it open a crack. Removing the cigarette from her ear, Olivia put it between her lips. Andrea cupped her hand, sparked her oil lighter to life, held the flame up, and lit Olivia's cigarette. She took a long drag as Andrea lit her own.

"She usually hang around in the doorway like that?" Olivia asked.

"Sometimes. A lot of people freak out their first night in the shelter and just run away. I think she's just watching out for you," Andrea answered, looking over to Magdalene.

"Thanks for talking to me, Andrea. You have no idea how much it meant," Olivia told Andrea.

Before Andrea could respond, and without any ceremony, Olivia walked calmly but quickly toward the canal. Once she was about twenty feet away, she broke into a run and didn't stop.

"Jane…" Andrea had turned to find Olivia gone.

"Jane! Jane! It's freezing. Don't do this…" Magdalene called into the night after Olivia but didn't give chase.

Running at full speed into the uncertain night, Olivia didn't look behind.

WEAKNESS

For the second time that night, respite had been cruelly snatched away. This is how they wanted her, isolated, alone, nowhere to turn for help. Not just the men chasing her, but the government, too. It was all part of a plan, cut off any support, cripple any organization that might help, tighten the noose.

This time, at least, she'd kept a bearing on her location. She'd run straight up the canal and taken a left over a tiny footbridge onto a deserted street that led to the river. It was at least a mile before legs and lungs gave up. She slumped down on a wooden bench to plan her next move. Her feet were freezing again. The heat gained at the shelter was already almost spent.

The enormous dome of the train station could be seen floodlit in the near distance. Under ordinary circumstances, she could have just hung around in the atrium for a few hours, but that would draw too much attention. There might be someone watching. Olivia put her head in her hands in frustration.

Can't go to a shelter. Don't have cash for a hotel. Can't book one with the card as I'd have to use my real last name. Can't go to the decoy hotel 'cause that's suicide. Won't survive the night in a phone box, not without a sleeping bag. I could steal one from that bum. He kinda deserves it for sending me to that shelter. No, you need decent shelter with heat. Think. Think...

Footsteps broke her chain of thought again, two people, relatively light-footed. Olivia gripped the bottle in her pocket as a precaution as they approached. *Don't freak out like at the phonebooth. They're probably just regular people.* The men slowed and stopped in front of the bench. Olivia looked up. Two young men wrapped up against the cold, faces half-covered. Exhausted, she wouldn't get far running now even if she tried.

"Wallet," demanded one of the young men.

"What?" Olivia asked, half-confused.

"Give us your fuckin' wallet, bitch," demanded the second young man.

Olivia took a quick measure of the two would-be thieves. One was about her height, the other a little shorter, but he gained an inch or two in heavy snow boots. Young, not particularly well built, but they might still be dangerous. It didn't matter. Her train ticket was in that wallet. She wasn't giving it up. Her life depended on it.

"You have a knife or a gun?" Olivia asked them.

"Give us the fucking wallet, now," the first one demanded again, clenching his fist.

"I'll take that as a no," Olivia began. "So, you're just tryin' rob me with what? Intimidation? Don't you need to be intimidating for that?"

Angry now, the young men didn't want to back down, but Olivia had their card marked. She stayed calmly seated. They were amateurs. They hadn't done this many times before, and when they had, they'd always preyed on someone weak, a girl by herself, an old lady.

"Give us the wallet or—"

"Or what, pussy?" Olivia goaded the taller one.

The insult provoked the exact reaction expected. The taller thief threw a decent right hook, but Olivia was ready for it, lurched to his left, and quickly got to her feet. As his fist swung past her face, she quickly pulled out the bottle and swung it into the back of his head with force. It didn't break. He stumbled but didn't fall.

Olivia wasn't in the mood to allow him a second attempt. She swung the bottle again. This time, it hit its target more cleanly. It shattered over the thief's head. He crumpled to the ground like paper, holding the wound.

The accomplice was frozen in fear by the ferocity of Olivia's attack, who now stood over the injured man holding a jagged bottle neck. Still conscious, he managed to stumble to his feet somehow. Blood poured from the gash in his head, trickling down through his hair and dripping into the snow. Olivia's eyes grew like saucers at the sight of the blood. Her breathing became louder, like an animal. She surveyed the two would-be thieves again, this time with new eyes. They were terrified.

"Your boots," Olivia said to the uninjured man, her voice a growl.

"What?"

"Give me your boots," she demanded.

"What? My—"

"Give her the fucking boots, man. Ain't you seen the videos? Look at her eyes," the wounded man urged.

A look of sudden realization came over the uninjured man's face. He understood now what he was really dealing with. The boots were ripped off without unlacing and tossed over to Olivia, who held one with her free hand to check the size against her sneaker.

"Perfect fit. My lucky day," Olivia joked. Her captives didn't see the funny side. "Money."

"We don't have any," answered the uninjured man, his voice shaking.

Olivia regarded the two for a moment, then took off her sneakers and tossed them to the man she'd taken the boots from.

"Go," she ordered.

They didn't question it. The shoeless man quickly slid into the sneakers and helped his wounded friend. Better to give them the sneakers. They'd put more distance between her and them that way. The two hobbled toward the river as fast as they could move, Olivia watched them as they disappeared into the darkness.

Sitting back on the bench, she put the jagged bottle neck in her pocket. Slipping on the boots, she opened the laces and retied them tighter. They were still toasty warm from their previous occupant and overall a pretty good fit.

Getting up to leave, her vision zeroed in on a small patch of bloody snow, a parting gift from the injured man. Before she knew it, Olivia was on her knees, face inches from the patch of dark red snow, panting like a wild dog. *Fight it. Fight it.* Pulling away took immense strength, but she managed to overcome it. She kicked the blood-tainted snow, then sprinted away toward the canal.

Whatever urge had gripped her was powerful. How long before she couldn't control it any longer? Nurse Ramirez had been wrong, or maybe just misinformed. The changes were coming sooner, stronger. *Gotta make it to the border, gotta survive, gotta get answers.*

Olivia trudged on through the snow, up the canal toward the train station, still half-frozen, no plan in mind. Maybe taking the blood would have kept her warm till morning. It was less diluted than at the fountain. No, better not. Who knew what effect undiluted blood might have. She might become savage, uncontrollable. *At least I got some new boots.*

As the canal grew nearer the center of the city, the walls raised in height. A set of steps continued the pedestrian sidewalk up to a higher level. Judging by how close the train station dome was if she followed the sidewalk, she'd probably make it to the bustling old town center in less than a mile. But something caught her attention. On the inside wall of the canal was a small, cobbled footpath cordoned off by a chain.

Curiosity piqued, Olivia stepped over the chain to see where the path led. All up one side of the canal were cave-like alcoves boarded up with plywood. Following instinct, she walked along the narrow path up the canal. The plywood barricades didn't look particularly solid but, without tools, there was little hope of getting one open.

Farther up the path, Olivia came across a side tunnel that undercut the street. It had four alcoves, also boarded up, but a flicker of firelight twinkled through the crack near the wall of the furthest one. *Someone lives down here.*

Getting close to the final alcove, it became obvious the barricade had been breached. A fabric tarp hung over a door-sized hole in the plywood and a thin plume of smoke poured out through the side. Olivia removed the broken bottle from her pocket, parted the tarp with it, and cautiously entered the opening.

The alcove looked bigger than expected. An old oil barrel containing a dying fire sat at its center, illuminating a small circle. The rest of the space was shrouded in darkness. As her eyes adjusted, the outline of a person could be made out, lurking just on the edge of the darkness.

"I haven't got anything worth stealing. Get the hell out of here," came a woman's voice from the penumbra.

"Only thing I wanna steal is some heat for a few hours," Olivia told her.

The figure stepped into the light of the fire barrel. A vagrant lady, dark hair with streaks of gray. Clothes old and worn but not tattered or filthy, she still took some pride in her appearance. She might have been anything from thirty-five to fifty. It was hard to tell with homeless folk. Living on the streets aged people prematurely.

Gripped in her left hand was a Phillips-head screwdriver, the point glinting in the firelight. Olivia eyed the weapon and the woman holding it cautiously. After two previous encounters that night, she wasn't going to walk away from heat and shelter, not without trying. The woman stood her ground but kept glancing nervously at the jagged bottle neck in Olivia's hand.

She's just afraid.

In a calculated gesture of goodwill, Olivia placed the broken bottle neck on the ground. The woman lowered the screwdriver to her side but kept a tight hold of it.

"You got any money?"

"A couple of singles, none I can spare. But…" Olivia rooted in her parka pocket. The woman raised the screwdriver before dropping it again when the pack of cigarettes was produced. "There's eight left. You can have half."

Four of the cigarettes were pulled from the pack and held out to the woman. Quickly but cautiously, the woman snatched them from Olivia's open hand.

"OK, you can stay till morning. But don't cause me any trouble."

"Don't worry, I won't. Sorry, I don't have a light. The gas ran out."

The woman slipped the screwdriver into her back pocket, then put one of the cigarettes in her mouth. She picked up a tiny twig from the ground and held it to the dying embers. Lighting her cigarette, she then held the taper out to Olivia, who did the same.

Smoking in silence for a time, the two heated themselves by the dying fire. It was obvious why a homeless person would take up residence in the alcove, sheltered as it was from the elements and prying eyes. It also seemed to retain a decent amount of heat, maybe because it was below street level. Picking up a small piece of broken tree branch, the woman added it to the barrel. A flurry of sparks emerged, and the fire glowed brighter.

"Last piece," said the woman.

With the extra light from the fire, more of the alcove was revealed. It was about the size of a small living room, a bedroll in one corner with some personal effects and old sofa chair in the other. Olivia looked at the heavy-looking sofa chair, then glanced near the entranceway in confusion.

"How'd you even get that down here?"

The woman laughed.

"Once in a while, the canal freezes so hard you can just slide heavy stuff down it.

"Handy, I guess."

"Butler's Lights, you're a rich kid, not from Ashtown but somewhere nice," the woman said.

"Is it that obvious?"

"It's the little things that give you away, I suppose."

"Where are you from?" asked Olivia.

The woman was a little shocked, clearly not accustomed to being asked personal questions.

"A tiny town in Wildplanes you've never heard of, where they grow corn, and nothing ever happens."

"How'd you end up here?"

"Came to the city to find work. Didn't find any. Partied too much, ran up some drug debts…" The woman took a long drag of her cigarette before continuing, "Guy I knew suggested I could pay off the debt by making some adult movies."

Olivia looked up at the woman as she described how her life had turned to ash.

"That industry chews you up and spits you out pretty quick. The drug problem got worse and, since then, I've been on the streets."

"Oh."

"Sorry you asked?"

"No. People do what they have to survive," Olivia answered. "Can't you go back? To Wildplanes I mean. Do you have family?"

"Thought about it…but I'm too far gone I guess."

Both women stared into the fire in silence again, the flames hypnotic. The warmth was returning to Olivia's body.

"What about you?" the woman asked.

"Would you believe me if I said drugs, too?"

"No."

"Why?"

"Kids on harder drugs have a dead look in their eyes like they can't wait for the grave," the woman stared into Olivia's blue eyes as she spoke. "But there's a rage in your eyes. I bet if I tried to rat you out, you'd cut right through me and keep moving."

Olivia nodded in somber acknowledgment. Both continued to smoke.

"I'm guessing you can't go back to wherever you're from?" the woman asked.

"No. Too far gone, I guess."

The woman seemed to understand. Maybe she didn't guess exactly what Olivia was but knew enough not to probe further. The fire was getting low again, darkness reclaiming the room.

"I'm gonna get back to sleep. There's an old chair in the corner you can use till morning."

"Hey, you have a watch or an alarm?"

"Got an old digital watch, why?"

"Can I borrow it till morning?"

"Everything costs something on the streets," the woman told her.

Olivia took any remaining items out of her parka, pulled it off, and held it out to the woman.

"I'd wash the sleeve before you try and sell it."

"Why wouldn't I wear it?" the woman asked, taking the parka.

"It's the little things that give you away," Olivia answered.

The woman noticed the blood on the parka sleeve, nodding in acknowledgement of the warning. She took the watch from her pocket and tossed it over to Olivia, who caught it without a fumble.

"Thanks. What's your name?" Olivia asked.

"It's Cara. I won't ask yours. Goodnight."

Olivia nodded. The woman slunk away into the darkness. The rustle of a sleeping bag was heard. It wasn't a great trade, but the parka was a liability. David had seen it. Better to double up with the hoodies.

Cigarette finished, Olivia flicked the butt into the barrel. She picked up the broken bottle neck and put it in her hoodie pocket, then took a tiny twig from the floor and lit another cigarette. *Two left. One for the train, and one for when you've made it to the border.*

Crossing the darkened space, Olivia slumped into the old sofa chair. Comfortable enough, it wasn't damp despite the location. The alcove was too warm and dry to be solely heated by the barrel fire. One of the walls must have backed onto a building's basement, maybe a generator or boiler pumping out heat, the alcove leeching just enough to make the place habitable. A subterranean palace, ruled by a fallen queen.

The watch had an old eight-digit style display that glowed green. It read 4:15 AM. Cigarette hanging out of her mouth, Olivia managed to set a timer for 7 AM. The would-be thieves, one of them knew what she was. *Ain't you seen the videos.* Clearly, not the video Olivia had seen of the young girl being burned alive, but something else. Sometimes, there were stories about vampire videos doing the rounds in the private message groups at school.

Olivia had never paid attention, figured it was viral marketing for some found footage movie. What was in those videos? What had the thieves seen that put such an unholy fear into them? One thing for certain, she'd learned that night violence was a blunt instrument. Intimidation was more as powerful a tool. She'd seen the weak buckle under its weight.

A quick movement broke Olivia's chain of thought. Scampering carefully along the corner of the wall toward her was a small rat. Despite the dying light, she could make out the rat's silhouette perfectly. It stopped to chew on something a few feet away. She carefully observed it for a time.

As the light of the fire grew weaker and weaker, her vision grew stronger, clearer. She couldn't see in the dark as much as she could see objects in the dark. The darkness was still black, but the structure of the alcove could be seen as a faint outline. Every object now had its own outline, even down to small stones on the ground, but clearest of all were the living things. The rat with its tiny blue glowing outline, and across the room, the thin figure of Cara, rhythmically breathing in her sleeping bag, giving off a perfect blue silhouette.

Gnawing away at a small root, the rat irritated Olivia. Rising from the chair without a sound, she crept toward the hapless rodent. Following some base instinct, in one swift movement, she snatched the rat from the ground and held it in a talon-like grip. Head held fast, the rat let out a tiny squeal and clawed furiously with its hind legs, its life depending on this titanic struggle.

Relenting, Olivia dropped her prey, and it scuttled its way across the ground toward the alcove entrance. Smiling, she returned to the sofa chair and sat down as silently as she'd risen. Cara hadn't heard a thing. It was unlikely the woman would try to sneak out and inform on Olivia, but it was reassuring to know she wouldn't get far if she tried.

How can you see like this? Move so quietly? Strike so quickly? Did the blood-tainted water at the statue speed things up, or just make my senses temporarily sharper? How long do I have left? They were all good questions, but they were questions for when the border had been crossed not before. Olivia generally hated thinking about the past but, in that moment, it was a good way to drown out the questions of the future. The memory her mind chose was a curious one, sparked by her conversation with Cara.

Thirteen or maybe fourteen, Olivia sat straight-backed at an upright piano in a spare room of her home, her mother watching over. Slowly and deliberately, Olivia’s fingers played out a melody. The tune was simple, but it still took concentration to get it right.

As the piece progressed, it became slightly more complex. Olivia subtly but deliberately lost her timing, and the tune descended into a discordant mess. Her mother looked disappointed but still smiled at Olivia as she finished the piece.

"I want to stop," said Olivia.

"Sure, you've practiced enough for today, sweetie," her mother told her.

"No, I want to stop piano for good. I hate it."

"But you're getting so good. Even I can hear you're improving,"

Olivia closed the lid on the piano with just enough force that the instrument let out an off note in protest.

"Olivia, this instrument was expensive. You need to treat it with more care." Her mother ran her hand along the polished hardwood.

"Why is it so important to you that I learn the piano. If you love it so much, why don't you learn to play it?" Olivia asked her in frustration, the first signs of teenage rebellion breaking through.

"As you get older, it gets harder to learn new things. I would have loved to learn piano when I was your age."

"So, why didn't you then? Maybe you wouldn't be torturing me with it now," Olivia said.

Back then, her mother didn't get as angry. She just looked deeply disappointed.

"You think everyone can afford expensive pianos and private lessons, Olivia?"

"No," Olivia conceded.

"No." Her mother nodded. "We spoil you a little, and some of that's my fault. Look, some kids have to grow up fast. There's no time or money for things like piano."

"I know, after your mom got sick…" Olivia began softly. It was always a difficult subject to broach with her mother.

"Sick," her mother let out a small scoff. "Yeah, it was a sickness of a sort, I suppose. She liked to drink. When I was eight, she ran off with the husband of a woman down the street, left me and daddy all alone. Our little family was the talk of the town. I was the kid whose mamma ran away."

Her mother's voice changed ever so slightly as she spoke. It became less formal, less practiced. The hint of a more rural twang even broke through. Olivia's grandfather had died when she was six. She remembered it clear as day. Her mother cried for days, but was her grandmother still alive out there somewhere?

"Is she still a—" Olivia began.

"No. We got a call a few years later. She was dead. She'd taken to something harder than booze. The fella she'd run off with wasn't around anymore. We didn't have money for things like pianos, but my daddy being a Godfearing man still found the money to bury the woman who ran out on us."

Olivia couldn't speak. Her mother was a stranger to her in that moment, there was hatred in her voice, teeth gritted, angry, the mask was pulled away just enough to reveal the poor angry kid from the rural west. Then like a light switch, her mother's face returned to normal.

"Me and daddy didn't have much, Olivia," her mother began, voice now with no trace of the rural accent it had moments earlier, "but we had each other, and we had our faith in God, and he watched over us."

After the revelation, Olivia persevered with playing the piano for another six months out of respect to her mother, or maybe it was out of respect to the poor kid from the rural west who couldn't afford those kinds of things, she wasn't sure which. Either way, eventually, she gave up the ghost.

The memory couldn't be indulged any longer. The past was the past, and Olivia had to focus on the present. Looking down at the watch, the glowing digits on its face read 4:40 AM. She slipped it into her jeans pocket, closed her eyes, and tried to clear her mind of all thought. *No memories, no thinking, no questions, just sleep.*

The mantra must have been repeated fifty times before it took effect. Finally, she slipped into a restless slumber.

Morning

Shafts of morning light spilled into the tunnel through cracks around the plywood barrier. Olivia woke in a panic, frantically checking her pockets before remembering she'd destroyed her cellphone. Brain catching up, she produced the small digital watch. The alarm hadn't gone off yet, and it wouldn't for another ten minutes. The sun had woken her early.

Good.

Preparing quickly, she took out the spare hoodie and threw it on over the existing one, then threw up both hoods. It was a stretch to imagine Cara had managed to rob her during the night, but she couldn't leave anything to chance. A cursory check of her bag showed nothing had been taken. She did the same with her wallet. The only thing in it worth stealing was the train ticket to Overton, and it was still there. Olivia gave it a quick kiss for good luck.

Now in the sunlight, only Cara's head was visible out the top of the sleeping bag. Olivia walked over and stood watching her for a moment. Face narrow, gaunt, how long would Cara survive eking out an existence on the streets? How many winters did she have left before one finished her off? Taking one of the little sponge cakes from her bag, Olivia set it next to the sleeping bag, along with the digital watch. She wished she had more to give, but everything else was necessary for her survival.

"Thanks, Cara," Olivia whispered almost inaudibly.

Moving silently, Olivia walked to the tarp, parted it, and stepped out into the crisp morning air. She moved along the edge of the waterway and up toward the street. Snow swirled gently in small eddies, the calm before the storm. Voices could be heard, the chatter of an early morning worker on his cellphone, a delivery driver dropping off goods.

In the light of the morning sun, the city was docile, not the monster it had been only a few hours before. Olivia stepped over the chain barrier and emerged into the street. The dome of the train terminal dominated the skyline in front. Target in sight, she made a beeline for it, stopping for nothing.

Eventually emerging across the street from the terminal, Olivia took a quick scan of the entrance. She gripped the broken bottleneck in her hoodie pocket. Very few people were hanging around. Everyone wrapped up tight against the cold, faces occluded, it was impossible to spot a threat.

Best to keep moving. More suspicious to stop and linger. Subtly, she took the broken bottleneck from her pocket and dumped it in a trashcan. Nerves calm and steady but alert, she made her way across the street and marched toward the entrance. She almost expected a group of men to approach or an arm to grab from behind. Nothing. She walked through the large, automated doors without ceremony. *Maybe they took the bait.*

The atrium wasn't nearly as busy as the day before, but everyone seemed to be in a rush to get the last trains, zigzagging about like insects with some mission for the hive. Olivia's destination was the ticket kiosks, needing a reissued ticket. As she walked, she pulled down her hoods, not wanting attention from the security guards.

The thin smattering of commuters was spread across about ten kiosks, no real queue. Spotting the same clerk from the day before, Olivia decided to deal with the devil she knew.

"Hey, is the train to Overton running?" Olivia asked, taking the ticket from her wallet.

"It is. It leaves the station from platform seven at 8:00 AM."

A massive wave of euphoria washed over Olivia like a drug at the good news.

"We spoke yesterday. You said I could exchange my ticket."

"Of course. May I see your existing ticket?"

Olivia placed the train ticket in the metal draw like it was a bearer bond for a million dollars. The tray slid back to the clerk, who carefully examined the ticket, then punched it with a hole puncher that read 'void' in tiny circles.

"You won't have much company."

"What? Olivia asked.

"Very few people have come to exchange their tickets. Forecast is so bad most folks are afraid to risk the journey, I suppose."

"Guess I'll have room to put my feet up then."

"Yeah, but don't let the conductor see you do that."

Both women chuckled. The clerk typed on a clunky-looking old-fashioned electronic device set up beside her computer and ticket printer.

"Something wrong with the computers?" Olivia asked.

"Yeah, network went down sometime last night. Our computers are offline. Gotta do things the old-fashioned way."

The woman typed cautiously on the antiquated device. It didn't have a full keyboard, only about fifteen fat gray keys that were stained yellow. There was a slot on the side presumably where it printed the ticket. *Thing looks older than I am.* When the clerk finished typing, the device came to life. It screeched as it went about its work and eventually spat out a small, dark red ticket. Tearing it off, the clerk put it in the slot and slid it over to Olivia, who picked it up and eyed it suspiciously.

"This is it?" asked Olivia.

"Yes, all the necessary information is on there."

On closer inspection, the ticket was a deep maroon. It was printed on thick card paper and embossed with the Northern Star Railways logo as a security feature. The ticket read:

'Northern Star Railways - Ashtown-Overton -S -OW -E'

Most of the ticket was pre-printed, the clunky machine only printing the -S -OW -E, single, one-way and express. Crucially, it bore no name, a stroke of luck.

"You're sure they'll let me through security with this thing?" asked Olivia, unsure of the old-fashioned ticket.

"Yes. Enjoy your trip, ma'am."

"Great. I like your glasses, by the way," said Olivia.

"Thank you."

The clerk smiled at the compliment and readjusted the red-framed specs for effect. Olivia walked away, ticket in hand. Nothing would pry it from her grasp till she was sitting comfortably on a train headed north. Overhead, the signs guided her across the vast atrium toward platform seven.

It was highly unlikely her pursuers would try anything in such a public place, but they were brazen enough at the hotel, so nothing could be discounted. Every face and body was scanned for signs of danger. Every man with a hand in his pocket could be holding a knife, a gun, a syringe.

Eventually, the overhead signs led to a security screening station. Beyond it were platforms six to nine, the queue small but slow-moving. The screening station was manned by four security screeners but guarded by two soldiers with assault rifles. One stood a post, the other patrolling. Joining the queue, it seemed like one of the soldiers was eye-balling Olivia.

He doesn't know shit, keep calm.

As the solder walked within inches of her, Olivia noticed something, something she wouldn't have noticed even a few days ago.

The soldier had several magazines in some kind of a tactical vest. Two magazines had blue tape strapped around them, the same as the magazine in the rifle. The other two spare magazines had red tape. Documentaries about the Final War were more like propaganda, and very little actual combat was shown, or what the vampires actually fought like, but they always had stock footage of the brave soldiers of the NSC, smiling broadly, holding their old rifles.

The magazines always had red tape around them. *Splinter rounds*. Olivia didn't know how they worked, but she knew they were some type of anti-vampire round for certain. Which meant the blue magazines had to be for humans, vampire sympathizers, or some other threat they didn't talk about on the news.

They're not looking for you. They're not prepared for you. You're a needle in a haystack. The soldier walked past again. It was just paranoia. His eyes scanned everyone the same.

Eventually, Olivia arrived at the front of the queue. She put her backpack and wallet in a plastic tray and slid it toward the x-ray scanner, her ticket firmly in her grasp. One of the screeners gestured for her to step forward through the metal detector. It gave no protest as Olivia stepped through. Trays came rolling through the x-ray scanner. Olivia's emerged and was picked up by a security screener. *Shit.*

"Whose bag is this?"

"Mine," Olivia answered.

The screener walked the tray over to an inspection table and placed it down. She had a stern face and wore black nitrile gloves. Olivia's face was calm, but her mind raced. Was there something incriminating in the bag?

"Did you pack the bag yourself, ma'am?"

"Yes."

"Any weapons or sharp implements?"

"No."

Unzipping a side pocket and reaching into a pouch, the screener seemed to know exactly what she was looking for. Racking her brains, Olivia couldn't think of a single incriminating thing that might be in the bag. The second soldier who stood guard overlooked the procedure, expressionless.

They know. They're planting evidence to keep you detained. The screener produced the hair scissors with a look that said, 'Mind explaining this.' Olivia had put them into her bag before going to bed in the hotel and forgotten about them.

"Oh, my God. I honestly forgot those were in there."

"You're lucky. These aren't considered a weapon, but you still can't take them aboard."

"Sorry."

Olivia put on the most sheepishly contrite face possible. The screener dumped the scissors into a bin containing other sharp implements, clearly a common enough mistake.

"Just be more careful in future, ma'am."

"I will, of course."

With that, the screener walked away, and the soldier turned his attention back to watching the rest of the crowd. Olivia zipped up her backpack, put her wallet in her pocket, and walked toward platform seven.

You're a needle in a haystack. A retarded needle drawing unwanted attention to herself.

Ticket still gripped in hand, she afforded herself a little grin of relief. There were no more barriers between her and the train. As long as it left the station, she'd be on it.

The corridor leading to the platforms was wide but narrowed as it came to a set of automatic doors. A couple of passengers ahead braced themselves as the doors opened and let in a gust of frigid air. Olivia followed suit, pulling up her hoods and putting her ticket safely into her wallet before stepping out. The platforms were sheltered under a high wrought iron and glass tunnel ceiling but were uncovered at both ends.

A cutting wind gave a low howl as it blew through the tunnel, bringing with it a flurry of snow. The signs above showed that platform six was the furthest away, and an ornate iron footbridge spanned the tracks. Crossing with a handful of others, she arrived at the platform. There couldn't have been more than twenty-five people in total waiting. Everyone had their faces shielded against the cold. It was impossible to tell who might be a threat. The platform was monitored by security cameras, which gave her some reassurance.

An electronic timetable board showed the arriving trains. 'Ashtown to Overton Express 08:00 - On Time.'

On time, the two sweetest words in the world. The clock on the timetable board read 07:46. It was freezing cold. The train couldn't come soon enough.

Scanning up and down the platform, Olivia noticed a payphone bolted to the wall under a small plastic shelter hood. Her eyes held on it for a while. There were no other passengers near it. Rummaging in her jeans pocket, the last of her small change was produced, a couple of dollars at best. She moved her hand up and down as if weighing the coins.

This is probably the last chance you're gonna get before you cross the border, if you make it across that is. You got anything to say, now's the time. Decision made, she closed her fist around the coins and walked up the platform to the payphone.

The stained plastic hood offered some protection from the wind. Olivia picked up the receiver and checked for a dial-tone. It was present. After shoveling a few coins into the slot, she paused, working up the courage, or the words. She was unsure which. Finally, she punched the old metal buttons. The phone barely has a chance to ring even once before it was picked up.

"Olivia, is that you?" her mother's frantic voice on the other end of a bad line.

Olivia didn't respond, didn't expect the phone to be picked up so quickly, hadn't formed a coherent thought, hadn't expected her mother's voice to sound so frightened.

"Please, Olivia, if it's you, say something. We're worried sick, please…please…" her mother pleaded. "Whatever trouble you're in, we can fix it, sweetie. We can fix it. Your father knows people."

She rested her head against the cold metal housing of the payphone, working up the courage. Finally, she spoke.

"All Daddy's connections can't fix this, Mom."

"Olivia, thank the Lord. Just tell us where you are, and we'll come and bring you home safe."

"I can't come home, Mom. I can't come home."

"Sweetie, why?"

"You know why."

Olivia left the statement hanging in the air. For what felt like an eternity, only the sound of breathing could be heard over the crackle of the phone line, then sobbing.

"No, don't say that. That's not true, it's a mistake…" her mother rambled through tears. "They've made a mistake. We can get a second opinion."

"No mistakes, Mom, no second opinions, no do-overs. This is the way it is."

"Please, sweetie. At least tell us where you are so we can say goodbye."

"I can't do it, I can't…"

"Please, Olivia," her mother's voice was broken now, begging. Olivia could barely hold herself together at the anguished sound.

"I'm afraid, Mama. I'm afraid, but I'm strong. Tell Jamie and Daddy I love them, and I love you, too, Mama."

Some of the other passengers were starting to stir. Glancing quickly up the tracks out of the station, Olivia could see a train slowly making its way toward the platform. She was running out of time.

"We know, Olivia, we know. But, please, just tell us where you are?"

"I'm sorry for everything, Mama." Tears welling in her eyes, Olivia hung up the phone before her mother could respond.

Before turning around, Olivia wiped her eyes with the sleeve of her hoodie, then returned her expression to one of blank nothingness. A distraught young woman might raise unwanted questions. She couldn't afford unwanted questions, so she bottled up every emotion she had and forced them to the back of her brain. *You're a needle in a haystack.*

As if on cue, salvation came rolling up to the platform in the shape of the train. The locomotive was a hulking metal beast with a faded blue paint job. The engine code on the side read 'DM-

TR-01' in large black letters. It pulled an enormous string of old-fashioned carriages, some of them mismatched. It certainly wasn't the sleek, streamlined, high-speed express train Olivia had been expecting. But sure enough, in a small window on each of the carriages was a mechanical display of plastic letters that read 'Overton Express.'

Several other passengers expressed their exasperation to each other at the state of the transport that had just arrived. Olivia didn't care about comfort. She was only concerned with whether or not the train would break down during the journey. Despite its age, the beast looked solid enough but, in truth, it didn't matter. She had to get onboard either way. There were no other viable alternatives left.

All that mattered was that it was going north before the storm hit, away from Ashtown, away from men who wanted her dead, toward the border. If the train failed somewhere halfway, well, that bridge would just have to be crossed when she came to it.

The train slowed to a crawl as it rolled up the platform before finally coming to a halt. Normally, the doors of the train would unlock automatically and open, but the train was so old the doors were manually operated. A conductor quickly made his way along the train and pulled each door open. The passengers all climbed aboard at different entrances, about forty anonymous people all wrapped up against the cold. Olivia boarded with them.

The Train

Although old and worn, the train's interior looked cozy, in an old, rundown pub sort of way. The carpeted floors had tracks worn into them from years of foot traffic. Old maroon drapes were tied up at the side of the windows. The carriage Olivia had entered had a very narrow corridor and was broken into several compartments with sliding doors. Each seemed to accommodate six people, all were still empty. Tempting as the compartments looked, she was apprehensive to sit in one. Too isolated, safer to wait till the train was moving, so she hung around in the narrow corridor.

It only took seconds for all the passengers to board, but the train still stood motionless on the tracks, waiting for its time to leave. It was only minutes, but agonizing minutes. With the outer train doors open, the corridor was cold, Olivia was desperate for the beast to start moving. The conductor came walking along the train and slid the outer doors closed but didn't lock them. Soon, a call was made over a loudspeaker outside the train.

"Last call for passengers for the Overton Express on platform 7. Last call."

A last-minute passenger wrapped up against the cold came running up the platform past Olivia's carriage. They boarded somewhere further up the train. As it wasn't a group of four or five burly men, she wasn't too concerned. The shrill pitch of a whistle from outside the train was heard, then the sweetest sound, the hiss of the hydraulic brakes releasing.

Movement, imperceptible at first, then the train gave a shudder. The locomotive's power dragged it forward unwillingly, like an old dog that needed some encouragement to get out of bed. The slow roll became a trot as the train chugged its way out of Ashtown station. A smile broadened across Olivia's face as the platform disappeared outside the window.

Still, she waited in the hallway, not able to relax, as if somehow not able to believe she was finally on her way, that she might actually make it. The door to the adjoining carriage slid open, and an elderly conductor came plodding through.

"May I see your ticket, ma'am."

Olivia handed him the small maroon ticket.

"Hey, can I ask you a question?"

"Of course," he answered as he punched the ticket with a manual hole punch.

"Will this train make it to Overton? It looks pretty old, and with the weather and everything…"

"These old Whitby class trains were built to last," he said. "She might not be as flashy as the newer trains, and she might take a couple of hours longer, but she'll get us there as long as we stay ahead of the storm."

"Slow and reliable is good. A couple of hours ain't gonna kill anyone," Olivia joked.

"True enough. You have a pleasant journey, ma'am."

With that, the conductor tipped his cap and squeezed past her down the hall toward the next carriage. A couple of extra hours wasn't a disaster, she had the time. Once in Overton, the last hop to the border was only a couple of miles at best. She'd crawl it if she had to. Outside the window, the scenery was speeding up, the tall brick buildings getting smaller as the train snaked its way out of Ashtown.

Olivia couldn't settle in yet, not till she'd done a quick walk-through of the train at least. Better to know in advance if there were any suspicious groups onboard. Making her way toward the locomotive, every carriage seemed to be mismatched, a slightly different color and décor in each.

Olivia's footsteps made almost no sound on the carpeted floors. There was an odd, eerie quiet you only get on a long-distance train. Only the sound of the machine itself and the weather outside seemed to make much noise as the passengers went about their business in near-complete silence.

Every carriage had a small hammer in a plastic holster attached to one of the windows, and an emergency stop lever protected behind a break glass unit. Both were possible options for a quick exit, but only if the train was somewhere beside a town or city. The hammer was useless as an impromptu weapon. It was attached to the holster by a thick wire tether. Two days ago, these were just objects, background details, but she noticed the details now. The details were what kept her alive.

Passing each compartment, she gave them a subtle, cursory glance. Most were unoccupied, some had a single occupant settling in for the long journey, and a few had couples chatting inaudibly behind the doors. So far, it was all good news. No large groups, no men with injured hands, no overly suspicious characters.

Doubling back, she passed the carriage she'd boarded at and kept going toward the back of the train. It was the same story, mostly empty compartments and a smattering of passengers in the rest: a lonely looking old lady reading a book, an arguing couple, a woman with her hood up and staring out the compartment window at the weather, a young mother trying to control an unruly child. Olivia took note of one carriage that was completely empty. That'd be where she'd set up shop on the way back.

Approaching the end of the train, a sign above a door had two icons, a crossed knife and fork, and a cigarette. Pulling the brass handle, Olivia emerged into the dining compartment. For such a long journey, it wasn't much worth talking about. A bar area to order drinks and hot food, some group seating areas, and a few standing tables.

Two men had already shed their winter coats. Clad in sharp clothing, they conversed over a coffee at one of the standing tables. One was maybe twenty-five, with slicked-back hair, the other a little older, graying. They could be a threat, but it seemed unlikely. They just looked to be your average rich douchebags. The only other passenger was a mother trying to feed her baby in a pram. Behind the bar was a bored-looking bartender in a waistcoat, settling in for the most uneventful day of his working life.

Approaching the bar, Olivia rummaged in her pocket, producing what was left of her loose change, a dollar-twenty was all she had left to her name. Not enough for a bus or a cab or anything substantial, she decided to splash the princely sum on some luxury.

"How much is a can of Z-Cola?"

"A dollar-seventy-five."

"You have anything for the more budget-minded consumer?" Olivia asked.

"We got Mega-Cola, it's a buck. It's Northern Star's sorta own brand cola."

"I'll take one of those. Knowing Northern Star, there's probably lemon and lime inside the can."

Taking the coins from her hand, the barman chuckled at the joke. On the corner of the countertop was a bowl of matchbooks bearing the Northern-Star logo.

"These free?" Olivia asked.

"Yeah, help yourself. But the smoking car won't open for a little while yet. It hasn't been cleaned up."

"That's fine."

Olivia snatched up three books of matches. She still had a couple of cigarettes left but no lighter. Plus, the matchbooks could always be set alight to trigger a fire alarm if necessary. The bartender placed the Mega-Cola on the counter, ice-cold dripping with condensation. She stuffed it into her hoodie pocket.

"Thanks."

Satisfied that the train seemed to be free of any large groups, Olivia exited the food car and made her way back to the empty carriage from earlier. She chose the second to last compartment. Sliding open the door, she slipped inside and closed it behind her. The compartment had a musty smell. There were privacy curtains on the windows to the hallway and on the exterior one, both held back by button ties. Outside the window, suburbia rolled past, identical rooftops carpeted with a thin layer of snow. The wind picked up, swirling large snowflakes in little dances. *Stay ahead of the storm, little train.*

For the first time since the hotel, Olivia was able to let her guard down if only a sliver. She took off her backpack and slumped into the corner window seat, then put her feet up on the seat opposite. The snow swirling outside the window was calming, almost hypnotic, while the narrow compartment was silent, warm, like a protective womb.

Deciding an inventory was in order, she opened her wallet. All that remained was her father's credit card and Anna Jankowski's ID. Neither was safe to use now. The credit card might raise a red flag, and her pursuers knew she was using the first name of Anna as an alias. At this point, they probably knew her real name, too.

Not wanting to dump either card just yet, but not wanting them to be found in the event of a search, she stuffed them into a used sock and put it at the bottom of the backpack. Glinting in the backpack was the nametag on the apron she'd stolen from the Sandman.

Guess I'm Mary now. Mary Smith? Too generic, sounds fake. Mary Karlsson? Yeah, Mary Karlsson sounds good. It was the best she had in a pinch. She hoped she wouldn't be questioned between here and the border.

Food-wise, only two sponge cakes remained. She had next to no appetite but forced one down anyway, then cracked open the can of Mega-Cola. The liquid sustenance was a lot easier to stomach. *Better get used to drinkin' my meals, I guess.*

Laughing at the absurdity of her situation, some of the cola spilled from her mouth before she regained her composure. The train hurtled Olivia toward a new life, no, a new existence. What if that new existence was the nightmare they made it out to be on the news?

She knew nothing of the land beyond the border with its terrifying placenames. What would she do there, who would she be, where would she live? Olivia tried to form pictures in her head of what the Vampire Union might look like, but her mind kept conjuring up old medieval castles and dank caves, comical caricatures from old movies.

Shaking the images away, she tried to think logically. What did she know for certain? They had infrastructure. They didn't fight the NSC to a stalemate with their bare hands. There were a lot fewer vampires than humans, that's why they had to focus on mechanized warfare, tanks, planes. That meant engineers and scientists to design them, skilled workers to build them, colleges or schools to train those workers. It couldn't be the total hellscape they portrayed it as on the news.

After running through endless scenarios, Olivia became frustrated. Hellscape or utopia, the truth would probably be somewhere in between. In about twelve hours, give or take, she'd know firsthand. Better not to speculate any further.

Mega-Cola now empty, she crushed the can and put it on the narrow windowsill table. Outside, rolling hills covered in a blanket of snow drifted by. She'd been daydreaming for some time. The train was now well away from Ashtown and powering north at speed, but there was still a long journey ahead. Pulling the cigarette packet from her pocket, she shook it. The two remaining cigarettes came out of hiding. She took one out and put it behind her ear.

Not wanting to leave her backpack unattended, she put it on, got up, and slipped out of the compartment. Hours to kill, she walked toward the dining car in no particular rush, passing the microcosm of life in the other occupied compartments. The woman's child had fallen asleep, sprawled across two seats. The old woman was still reading her novel, the couple had clearly made up and were asleep in each other's arms, the solitary woman, hood up still stared out the window at the scenery rolling by.

Olivia pulled open the door to the dining car and entered. The two men with slicked hair were still propping up the bar, so to speak. On the corner wall, there was an information screen with a TV next to it. She hadn't noticed them on her first visit. She sat at one of the tables to take a look. It showed the list of stops. There were only eight in total on the long journey. The little red dot indicating the train's location was about two-thirds of the way toward the first stop. Estimated arrival time to Overton read: 8:45 PM. *Plenty of time. Plenty of time.*

"It's gonna be fuckin' chaos," one of the men said to the other.

"Don't knock chaos. A lot of opportunity in chaos," the older man responded.

"Yeah, for equities maybe. But tariffs are a nightmare for me. Rumor is, the retards in the CFU are gonna double down, put forty points on zinc and lumber coming south. The vamps are talkin' about twenty points on our coal and steel going north in reprisal. And the intermediaries are still gonna want their five percent on top."

Back turned to the men, Olivia continued to eavesdrop on the conversation. She wasn't aware of any trade with the Vampire Union. The men were discussing it openly. Odd. Maybe it just wasn't allowed to be mentioned on the news.

"They'll both back down, they always do."

Two other passengers walked past Olivia and out toward the smoking car. It was open now, but the conversation was worth listening to.

"I'm not so sure this time. So much bad blood right now, pun intended. There's talk they might even close the loophole."

"The CFU are probably just playing hardball to appease their more...puritanical elements. Trust me, there'll be a compromise. There always is."

"Maybe."

"Stop worrying about it. These are Monday problems. I'm heading back to the compartment. Gonna try and relax. You coming?"

"Yeah."

The two men crushed their cups, then threw them in the trash and left the carriage. It felt like the farther north Olivia got, the more she learned the relationship with the Vampire Union wasn't exactly as black and white as made out down south. There was some form of trade at the very least, although she wasn't sure exactly how it worked. Taking the cigarette from her ear, she got up and walked to the smoking car.

The car was markedly different from the others. Looking more like a subway car, it had uncomfortable-looking molded plastic seats with little ashtrays built into the arms. The entire décor was a faded shade of turquoise, and everything was stained with the smoke of a million cigarettes. A sign on the door at the far end indicated an outdoor smoking area beyond. Olivia decided smoking in the cold was preferable to the depression-fest of the smoking car.

Passing through the double doors leading to the very tail of the train, the small outdoor area was the width of the train and about ten feet long. A metal railing stopped people from falling over the back. Two other passengers, an older man in a big coat and hat, and a woman with her hood up, leaned against the rail smoking, looking out at the countryside whizzing past.

Olivia put the cigarette in her mouth and leaned on the railing near the other two. Visibility was poor, the snow a little heavier now, shrouding everything. The train tracks were consumed by the gloom of the oncoming storm before they got a chance to disappear over the horizon. The effect of staring into the void was calming, though. She stared out at it for a few seconds.

Taking one of the matchbooks from her pocket, Olivia tried to light the cigarette in vain. The wind snuffed the matches out in a heartbeat. In frustration, she turned to the man to her left, but before she had a chance to speak, he'd finished his cigarette. He flicked the butt over the railing and went back inside. Only the woman remained, taking long draws of her cigarette, shrouded in a thick winter parka with the hood up.

"Could I bother you for a light?" Olivia had to shout over the roar of the wind.

The woman remained silent but stopped smoking. She'd clearly heard Olivia.

"I only have matches. They're not really cutting it today," Olivia joked.

Silently, the woman reached into her pocket and produced a lighter. She held it in her outstretched arm to Olivia. The entire time, the woman didn't turn to face her or acknowledge her in any other way.

"Thanks," Olivia shouted to her as she took the lighter.

She clicked the button on the lighter, and it produced a sharp blue spike of flame, impervious to the storm. Lighting the cigarette, she took a big drag before looking at the unusual lighter.

"You recognize it?" the woman shouted over the wind, still not turning around.

"What, the lighter?"

"Yeah, you should. You bought it for me."

Olivia didn't panic or try to run anywhere. She recognized the voice now, even over the storm.

"For your birthday."

The figure turned to face Olivia and pulled down her hood to reveal herself. Angie McAvoy, red hair tied back, pale freckled face windswept from the freezing wind, piercing green eyes narrowed against the elements seemed to hide a quiet rage. Tall and broad-shouldered in the tiny confines of the outdoor area, Angie cut an intimidating figure. She pulled the hood back up to protect against the cold.

"Back when we used to call each other friends," Angie added.

"Why are you here?"

"Looking for you."

"Why?"

Angie didn't answer. The two young women stood a few feet apart. Angie had one hand in her pocket. Olivia eyed her with suspicion.

"Relax. I had the drop on you. I coulda thrown you over the railing and got off at the next stop if I'd wanted to." She removed her hand from her pocket as a gesture.

"You coulda tried. You didn't answer my question. Why are you looking for me?"

"I'm not even sure myself. Look…can we go somewhere a little quieter."

Olivia stared at Angie for a long time. What did she want, why was she there? Revenge for abandoning her after her brother went missing? Handing Olivia over to whoever was hunting her would certainly ingratiate her and her family to the powers that be, but that wasn't Angie's style. But did she even know Angie anymore?

For the past nine months, she'd been a ghost with a papier-mâché exterior, a brick wall. Nobody knew what was going on in her head when she came to school dressed like a forty-year-old librarian. But Olivia could see something in Angie's eyes. Anger certainly, but pity, too.

"OK, but you go first," Olivia ordered her. "I'll walk behind. I've become less trusting these last few days."

"OK."

"And keep your hands out of your pockets."

Both women threw their half-finished cigarettes off the back of the train. Angie walked through the double doors, and Olivia followed. Not a single word was uttered by either as they passed through the cars. Filing along the narrow corridors beside the compartments, they arrived at Olivia's.

"This one," Olivia told her.

Angie pulled open the door, went inside, and held it for Olivia to enter, who refused, instead gesturing for Angie to sit in one of the seats. Angie complied. Taking the left-hand window seat, she pulled down her hood and kept her hands visible, only then did Olivia enter the compartment and sit opposite her. And there they sat, for a minute or more, staring at each other.

The only time Olivia saw Angie in the past nine months was at school dressed in her oddly formal clothes. Today, she looked different, not the same Angie from before her brother disappeared, but something else, colder, harder. Two days ago, Olivia would have been deeply intimidated by the confrontation, but she was a different person now herself.

"Talk," Olivia finally broke the silence.

Angie didn't immediately respond, as if the words were there, but she was stewing them over before speaking.

"You're the one who messaged me the other day. Told me to get rid of my phone," said Olivia, Angie gave a tiny nod of confirmation.

"Why? Why stick your neck out for me?" Olivia asked.

"You're a real piece of work," Angie finally broke her silence.

"What do you want me to say?" Olivia asked.

"An apology."

"You came all this way for an apology?" Olivia asked in disbelief.

"Sorry for what happened to your brother," Angie began her rant. "Sorry I abandoned you when you needed a friend the most. Sorry I treated you like dog shit the past year with all my cunt friends."

Eyes burning with fury, teeth clenched in a rage, Angie had probably been practicing the speech in her mind for months. How often had she run it through her head? Had she imagined confronting Olivia in different scenarios, spitting venom at her after school some evening, or calling around to her house? Nine months of hatred released, she could barely look at Angie with the shame of it. Like a submissive dog, Olivia averted her gaze to the ground.

"Look, I—" Olivia began.

"Say it!"

"I'm sorry."

"For what? Say it!"

"I'm sorry for what happened to Simon," Olivia said, raising her head to look Angie in the eye. "I'm sorry I abandoned you when you needed me the most, and I'm sorry I treated you like dog shit."

"With my cunt friends," Angie prompted her.

"With my cunt friends."

Olivia returned her gaze to the carpeted floor. For a time, there was near-total silence, only the sound of the wind and the rhythmic movement of the train breaking through to the compartment womb.

"I forgive you," said Angie, much of the poison drained from her voice.

Looking up at Angie's face, Olivia could see there was still anger, but a small amount of warmth broke through.

"Thank you," Olivia said, a shake in her voice.

"I almost didn't recognize you. You look like shit. You take a bread knife to your hair or something?" Angie asked.

"I've had a rough few days."

"You run into any trouble?"

"Yeah, you could say that."

"Purification squad?" Angie asked.

"I think so. They didn't exactly show a badge when they broke down the door."

"You obviously got away OK. You do any damage?"

"One of them might need some help cutting up his steak from now on, but he'll live."

Angie gave a gleeful little cackle at the violence inflicted on the purification squad. Olivia joined her, some of the tension cooled.

"How'd you get here, bus?" Olivia asked her.

"Borrowed slash stole my mom's car. Left it in a parking garage in Ashtown."

"Won't your mom freak out when she finds it missing?"

"Yeah, I left a note. She'll understand. She's more understanding of a lot of things since…since my brother."

"I see."

"I searched for you in Ashtown, you know," Angie quickly changed the subject. "Figured you'd go north by a city you knew at least a little. Obvious choice, but not the safest."

"Coming from Greenfields, the routes are limited."

"I went round a bunch of hotels, rang at least two dozen more. Asked under the name on your fake ID, Anna Jankowski."

"You remembered that?"

"I remember laughing for ten minutes solid when you first got the damn thing."

"You didn't find me. How'd you know I'd be on the train?"

"You can't drive last I remembered. So, it was train, bus, or ferry. Bus is too slow, too many transfers. Train was the most direct route, but also the most obvious. Others might have guessed that, too."

"Hold on, back up. How'd you even know I was running in the first place?"

"Thursday evening in the bathrooms at school. I was in one of the cubicles. I heard you, and you sounded rattled, afraid."

"Not exactly hard evidence. You came all this way on that?"

"No, not just that," Angie said. “Francesca messaged me, told me she saw you on her bus Friday morning, that you looked spooked, that you didn't get off for school, that you kept riding for the bus terminal and had a decent-sized backpack with you. I still wasn't a hundred percent sure, but I rolled the dice, skipped out of school at recess."

"Slow down, Francesca Bianchi? Why the hell would she message you about me?"

"We hang out sometimes. She knew we used to be good friends, so she let me know."

"I didn't think anyone still hung out with you."

"Yeah, well, Francesca does. Not in public obviously, what with me being a pariah and all and we send out messages through an encrypted chat app."

Angie said the word pariah like it was a badge of honor. She was stronger than Olivia. There was no shame in her. She was proud society had cast her out after her brother went missing.

"Still, it's a massive risk for her even meeting you in private. It could cause her a bunch of problems if people found out."

"We're careful, and she's willing to take the risk," Angie told her.

"That's a big risk to just to hang ou… Oh."

"You were always a little slow on the uptake, Olivia."

"She's pretty. I didn't think she'd be your type. I guess I don't really know what your type is…"

"Please, stop talking, Olivia."

"OK."

Silence reigned over the compartment again, only the wind speaking. The train rocked side to side a little with the force of the gusts.

"She's willing to put her neck on the line for you," Olivia began. "Which is more than your best friend was willing to do."

"True."

"She make you happy?"

"Yeah."

"That's all that matters, I suppose."

Another awkward pause lingered over the conversation. Olivia wanted to ask a dozen questions, but all were left unspoken. Reaching into her pocket, Angie produced a small wad of cash held together with two hair clips. She held it out to Olivia.

"Here, take it."

"What, why?"

"How much money you got left?" Angie asked.

"Less than a dollar."

"Then you need it. You might need to bribe someone or get a cab if the train has to stop before the last station."

Olivia bit her lower lip and gave a nod as she took the money, she wasn't accustomed to needing charity.

"You came here to help me, even after everything?" Olivia asked.

"Yeah."

"Thanks."

"You have a weapon?" Angie asked.

"Had. The blade snapped. I wouldn't have got it past the metal detectors anyway."

Getting up, Angie pulled the compartment drapes shut, and then sat back down. If it was any other person, Olivia would have assumed danger at this action, but she could see the disgust Angie had for the purification squads. Hatred and sadness dripped from her voice every time she mentioned her brother. It wasn't just about helping Olivia, it was about getting one over on them. Slipping off her left boot, Angie pulled up the insole and removed something, then she slipped the boot back on.

Cupped in hand, Angie palmed the object over to Olivia. Holding the object down near her right leg, hidden from view if someone were to unexpectedly enter the compartment, Olivia inspected the object. It was a folding blade made of an odd, patterned material. She extended the blade with her thumb. Razor-sharp, the knife was made of the same unusual material as the handle.

"How'd you get this past security? Is it ceramic or something?" Olivia asked, admiring the blade.

"No, they put sprinkles of metal in ceramic blades so they set off metal detectors. That's a carbon-fiber, black-market, lot harder to detect."

"Illegal?"

"Highly, not just on the streets, but having one for any reason."

"How'd you get a black-market knife at such short notice?"

"I didn't."

"So, why'd you have it?" Olivia asked.

Angie sighed and looked at Olivia like a frustrated teacher who just can't get a simple concept through to a dim student.

"You still haven't worked it out?" Angie asked her.

"Fine, I'm stupid. What am I not understanding?"

"I've been planning to make this trip for months," said Angie. "Ever since my brother disappeared, and we got the call from the government."

"But you're not—" Olivia was cut off.

"Do you know how many kids dream that what's happened to you right now would happen to them?"

"A few, I don't know."

"Thousands. It's the kids who get bullied and abused that dream of it, Olivia," Angie said. "They fuckin' pray for it day and night, anything to break them out of their shitty lives and having to deal with kids like you."

Voice shaking, the anger from before had returned to Angie's voice. Anger at the kids in her school, the government, the entire system. Olivia was just the receiver for a broadcast that should have addressed a nation.

"I'm never gonna see any of my family or friends again. I'd swap with any of those kids in a heartbeat," Olivia told her.

"Of course, you would. You were one of the popular kids. You had a bright future and a nice rich family."

"You were one of the popular kids as well, in case you don't remember."

"Was I? Or was I just the kid you tolerated in your little clique."

"Look, I already said sorry. I know you're angry. I can't imagine…your brother…" Olivia spoke but stopped when she saw the anguished expression on Angie's face.

"About a month or so after my brother went missing, I had this constant daydream. I dreamed I got sick, and I went to the doctor and got the diagnosis. I even convinced myself I had the symptoms sometimes. I imagined making my way to the border, the hardship of it, the route I'd take, the supplies I'd need, the type of weapon I'd have. I was so convinced, I even prepared as it was really gonna happen."

Eyes red, tears rolled down Angie's face. The hardened exterior she showed to the world had fallen away to reveal a broken young woman. Olivia kept eye contact with her as she poured out her anguished lament. She owed her that much at least.

"In the dream, I always made it to the border. When I got across, I'd find my brother. He'd be already set up. He'd have an apartment he shared with a friend. I'd sleep on the sofa till I found a place, and he'd tell me everything was gonna be OK because he was my big brother, and he'd look out for me. It's a whole new life he'd say…a whole new life."

The weight of Angie's tragedy shocked Olivia. Every name on the special page in the newspaper had a family left behind. Only now did Olivia truly understand the reality of it. Her own name would be printed that week, her family the ones left behind to pick up the pieces. Angie bowed her head, sobbing.

"When I get past the border, I'll do everything I can to find your brother. I'll make sure he knows what you did for me. I can pass him a messag—"

"He didn't make it," said Angie, raising her head, voice barely a whisper.

"What?"

"He never made it to the border. He's dead."

"How can you be sure?"

"The Vampire Union has a sort of unofficial consulate number you can call, for families. They can only tell you if someone crossed and registered at the border and gave you as next of kin, but that's it. They can't give any other information."

"Your brother never registered?"

"No."

"Maybe it was a mistake."

"No, we called again and again, nothing."

"Maybe he just didn't give a next of kin?" Olivia suggested.

"You're doing what I did at first, clutching at straws. He's dead, murdered, buried in some unmarked grave like fuckin' a dog."

A lump rose in Olivia's throat. People had always assumed Simon McAvoy had made it. That was the rumor around town anyway. A guy, who knew a guy, who's cousin worked at the border crossing at Freefort, had seen him cross. Lies, hearsay, and rumor. Maybe if people knew the truth, they wouldn't have treated Angie as badly.

A lot of the hate directed at her was because people thought her brother did make it, he was one of them now, an abomination, a traitor. Olivia was just as guilty, buying all the bullshit. If she'd taken even a moment to talk to Angie in private, she'd have learned the truth long ago. Angie could have set people straight publicly but never did. Her brother was murdered, and she just took the hate, took the punishment, fed on it.

"There's videos online, the purification squads…" Olivia began.

"I know. I must have watched over a hundred. My brother wasn't in any of ‘em."

"Maybe he put up a fight, and they couldn't make their little propaganda film."

"Yeah, I hope so. Maybe he took one of ‘em with him," said Angie, a sad smile breaking through.

Angie wiped the tears from her eyes and quickly regained her composure, face returning to one of almost no emotion. It was clearly a well-practiced routine, a blank slate shown in public.

"You ever hear about the fence?" Angie asked.

"Fence?"

"I don't know much myself. Supposed to be a couple hundred-mile stretch in the border that's double-fenced, hard to police. People can talk through it. It's how a lot of contraband goes north and south. Might be worth checking out if you make it."

"How do you contact people to meet?"

"I honestly don't know the details of how it works. The guy who sold me the blade said it came from north of the border. Maybe he was full of shit."

"Thanks for the info either way," said Olivia. "Are you riding all the way?"

"No, I'm getting off at the next stop, try to get back to Ashtown before the storm fully hits. Also, if I got stuck in Overton and you crossed successfully, I might get accused of aiding a vampire."

"Wouldn't wanna get accused of that." Olivia tapped the blade on her knee. They both gave a small laugh.

"Here, before I forget." Angie took off her thick winter parka and held it out to Olivia.

"I can't take your fucking jacket," Olivia protested.

"You can, and you will. Winter's on the way, and it's damn cold where you're going. Once I make it back to Ashtown, I'll have the car heater to keep me warm."

"What if you don't make it back to Ashtown?"

"I'll stay in a cheap hotel in Springvale. Don't worry about me."

Grudgingly, Olivia took the winter coat. Thick and heavy, it felt expensive.

"I can never repay this," Olivia said.

"Make it across the border. That'll be payment enough for me."

Maybe their friendship died a long time ago, or maybe a tiny sliver of affection still lingered in Angie's heart despite everything Olivia had done. Or maybe Angie didn't care. Helping Olivia to get across the border was just a massive fuck you to the people who murdered her brother and the government that allowed it to happen. Or maybe she was just a good person, helping someone in need. A better person than Olivia.

"There's one last thing I have to give you," Angie's tone suddenly deadly serious.

"Oh, yeah?"

"A warning."

"About what?"

"Don't trust Sara," Angie told her.

"Look, I know you and her never really saw eye to eye…"

"Don't trust her."

"What does it matter. It's not like she's gonna magically show up," said Olivia.

"I did," Angie said. "This is a train, trains make stops. If she gets on at one of those stops or is magically waiting for you at the platform in Overton, be on your guard."

"Where's all this coming from. I know she treats you like shit, but…"

"I don't care about her treating me like garbage or throwing shit at me."

"So, what is it then?"

"She never told you about my brother?" Angie asked, carefully studying Olivia's reaction.

"I suspected they were seeing each other at some point, maybe a one-off thing. She got mad when I brought up the possibility."

Like some inhuman machine, Angie seemed to analyze Olivia's response, watching every eye movement, listening for any odd inflection in her voice that might indicate she wasn't telling the complete truth. After Olivia finished speaking, Angie's face relaxed, and she sat back in her chair, satisfied no information was being held back.

"Sara was the last person to speak to my brother before he disappeared. She may have been the last person to see him alive."

"How do you know that?"

"I didn't, until recently."

"What changed?"

"When he went missing, the cops didn't really do any kind of investigation. Why would they? My parents begged them to at least request the passwords for his social media accounts and whatnot. They just wanted a shred of hope he might have made it. The cops refused, said it was against procedure."

"But you got access?"

"About a month ago, we finally decided to clear out Simon's room. My parents couldn't face it, so the task fell to me. I found this old handheld games console. Thing must have been eight or nine years old, junk really. He used to let me play it sometimes when we were kids. I tried to turn it on, but the batteries were dead. So, I opened the compartment. Under the lid, there was something faint. I could barely make it out, written in marker years before, the password to unlock it."

"He'd been using the same password most of his life."

"Yeah, but not for everything, and the social media sites wipe the profiles of people who get the diagnosis after a couple of months."

"So, what were you able to access?" Olivia asked on tenterhooks.

"All his cellphone records, call logs, instant messages, they were all backed up to the cloud."

"And?"

"Sara and my brother were an item, so to speak."

"You sure?"

"Yeah, they were sexting each other, shit I wished I didn't have to read. But the last message was different."

"What it say?"

"'Babe, I'm in trouble.' That was followed by a single phone call, twenty minutes long. Then another call three hours later, only two minutes long. They're the last events listed. After that, no more calls, no more messages, nothing."

Olivia took a moment to digest the information, thinking of possible scenarios. There were plenty of plausible explanations.

"I know you want someone to blame, someone you can put your hands on, someone you know, not just some random purification squad. Sure, they were seeing each other. Maybe he told her about his diagnosis, maybe she told him to destroy his phone and run. Maybe they even met one last time before he left town, but that doesn't mean she was involved in his disappearing."

"Why not come to me after in secret, tell me what happened?" Angie asked.

"People get scared. Maybe when he disappeared, she was terrified they might come after her too just for meeting with him, just for knowing. Maybe she treated you like shit to keep up a front. People wouldn't suspect she and Simon had a thing if she treated you like garbage. People do a lot of strange things out of fear, Angie. Believe me, I know."

"Maybe, maybe, maybe. Maybe is the only reason I haven't driven a knife into the back of her skull. I can't kill someone on a maybe," Angie said.

"I know you hate her, and you have every reason to, but Sara's my friend. I just don't think she's capable of that," said Olivia.

"You of all people should know what people are capable of given the right circumstances. Her family's pretty religious right? Her uncle, he's a local CFU councilor."

"Yeah, but Sara drinks, she smokes."

"So?"

"So, she's not like her family."

"You sure?"

"Yeah."

Olivia answered with as much confidence as she could but failed to be one hundred percent convincing to herself or Angie.

"Sure enough to bet your life on it?" Angie asked.

Olivia didn't respond. Instead, she studied Angie's pale, freckled face. Angie was holding something back, just for effect, waiting to see if Olivia would ask the right question before being spoon-fed the answer. The cogs of Olivia's brain turned slowly but eventually came up to speed.

"Was Sara in school Friday morning?" Olivia asked.

"She cut class after first period. Even before I got a chance to leave."

Angie's words had the desired impact. Olivia fell silent as she processed them. Harsh static feedback came through over a small speaker mounted on the roof of the compartment, startling the two young women.

"Ladies and gentlemen, we will soon be stopping in Springvale station. All alight at the next stop for Springvale and westbound transfers."

"This is where I get off," said Angie, rising from the seat. Olivia stood to join her.

"I'll walk you out."

The two young women filed out into the corridor and stood at the end of the car near the exit doors. Both seemed to have said all they were going to say, and a stony silence sat over them as the train slowed to a crawl into Springvale station. A loud hiss signaled the brakes had been engaged. Angie reached out to slide the door open but was interrupted by Olivia giving her a sudden bear hug.

"Thanks for everything," Olivia whispered, almost on the verge of tears.

Angie didn't respond. She just hugged Olivia tightly then broke away. Sliding the door open, Angie disembarked onto the deserted Springvale platform, a light hoodie her only protection against the elements. Standing in the doorway, Olivia held the door open to see her off. Snow swirled around in currents, and the wind battered her, but Angie stood there, steadfast. Brakes hissed again, and the train began to move.

"Remember what I told you," Angie called to her as the train pulled away.

Only black sky was visible above the open platform. The storm was consuming everything as it rolled in from the east. As the train pulled away from the station, the solitary figure of Angie stood like a dolmen, then she, too, disappeared, consumed by the storm.

Olivia closed the door and returned to the compartment. The heavy winter coat gifted from Angie lay across the seat. She tried it on for size. Lengthwise, it was perfect, but it was bigger in the shoulders than Olivia needed. It was heavily insulated and of good quality. She'd have murdered someone for a coat like it the night before.

Checking the pockets revealed something: a pack of cigarettes. It was a hard pack. A caricature of a woman adorned the front, cleavage spilling out of a red cocktail dress. The writing on the front was indecipherable. Foreign cigarettes, Simonian by the looks of them. Where the hell had Angie picked them up? She was a mystery now.

Kids at school were still busy being teenagers, but Angie had to grow up fast, become someone new. Olivia would have to do that, too. Opening the pack revealed about ten cigarettes and the storm lighter. Had Angie left it deliberately? An end to their friendship, or was it just a parting gift?

Putting the cigarettes away, she double-checked the money. One hundred and eighty-five dollars. More than needed. She put the five-dollar bill in her jeans and the rest in her wallet. Next, she took off one of the hoodies and stuffed it into the bottom of the backpack. The winter parka was plenty of protection against the cold.

Wanting the knife available at all times but afraid it might fall out of her pocket, she hid the weapon in a sleeve section of the pocket of her backpack that contained the tampons. Preparations complete, Olivia opened the drapes on the compartment window leading to the corridor. She wanted to see everyone who went by.

Outside the window, barely visible, small towns bisected by rivers floated by in the distance, their tallest point always the three peaks of the chapel spires. The church's power bases. The hate spewed in sermons trickled down, reaffirmed people's existing prejudices, justified violent actions. It wasn't always like that. Olivia remembered church services as a child. The sermons were different, less extreme, filled with a spirit of hope and forgiveness.

There was an old pastor, Hume. All he used to talk about was tolerance and forgiveness, he was part of a movement to get rid of the three-day law, the movement was even gathering steam, then the CFU came back to power. The older pastors weren't exactly retired, just pushed aside, replaced with younger ones, all fire and brimstone.

The CFU had only managed to win the election because of the support of the youth movement in the church. They had to be rewarded with positions of power. In the NSC, it was hard to tell which was the dog and which was the tail, and which wagged which. Maybe they wagged each other in an ever-degenerating cycle, a vortex of hate that sucked everyone in whether they liked it or not.

Deciding she couldn't think about it any further, Olivia dragged her weary body to the food car. The place was deserted, save for the waiter still standing at the bar. The information screen showed the little red dot of the train farther along its journey, halfway between the second and third stops.

She bought another can of Mega-Cola and slumped in a corner seat near the window. Playing on the TV was an old noir movie, a private detective holding a gun on a man across a desk. The sound was down so low it made it impossible to tell who the good guy was and who was bad. Olivia tried to follow the plot, but her brain was fried, body crashing from exhaustion.

Lack of sleep from the night before finally took hold, like a vise tightening around her body. Fighting it was futile. She'd have to rest at some point before hitting Overton, and it was safer to do it in a public part of the train than alone in her compartment.

Sleep didn't come quickly. It was a half-sleep at first, the kind where you're semi-conscious but somehow dreaming, the kind of sleep that only comes with severe stress. Eventually, she drifted off into a world of horror. Olivia could see herself in the third person, standing in a dark cathedral, candlelight the only source of illumination. Hovering in the air like specters were men in dark purple vestments, their faces disfigured, teeth malformed and razor-sharp.

Their arms and hands freakishly elongated, fingernails a foot long. They were without legs, their torsos cut off at the abdomen, black entrails hanging down several feet. There was no attack, they didn't move toward her, they only hovered up and down slowly. Vacant blue eyes like a blind man, somehow still watching, judging.

A sudden jerking movement slammed Olivia's head against the tabletop, followed by a loud screech of brakes.

"Fuck," said Olivia, suddenly awake.

It took a second to remember where she was. Looking over to the waiter, he looked as frightened by the sudden jerking movement of the train as she was. Some glasses smashed as they were thrown from the bar. Were they crashing?

Looking out the window, Olivia could see a sheer decline to a river. For a split second, her stomach dropped, assuming the train had derailed and was about to fall into the valley below. Then she saw they were simply on a narrow rail bridge. The train was slowing to a stop and seemed to be stuck on the tracks. Why the hell would the train stop on the middle of a bridge. *This is bad.*

"You know what's going on?" Olivia asked the bartender.

"I know as much as you." He looked petrified.

"How long have I been asleep?"

"Hours. I'm not sure exactly."

Olivia looked up to the information screen. The red icon for the train showed it was more than halfway along its journey. A black bar of text across the bottom of the screen read, 'Emergency Stop - Sorry for the Inconvenience'.

She looked out the window again. The weather wasn't too bad. They certainly hadn't been hit by the storm. It was getting dark. Although obscured by clouds, the sun was clearly going down.

"Well, let's go find out why we're stopped," Olivia told him.

Shaken, the young bartender seemed glad someone else had their head screwed on. He was happy to follow orders.

"The conductor, Jimmy, he'll know what's going on."

"Let's go talk to Jimmy then," said Olivia.

A train didn't just stop on a high-spanning bridge, not without a damn good reason. If she was discovered, there was nowhere to go, just a straight run along the tracks until you hit the other end of the bridge.

Olivia let the bartender lead the way. If anything went wrong, he was another body blocking the way in the narrow corridors of the train. Other passengers stuck their heads out of their compartments in various states of alarm.

"What's going on?" the young mother asked.

"I'm on my way to find out," the bartender told her. "Please, remain in your compartments."

The other passengers pulled their heads back inside. Some nervously looked out the windows at the massive drop to the river below. Both Olivia and the bartender picked up the pace, reassuring the smattering of passengers as they went. Eventually, they reached

Jimmy, his ear pressed to an emergency telephone on the wall. He listened intently, a finger held in his other ear so he could hear better. Eventually, he nodded and hung up the receiver with a *clang*. He sighed heavily, then gestured for the young bartender to come over. The old conductor whispered in his ear, and the young man's face turned white.

"Go," the conductor finally ordered him.

Moving at a pace, the young bartender doubled back the way they'd come. Jimmy went the other way. Olivia sprinted after him.

"Hey," Olivia called, but the old conductor didn't stop.

"Hey, Jimmy, wait," she called again.

Surprised to hear his name called, he turned to face Olivia.

"Please, return to your cabin and remain there, ma'am."

"Please." She caught up and stopped him. "Listen, Jimmy, my dad, he's not got long left, and there's some shit I need to say to him before… I gotta get to Overton. How long are we gonna be stuck here?"

"Look, it's a bomb threat," the conductor whispered. "We get them sometimes, but we haven't had one in about six months. We won't be stopped long."

"What about yesterday? Wasn't there some sabotage yesterday as well?"

"No. An embankment partially collapsed under the line. It was the company covering for poor maintenance."

"So, how do you even know this one's a genuine threat?" Olivia asked.

"We don't, but we have to take all threats seriously," he said. "They used a recognized code-word, vampire sympathizers, apparently."

The aging conductor raised his eyebrow. Olivia did the same.

"Seems unlikely on lines going north," Olivia suggested.

"Yeah, but they gotta check all the same," said the conductor. "Return to your cabin. We'll be back underway as soon as possible. We'll get you to your dad, don't worry."

The old conductor put a comforting arm on her shoulder for a moment, then went up the train corralling passengers into their compartments. Olivia returned to her den and sat down. A message finally came over the loudspeaker, warning everyone to stay in their compartments. Was this a trick? Had the friendly old conductor marked her card? Would the cops come to drag her off the train kicking and screaming?

Get off the train and run! Run where, idiot? The end of the tracks, then where? Sit tight. You'll only make yourself look like a suspect. Paranoia gripped hold of her again. The border was so close she could almost taste it.

Spiders in her guts, time passed as Olivia stared down the precipice outside the window. Unexpectedly, a head went floating past outside. A soldier walked along the narrow space between the train and the edge of the bridge. Clad in a ski mask, he was inspecting the underside of the train with a mirror on a telescopic rod.

Hurry the fuck up.

Pressing her head against the window, Olivia watched him go up the train. A loud knock came on the window leading to the corridor. Startled, Olivia turned to find two soldiers looking in. The knock was a courtesy. They were coming in either way.

Sliding the door open, the two men stepped into the cramped compartment, along with a large tundra dog with pointed ears. Both soldiers were young. One was tall, black, and well built, barely older than Olivia. The other was much shorter but a little older, with a scar down his face. They both had rifles slung across their chests and the same icons on their shoulder, two small crosses. Olivia wasn't sure what rank they were, but she guessed low enough. The dog sat dead-eyed. Olivia didn't move.

"Evening, ma'am. Where you headed?" asked the shorter soldier.

"Overton."

"Your name?"

"Mary. Mary Karlsson."

"You got business in Overton, Mary?"

"My father's not well, cancer."

"Sorry to hear that. What kind?"

The question threw Olivia a little, but that was the point, probing. The questions didn't really matter, it was how you answered them. She decided to lie with everything she knew from when her father's friend Sigurd got sick.

"Bowel, but it's in some of his lymph nodes as well."

"Yeah, it's tough. My uncle got it in his prostate a few years ago, but—" the soldier began.

"If it was prostate cancer, I wouldn't be on a train with the storm of the century bearing down on me," Olivia cut him off.

The soldier held his hand up in apology. The massive dog watched on, dead eyes waiting on orders. A barely subjugated wolf on a leash.

"You got some ID we can see, ma'am," the younger soldier asked.

"Sure," Olivia replied.

Fumbling with the wallet, she mocked surprise that the ID wasn't inside.

"Ah, shoot. I must have left it at my apartment in Ashtown. I had it when I bought my ticket, but the train got canceled."

Both soldiers sighed in frustration. The situation must have been a regular enough occurrence.

"May we see your ticket?"

"Sure," Olivia handed over the replacement ticket.

The two men regarded it harshly. Her story was already threadbare. Without ID, the ticket, although legitimate, looked more suspect.

"There's no name on here," said the shorter soldier.

"Yeah, it was reissued. The computers were down."

"Radio the lieutenant," the shorter soldier instructed.

Stepping out of the compartment, the taller soldier spoke into his radio, only audible as incomprehensible chatter to Olivia through the glass. She sat in silence, exterior calm, looking into the dog's massive brown eyes. *Don't rat me out.*

There was nowhere to run this time. It was better to keep up the lie, wait for a better opportunity to escape if things got worse. After about thirty seconds, the taller soldier reentered in a hurry.

"Lieutenant says more than half the people they checked so far have these reissued tickets, the ones who got on at Overton and don't have ID or the wrong type. He said it's not what we're here for, we're not cops and to just check the bags and do that other thing. He also said to hurry the fuck up, so we don't get stranded in the storm."

A fire lit under both men set them to action. Inside, Olivia did a little dance of joy that the interrogation had to be cut short, then she remembered the blade hidden in the backpack.

"Can you open the bag, please, ma'am," the shorter soldier asked.

"Sure," Olivia answered, opening the bag's main compartment.

"Otto," the shorter solder commanded the dog with a little click of his tongue.

The massive dog sniffed the bag. A wave of relief washed over Olivia. The bomb threat! It was an explosives dog. The soldiers wouldn't manually search the bag. The dog prodded and probed his nose in and around the bag. Finding nothing in the main compartment, he sniffed the side pockets and zeroed in on the one with the knife, then sat. *Shit.*

The taller soldier stepped forward and fished in the main area of the bag but found only clothes. He took note of the apron with the nametag. It was flimsy, but it backed her story. It wouldn't help if they found the knife, though. Confused, the soldier opened the small pocket indicated by the dog.

Reaching his hands inside, he produced a sanitary napkin and some tampons, but he didn't find the knife in the sleeve section. Olivia's exterior was calm as a mountain lake, but inside her veins, adrenaline rushed like a tidal wave. Both men threw their eyes up to Heaven at the contents of the pocket.

"Sorry, ma'am. Sometimes, they put perfuming agents on these sanitary products. It messes with the dogs a little. We get some false positives," the taller soldier told her.

Both men seemed satisfied, not just that she didn't have any explosives, but that there was at least some evidence she was who she claimed, however flimsy. If they were in less of a hurry, she wouldn't have been so lucky. Olivia closed her bag.

"Sorry for the trouble, ma'am. Hope you get to your dad in time."

The shorter soldier now seemed genuinely apologetic they had taken up so much of her time. Olivia nodded in acknowledgment.

"Bye, Otto," said Olivia. The tampon-sniffing dog didn't seem to care.

Both soldiers walked out of the compartment, dog in tow. Holding the door open at the last second, the younger soldier took something out of his pocket, a piece of paper.

"Oh, real quick. We were asked to show this photo during our inspection..."

Unfolding the paper, he held it out for Olivia to view. The photo was printed in poor quality. The ink must have been running out, causing the colors to be off, but Olivia could recognize the face. It was her own. *Was* being the operative word.

The photo was old, a least six months, and the Olivia in the photo looked much younger, long brown hair with fuller cheeks. Of course, the soldiers didn't recognize her. The photo was of a young girl, not the woman sitting in the compartment before them. She scarcely recognized herself those past few days.

"This kid, she's missing."

"Come on, man," the shorter soldier called from the corridor, not wanting to waste any more time.

"The photo isn't great quality, but I'm sorry, I don't think I've seen her," said Olivia.

"Yeah, the barracks printer is on the fritz. Thanks for your time, ma'am." He folded up the paper.

"Must be tough on her family. She looks so young."

"Nine times out of ten, they show up, just a cry for attention."

With that, the soldier nodded in acknowledgment and walked out and along the corridor. The door slid closed. Entire nervous system charged with electricity, Olivia couldn't relax. Would they show the photo to everyone on the train? The conductor had got a pretty good look at her. Even if he suggested Olivia was the girl in the photo, would it overrule what their eyes had already decided?

Time slowed to a tenth speed as the soldiers inspected the train. Statuesque, patient, Olivia sat like that dog waiting on the order to relax from some unknown governing force. Eventually, the soldiers filed past again. They were leaving the train.

"Ladies and gentlemen, please secure your belongings, we will soon be departing," the voice came over the loudspeaker.

Still, she sat. Five minutes might as well have been five hours, but time passed and, sure enough, the blissful sound of pneumatic brakes releasing was heard once again. The steel beast lumbered forward, forward to Overton, forward to the border, forward to Vampire's Rest, forward to freedom. The train sped up. The gorge outside the window was no longer visible, the night and the approaching storm consuming all.

Olivia transferred the knife to the parka pocket. It wouldn't leave her side till Overton. Fully awake now, there'd be no more sleep till the border was crossed. She ambled her way to the food car. Studying the information screen, the train icon was three stops from Overton: Murnauville, Rushing Creak, and Shallow Crossing. The estimated time to arrival in Overton had changed to 11:20 PM. A few hours had been lost, but nothing critical. Of more concern was the bomb threat.

Her pursuers clearly realized they'd been sold a lie. In desperation, they tried to delay the train for a few critical hours in the hope of stranding her in the storm, the last sting of a dying wasp perhaps. If that was the plan, it hadn't been successful. Like Jimmy had promised, the old train was built to last. Its cars shook in the wind, but it continued regardless. It had been built strong for these very conditions.

Almost on top of Murnauville already, there was maybe a third of the journey left. The last hop from Shallow Crossing to Overton looked short. It must have been a suburb or a commuter town. Olivia stared at the information screen, picturing the stops being utterly uneventful. Would her pursuers try again? A second bomb threat probably wouldn't be entertained in the same night.

Unless they had people waiting for her in Overton, she was safe until there, at least. Even then, they weren't sure what she looked like now, how she was dressed. But if they were going to hit her, that's where they'd do it. They wouldn't be able to do it in the station, though, too many eyes and ears, security cameras, and probably soldiers, too. Money wasn't a problem now. She only needed to make it to a cab alive.

Deciding a smoke was in order to calm her nerves, Olivia entered the smoking car. After her encounter with Angie, Olivia decided the interior area was a lot safer. She sat in solitude on one of the depressing molded plastic seats. Deciding to save her last cigarette for when she crossed the border, she lit one of Angie's foreign cigarettes.

She took a long drag. It tasted foul, and the harshness of it cut her throat. They weren't a teenage girl's cigarettes, but nicotine encouraged her to persist all the same, as nicotine is wont to do. Murnauville came and went without incident. The place was a tomb. Nobody got off, nobody got on.

The hour was getting late. The train seemed to be moving in a black void. Nothing was visible outside the windows except the storm, and even it only allowed a foot or so of visibility into its swirling mass. Olivia killed the time by alternating between her compartment and the smoking car, adding to a small chain of Mega-Cola cans and an ashtray of cigarette butts. A book would have been nice.

Arriving in Rushing Creek, the train halted for a while, but not long. The arguing couple got off and were replaced by an elderly woman. The sweet-looking woman didn't seem like much of a treat, and if she was, Olivia was confident she could best her in a fight to the death. More cigarettes were smoked, lungs cut up Olivia gave it a rest for a while and returned to her compartment.

As she watched, ice formed on the windows like a picture frame. Mercury rapidly dropping, even the mighty diesel engine couldn't keep the windows from frosting over. The interior of the cars was colder now, not freezing, but not comfortable, either. Olivia could see her breath with every exhalation. The train was truly in the grip of the vortex now. Cold like this was foreign to her. How did people live in it? How would she live in it?

Gripping the small side table, Olivia steadied herself. The lights flickered as the car shook, buffeted by the wind. *Keep going, old train, keep going.* The train was clearly as stubborn as its fugitive occupant, plowing forward, cutting through the night, nothing in the world mattering but the destination. As time passed, the frost framing the windows eventually consumed the glass entirely. Opaque now, not even the storm could be seen.

Getting closer to the border, Olivia became twitchy. *Almost there. Almost there.* The train had to be close to its final stop before Overton. Getting up, she stamped her feet to warm herself, and then walked out the door. Whatever way the heating system was set up seemed to prioritize certain areas. The corridors were even colder than the compartments.

She walked through the frigid tunnels and into the food car. It was warmer than the others but still nippy. The bartender even wore a coat. The information screen confirmed her gut instinct. The icon was almost on top of Shallow Crossing. Nodding to the bartender, she exited for a smoke.

The smoking car felt like a meat locker, but Olivia didn't care. She sat and started to smoke one of the harsh cigarettes. *Not long now. Not long.* What would she say when she got there? Would they ask any questions? Could she be denied entry? With her phone gone, there were too many questions and no internet to answer them even if she'd been able to get a signal in the storm.

Slowing, the train came to a halt.

"Shallow Crossing," came the voice over the speaker.

Within about a minute, the train started again. Windows completely frosted over, it was impossible to see if anyone got on or off, but Olivia guessed it was unlikely given they stopped for such a short amount of time. The train picked up speed again. *Next stop, Overton.*

Olivia took a massive celebratory drag on the cigarette, then coughed as the acrid smoke cut into her lungs. Stubbing out the cigarette, she sat in the freezing cold for a few minutes, like the statue of Lang in Ashtown, just enduring it.

Get back to the compartment. Get ready. Practice what you're going to say when you get there.

Rising, she left the smoking car. Passing the bartender, she gave him a nod. It would be the last in their brief friendship. She planned to stay in her compartment till Overton. As she exited the food car, a set of arms suddenly wrapped around her. Instinctively, her hand gripped the knife in her pocket.

"Oh, my God. I was worried sick," said a voice on her shoulder.

It was a voice she recognized all too well. It was Sara. Olivia loosened her death-grip on the knife but kept her hand in the pocket. The soft embrace was broken, and Sara looked into her eyes. Olivia smiled at her as if she was happy to see a familiar face. Inside her brain, every neuron fired, trying to formulate plausible lies and cover stories.

"You wanna go somewhere to talk? The corridors are freezing," Olivia asked.

Better to be on the turf of her choosing than someone else's. Sara smiled a warm, beaming smile in response.

"Sure, yeah."

"My compartment is down the train a bit." Olivia gestured Sara forward. She wanted her in front. Sara didn't argue.

Sara was dressed well against the cold, wearing a thick red puffer jacket with a hoodie underneath and heavy boots. She was better equipped than Olivia had been before running into Angie. Walking in silence, Olivia glanced into each compartment they passed, half-expecting to see one containing a group of men, there were none. Finally, they reached her compartment.

"This is me," Olivia told her.

Sliding open the door, Sara slipped in and sat down on the right-hand side of the compartment, Olivia followed her and sat on the left, directly facing her.

"It's a lot warmer in the compartments, I think..." Olivia began.

"Cut the crap! What the hell have you gotten yourself into, dumbass?" Sara cut her off.

"Does it matter?"

"Of course, it fucking matters. Look where we are."

Olivia took a moment, looking deep into Sara's hazel eyes. She tried to read her while also attempting to shroud her own emotions from view. Compassion, pity, empathy, all looked present in her best friend's eyes, but was it a front?

Sara's mood could turn on a dime at the best of times, a heartfelt comment followed by a cutting blow or backhanded compliment. How well did she really know Sara? What made her tick? They called each other best friends, but what did that mean in a country where people's own family betrayed them to the mercy of the state? *Lie through your teeth.*

"I'm pregnant," Olivia spluttered, her voice wavering on the words like it was an emotional struggle just to utter them.

Sara exhaled deeply, the breath expelled as fog, hung in the cold air. Some relief washed over her face.

"Who's the father?"

"It doesn't matter."

"Did you talk to the guy about it?"

"No, and I'm not going to, and when we leave this train, we're never gonna speak about it again."

Sara shook her head at the story, her mouth opening and closing as if trying to formulate words to articulate her thoughts.

"Why the fuck are you here, though?" Sara finally asked, gesturing to the antiquated train compartment.

Olivia bowed her head in shame before speaking, laying it on thick, hoping to sell the story.

"I had an appointment for a termination at a clinic in Ashtown," Olivia said. "They canceled it at the last second because of the storm coming in."

"What?" Sara asked, still confused but also upset.

"I had to ring everywhere like crazy. They're more used to this kind of weather in Overton so there was a clinic staying open despite the storm. I have a hotel booked for the night. The appointment's early tomorrow morning.

"Why not wait, get an appointment next week in Ashtown?"

"Because I'm running out of time. I didn't go to the doctor till it was late. I'm almost at the twelve-week cut-off."

"Oh…"

Eyes trained on the floor, Olivia welled up some convincing tears. They dropped onto the carpeted floor, making little *thud* sounds as they landed. She sobbed for some added effect.

Sara surveyed the specimen before her, then she stood and closed the curtains of the compartment leading to the corridor. *She knows.* While her back was turned, Olivia slipped her hand into her pocket and gripped the knife. Sara returned to her seat.

"Where's your phone? I've been trying to call you all day," Sara asked.

"It's in the bottom of my bag. The battery's dead."

Was Sara just curious, or was she probing for weaknesses in Olivia's story? Sara had always been the more accomplished liar. Maybe she didn't believe Olivia's story, but maybe she didn't care either way.

"How'd you know I was on this train?" Olivia asked.

"I thought you were a damn vampire, you idiot. I was gonna help you get to the border."

Olivia cocked her head back and let out a small laugh at the statement. *She knows.* Both women seemed to be studying each other's reactions for some sign of weakness or fault. Angie's story ran through Olivia's mind.

Sara was the last person who ever spoke to Simon McAvoy. She could be the last person to ever speak to Olivia. Both of their stories were ridiculous to the point of farce, but they were both holding their positions, waiting for the other to fail or fracture.

"Honestly, some nights over the past week I wished it was that," Olivia said. "I wouldn't have spent my nights lying awake deciding what to do."

"So, what are you gonna do? You really gonna get an abortion?" Sara asked, a tone of judgment in her voice.

"Look, I know your family are pretty hard on this kinda thing, so are mine, but I don't need a lecture right now, Sara. I need a friend."

Olivia was selling the story hard, but was Sara buying it? Probably not. A bizarre stage play between two liars, both trying to convince each other of a ludicrous narrative that had them on a train bound for the border with a once in a decade storm barreling toward them. The wind shook the train car as if to remind them both. The lights flickered.

Sara took a deep breath before finally speaking, "You're my best friend, so I'm not judging. I'm not like my family." Sara said. “Whatever you decide when you get off this train, I'll support you."

"And you won't tell a soul?" Olivia asked.

"And I won't tell a soul."

"Thank you," Olivia said, tears in her eyes.

The two women sat in silence for a few moments, surveying each other, wondering how long the charade would continue. Overconfidence, that was always Sara's failing; in school, with boys, lying to her parents. They were both lying, but was Sara foolish enough to think her lies had been successful? Maybe. *Overconfidence.*

"How did you even get here?" Olivia asked in as non-nonchalant a way as possible.

"My cousin Sam. You know Sam, right? She owed me a favor, so she drove me."

"Yeah, I remember Sam. She's the one in the terrible rock band, right?"

"Yeah. Don't say that to her, though," Sara answered, laughing. "I wasn't sure if you'd be on the train, so I told her to meet me in Overton. I can give her a call. She can give us a ride to your hotel if you want. We don't have to tell her what's going on with you."

Reaching into her pocket, Sara fumbled for her phone.

"Don't bother. Signal on the train is bad enough, and with the storm kicking up, it's non-existent," Olivia said. "But a ride to the hotel would be great. What kinda car does she drive?"

Taken aback at the inconsequential question, Sara stumbled and apparently had to think for a second.

"I'm not sure, it's a small van…for her instruments."

"Yeah, I remember. She plays drums, right?"

"Yeah."

Before you slaughter an animal, you make sure it only sees the blade at the last second, when it's already too late. The mention of the van was all it took for Olivia. Sara knew Olivia would see the van eventually, maybe panic when it wasn't a car like she was expecting, so she must have decided it was better to try a convincing lie now when asked. It was an amateur mistake. Sara had shown her hand too early. Now, she had a wild animal to subdue.

"You never mentioned my hair," Olivia said.

"What?"

"My hair. I cut and dyed it."

"Oh, yeah. Well, I figured you had bigger problems so I wasn't gonna mention the bad haircut."

Sara laughed, trying to cover for her mistakes. Olivia didn't see the joke and stared into her hazel eyes like a hawk intimidating some lesser bird. Silence reigned in the cold compartment and, for a time, neither young woman spoke or moved.

"Do you think it'll be easier or harder with me than it was with Simon McAvoy?" Olivia asked.

"What the hell are you talking about?"

"What did you tell him in that last call? Did you promise him you'd help him, too? Did he climb into the same van waiting for me in Overton?"

All pretense fell from Sara's face and it turned to a flat expression, her mood turning on a dime. This was the Sara that Olivia knew, she just never wanted to admit it was the true character of a person she called a friend. Silence returned. Sara took her time before opening her mouth.

"It was unexpected with Simon. We weren't dating, not really, just fooling around, you know. I was shocked when he messaged me. He coulda talked to one of his friends, maybe his sister, anyone."

"He was falling for you," Olivia said. "Maybe even thought he loved you. Thought he could trust you."

"At first, I wanted to help him, but I got scared. What the hell would happen to my life when people found out?"

"So, you blabbed, told someone else."

"That night, I told my mom. Expected her to freak out like usual, ya know. But she was calm. She just smiled at me, took my phone, and told me to wait in my room. Within the hour, some men arrived at the house. One was friendly, well-spoken, told me I'd done the right thing, that it took a lot of strength of character to do what I'd done.

First time in my life my mother ever looked at me with pride in her eyes. The man told me all I had to do was make a phone call, and they'd even tell me what to say. At first, I didn't want to do it, but he was persuasive, made me see the dangers of your kind. Told me about a family who got butchered in their sleep by a vampire who changed before he made it to the border. Eventually, I did the right thing."

"Did the right thing?" Olivia's eyes burned with unbridled fury. “Did the right thing? Had Simon murdered, you mean."

"It's not the same, Olivia. You're not human. The Book of Truths—"

"Oh, fuck you! Since when do you give a fuck about the *Book of fucking Truths*?"

"You're dangerous, Olivia. You have to understand that, right? You've must have seen it in yourself already, at the hotel last night."

"Oh, that. How is he?" Olivia quipped.

"He'll live, but there was serious nerve damage to his hand. He'll never regain full use of it."

"What's he do for a living? I'm guessing hunting down frightened girls isn't his day job."

"He's a carpenter."

A burst of laughter emerged from Olivia. The answer was a punchline to a joke only funny to her, or maybe Angie if she'd been there.

"That's funny to you? It's his whole livelihood," Sara spat back.

"Yeah, that's funny to me. You'll forgive me if I don't feel any pity for a man who wanted to burn me alive."

"You're not alive, Olivia, not anymore. You're already dead, your soul gone."

"Oh, that's good. Who gave you that line? That silver-tongued guy who came to your house, or maybe that pretty boy, David?"

A tiny snarl of Sara's lip gave Olivia her answer. It was David. She knew him.

"Ah, so it was David, " Olivia said. "That his real name? He's a better liar than you. Smarter too. He didn’t get a good look at me at the hotel. He must have smelled the burning hair, knew I'd cut it, told you I'd look different. But your dumb ass forgot to mention it when you got here."

"Shut up."

Sara was clearly rattled. Nothing was going according to plan. How would she get Olivia into a waiting van now? Even before whatever transformation was happening to Olivia, Sara would have been no match for her physically. But there was still something intimidating about Sara. Maybe there always had been, a coldness, an unsettling ability to justify any behavior or action she took and not feel any guilt for it.

The train shook in the wind, and the lights flickered again. The two women kept their eyes trained on each other. Olivia wanted Sara riled up, wanted her angry, wanted her to do something stupid or reveal some important information about what waited at Overton station.

"You fucking him?" Olivia asked. “Why am I even asking? Of course, you're fucking him."

"We're waiting actually."

"You? Waiting? Wow, he must really have you wrapped around his little finger."

"I told you to shut up."

"So, how does this work, they send the pretty kids like you and David to be the welcoming party, then others do the dirty work? Where's your backup? Were they dumb enough to get the river ferry to Redhorn?"

Once again, Sara's face betrayed her, a twitch in her eye gave her away. Olivia was getting better at reading the subtleties; afraid but determined.

"They were," Olivia said. "No backup, just you and lover boy waiting at Overton station."

"You overdid it with your little diversion," Sara began. “The hotel booking was fine, but once David, saw the driver show up with a sign with your name on it, it was too much. He guessed something was up."

"But it was too late, the others were already aboard the ferry searching for me," Olivia said. “It was just you and David left at the hotel, the greenhorns. He must have been desperate to impress the others. Bringing me in. That'd show 'em what he was worth. I suppose the bomb threat was his idea."

"It was mine, actually."

"Smart. You wouldn't have caught up to the train otherwise. But it might have been smarter to just let me be the one who got away."

Considering Olivia's thinly-veiled threat, Sara surveyed her in silence with cold, heartless eyes. She cut an intimidating sight, but her hands betrayed her. They'd developed a slight tremor. Sara was clearly afraid but not intimidated. The backing of the church, the zealous mob, it made people feel powerful, empowered to take risks and actions they might otherwise never dream themselves capable of.

"In answer to your question," Sara began, "about it being easier with you or Simon McAvoy. It's the same. I liked Simon. I liked him a lot, but he died the day he got that diagnosis. And maybe you were my friend, but Olivia Thompson died the day she got that diagnosis, too. She's just been living on borrowed time these past couple of days. All I can do is help save her soul."

Sara had always been a tearaway, never caring much for following the more pious members of her family. But she'd been broken now. Whatever Kool-Aid David and his friends had been spewing out, Sara had been gulping down. A festering fanatic, one of the popular kids, who'd suspect her? A sleeper, playing the role of her former self, hearing every schoolyard rumor, who'd had a pregnancy scare, who was missing the past day, who'd been seen outside a medical clinic. There might have been a Sara in every school in the country.

"And what?" Olivia said. "I'm just gonna march my way into the back of some van with blacked-out windows like a fucking cow going to slaughter."

The wind howled as if to echo Olivia's anger. The train car shook, battered by the storm.

"That would be best. They prefer things to be clean."

Adrenaline coursed through Olivia's veins like liquid electricity. The time for talking had ended. She rose in a burst of movement and produced the carbon-fiber knife, thumb ready to extend the blade. Then she froze in place.

Still seated, Sara had produced a pistol from her pocket and trained it on Olivia's chest. Hands shaking, she held the weapon close to her body for fear Olivia might try to grab it. Jet-black, the weapon was small but looked heavy in Sara's hand. It had an odd, extended muzzle. Olivia didn't know much about guns, but she'd never seen one like this, not even in a movie.

"That even real?" Olivia asked.

"Yes. Drop the knife and sit down."

Something told Olivia that Sara was telling the truth. The weapon was all too real. The clear weight of it, the way Sara held it, afraid of the recoil, she wouldn't have come here with nothing to protect herself. Finger shaking on the trigger, Sara could have set the weapon off just through sheer nervousness. Olivia dropped the knife on the floor and sat back in her seat. Sara's hand steadied a little.

“How did you even get that past security?”

“Someone made a call. People support our cause, Olivia. It’s easier to turn a blind eye at the smaller stations.”

"What happened to clean?"

"It's just in case of emergencies. We're both getting off at Overton, and we're gonna walk to the van together. Clear?"

"What if I say no?"

"David tells me the gun makes almost no noise, and the storm will cover what little it does."

The tone of Sara's voice was deadly serious. The threat was real, but could she follow it through? Gun Olivia down and get off at Overton. Legally, it was still murder. It didn't matter that Olivia was turning into a vampire, she still had time left on her three days.

The government could drag a minor back home so their three days ran out. It could turn a blind eye to people going missing or killed in secret before their three days were up, but it couldn't sanction open murder without breaking the treaty with the Vampires and risking a war they might not be prepared for, politically or militarily.

Maybe Sara would turn herself in when she got to Overton, say it was self-defense. The gun was Olivia's. She'd managed to wrestle it from her. The law would go easy on her, maybe even cover the whole thing up. Or maybe she'd just get off and walk to the waiting van. When they found Olivia's body, Sara would already be long gone.

They wouldn't do much of an investigation when the autopsy showed Olivia had the diagnosis. All Olivia could tell with certainty from looking at her face was that there was a confidence she'd get away with it. *I'm not getting in that fucking van.* An unsettling smile broadened across Olivia's face before she spoke.

"David tells you it doesn't make much noise…you've never even fired it before, have you?"

All color left Sara's face. The comment had the desired effect, unsettling her for just a moment. She only had a split second to see the expression on Olivia's face change to one of malice, lip curled, eyes narrow. A violent gust of wind shook the train car and the lights flickered. Taking her chance, Olivia pounced at Sara, grabbing her gun hand before she could fire. They struggled for the weapon, Olivia the stronger of them, but it didn't matter.

Sara managed to point the gun in Olivia's direction just enough before pulling the trigger. A low snap, a clunking of metal, not even a bang, then a smell like fireworks. The weapon was real. A bullet had torn through Olivia's parka and into her side. The damage had been done, she could feel it, but adrenaline kept her fighting.

Whatever basic strength advantage Olivia had over her opponent was fading fast. They still struggled with the weapon, both with teeth bared. Sensing her advantage, Sara threw them both to the floor. Straddling Olivia, Sara managed to keep her pinned down. Holding Sara's arm in a death grip, Olivia fought for her life.

If she failed, the next bullet would be clean through her chest. The storm howled in the void outside the train, the car swaying so wildly in the wind it was a miracle it stayed on the tracks. The lights flickered one last time, then extinguished completely.

The struggle continued in almost total darkness, two silhouettes, one pinned atop the other, no words, only gritted teeth and the language of violence. The top silhouette was gaining the upper hand, the weapon inching toward the chest of the other, the other's strength to hold it away failing.

A sudden burst of illumination erupted, the cold blue flame of the storm lighter in Olivia's left hand held to Sara's face. The flame ignited Sara's hair and burned her cheek. A horrible scream of agony emerged from her mouth, but it was swallowed by the storm. Glowing in the blue flame, Olivia's face was savage, a cornered animal, snarling, desperate for survival.

Recoiling, Sara dropped the pistol. It slid into the corner under one of the seats. Desperately, Sara put out the fire in her hair. An uncontrollable fury gripped Olivia. She grabbed Sara and bit a chunk from her upper ear, spat it out, and threw her off. Blood poured from the open wound. Olivia's mouth was covered in it, and she swallowed hard. It coursed through her veins like a drug, strengthening her despite the bullet wound.

Sara reeled backward, roaring in pain. Taking her chance, Olivia dived to reach the pistol under the seat. But her opponent, fighting through the pain, managed to drive a kick into Olivia's wounded side. The pain was crippling. Another kick, then a third. Olivia writhed in pain, but the blood somehow sustained her, kept her conscious and focused.

Now free, her adversary reached for the pistol under the seat, but Olivia wasn't done. The carbon-fiber knife had slid in the shaking train car. It lay under the opposite seat. To Sara's eyes,

Olivia must have looked defeated, almost motionless on the floor. The gun was all Sara saw. Reaching out with a burst of strength, Olivia grabbed the knife at the same time Sara grabbed the gun. Turning with pistol in hand, Sara made to fire it point-blank into Olivia's torso. She was a split-second too late.

Olivia's thumb flicked the carbon-fiber blade open and drove it deep into the center of Sara's chest. Not even a fraction of a second passed and instinctively Olivia twisted the knife in one quick motion. The pistol fell from Sara's hand, and Olivia released her grip on the blade in horror. Sara slumped to the floor. Stumbling backward, the full gravity of what Olivia had just done struck her. Sara's lips moved as if to speak, but only a gurgling wheeze came out.

"I'm sorry, I'm sorry," Olivia said as she fell to the floor herself, slumping against the right-hand seat, holding the bullet wound.

Sara didn't respond. She couldn't. Her chest rose and fell twice more, and then rose no more. Her jaw went slack, saliva pouring from the corner of her mouth. It was all over in a couple of seconds, no more. She was dead. A circle of blood formed on Sara's hoodie, oozing out from around the knife. Olivia broke down. Sara's dead, glassy eyes stared at her in accusation.

"I'm sorry."

What now? Just wait for the train to stop in Overton, hand herself in? It would be there soon. There wouldn't be a long wait, assuming she lived that long. No idea how serious the wound in her side was, she was afraid to even look.

You've come too far, too far to stop now. It was her or you. Don't think about it. Get up. Move.

Despite what the logic of her mind advised, Olivia just sat there, slumped down, staring at her dead friend. The storm howled outside the window. The train seemed to be slowing ever so slightly.

"Ladies and gentlemen," the voice came over the speaker. "We will soon be arriving at Overton station. This is the terminal station for our journey. All passengers must alight the train. Thank you for traveling with Northern Star Railways."

Still, Olivia sat frozen. The bloodstain on Sara's chest had grown from where the knife was still embedded, staining the entire front of the hoodie a deep shade of crimson. The outer layer of her puffer jacket seemed to be the only thing stopping the blood from oozing out and onto the floor.

Olivia didn't lose control at the sight of the blood like before, perhaps because she'd just consumed some from Sara's ear, maybe just enough to stop her from losing it. *Get up, move. Do something.* A gust of wind battered the train so hard it shook everything in the car. It was strong enough to somehow snap Olivia out of her daze. *Get up, now.*

Uneasily, Olivia rose to her feet. Cradling her wound, she sat. Unzipping her parka and pulling up her hoodie, she examined the bullet wound. It was low down near her gut. The slug hadn't so much pierced through as it had torn a chunk of flesh and muscle from the side of her torso.

The wound was surrounded by a black powder burn, but only a relatively small amount of blood seeped from the wound. It was being soaked up by her hoodie. At a glance, it was nasty to look at, but it didn't look critical, not under normal circumstances anyway. *Just gotta hide it till you get to the border. First, deal with Sara.*

The carbon-fiber knife was still lodged deep in Sara's chest, Olivia's fingerprints being on it didn't matter, but some of Angie's might be on there, too, so it couldn't be left behind. Taking a deep breath, she kneeled over Sara's lifeless body, gripped the knife, and closed her eyes before pulling hard. It made a deeply unpleasant sound as it slid out, scraping bone.

She wiped the blade clean on the side of the seat, the blood barely visible on the ugly patterned material. Before folding up the knife, she wiped it clean of any fingerprints, then put it in her parka pocket. Blade now removed, blood pulsed more freely from Sara's chest. Olivia zipped up the puffer jacket to contain it as best possible.

It wasn't like at a funeral, where the person looked so serene they could be sleeping. No, that was after the undertakers had done their job. There Sara lay. Even with the wound concealed, her body looked like a comical marionette, eyes staring, empty, soulless. Olivia couldn't bear to look at her any longer. The body had to be hidden.

You have to do it.

Without any ceremony, Olivia pushed Sara's body under the seat as far as it would fit. The deadweight was hard to move, and she winced in pain with the effort of it. At a quick glance, the compartment would be empty, but anything more than that and the body would be spotted. Maybe with the storm, they'd be lax in checking.

Only two items of importance remained in the compartment, Olivia's backpack and the pistol, the latter still sitting where it had fallen from Sara's limp hand. Cautiously, Olivia picked the weapon up. A jolt of pain ran through her side as she did, a reminder of the wound. She was still human, for the most part. An inspection of the weapon would have to wait till she'd dealt with the injury. She slipped the gun into her jacket pocket.

Fumbling in the side pocket of the backpack, Olivia took out the tampons and pad, the closest thing she had to gauze. Deciding it would be too awkward to pack the wound with the tampons, she focused her efforts on the pad. The train was slowing more, not much time left before it came to a stop. Frantically, she tore open the plastic packet of the pad. Inside, there was a tiny piece of tape keeping it folded closed. Carefully, she took the tiny piece of tape and stuck it to the backpack.

Lifting up her hoodie, she took a good look at the wound, then took a deep breath. Biting the tape into two pieces, she stuck a piece on either side of the pad. She then applied the makeshift bandage to the open wound. The cotton making contact stung like hell without painkillers, but she persisted and held it in place with the tiny pieces of tape. It would only need to hold for a few seconds.

Finally taking a T-shirt out of her bag, she slung it around her without disturbing the bandage. She braced herself again, taking another deep breath as she pulled the T-shirt tight around her waist and tied it, holding the bandage in place, binding the wound.

The pain was excruciating, teeth gritted so hard she thought they might smash, but she endured it the same way she'd endured everything since Thursday morning. After about thirty seconds, the initial pain subsided. Not entirely but enough to function at least. Standing, she tried it out. The wound throbbed but didn't cripple her. She'd be able to walk off the train at least.

She pulled the hoodie down and zipped up the parka to hide the wound. Feeling around, she found where the bullet had entered and exited the parka. The entry was tiny, barely noticeable. The exit was a little bigger, but not by much. Flattening them both out, she hoped no one would notice. They were just tears in a jacket, and she only had to make it out of the station to a cab.

Slower now, the train must have been in Overton proper. With the windows frosted over, she couldn't tell for certain, but she knew the train had to be almost at the station. Putting all the wastepaper back in her backpack, she slung it over her shoulders. It would cover the exit wound at least. Only one task remained, an inspection of the weapon in her pocket.

Reaching in, she pulled it out with extreme caution. It felt sturdy, heavy in the hand. Its entire frame was made of machined metal. The unusual, elongated barrel had small horizontal holes cut in it. Careful to keep her finger away from the trigger, Olivia pressed a small button on the handle to release the magazine. The weapon must have been well-oiled. The magazine slid out without any extra encouragement.

Olivia knew little about guns but knew enough to know there'd still be a bullet in the chamber. Searching for a safety catch, puzzled, she found none and assumed the weapon must be ready to fire by default.

Inspecting the magazine, the top round was clearly visible. It was fat and shaped as she'd seen in the movies, but with one noticeable difference. The slug looked to be made of dark wood, banded together with metal strips for strength. Olivia looked over at the body of Sara, only the back of her puffer jacket visible under the seat.

Where did your friends get this?

Either way, the bullets were clearly deadly enough even to people who were still somewhat human. She slotted the magazine back into the weapon until it clicked home, then put it back in her pocket as carefully as possible.

There was no more preparation to be done, and nothing left to do but wait, endure the pain, and stare at Sara's body under the seat. Looking at the compartment, it seemed impossible to conceive the life and death struggle that had taken place only minutes before. Slower, slower, the train was crawling now. Almost, almost, then, finally, it stopped. Olivia didn't move. She had to be certain, didn't want to be hanging around in the corridor with a bullet hole in her jacket.

"Ladies and gentlemen, we have now arrived in Overton Station. Please, ensure you take all your belongings with you when you disembark the train. Thank you for traveling with Northern Star railways."

Like a robot, Olivia rose. She considered saying some final words to Sara, but it was hard to find genuine words of solace for someone after you've stuffed their corpse under a seat. Instead, Olivia wiped her eyes and pulled up her hood. She opened the door and wiped the handle on either side with her hoodie sleeve, hoping to smudge away any fingerprints Angie might have left behind from earlier.

Olivia slipped out into the corridor like nothing had happened. Walking as casual as possible with a gunshot wound, she made her way down the corridor and exited the train into Overton Station.

The Station

Overton station was small and rundown, but the platform was fully sheltered due to how far north it was. The two dozen or so passengers on the train disembarked, nowhere near enough people to disappear in the crowd if there was trouble. A red line on the cracked tiles pointed toward the main atrium.

Olivia didn't have time to think, she just powered forward as fast as the wound in her side would allow. A steep escalator ferried her up to the atrium. How soon would they find Sara's body? They'd do a check of the train to ensure everyone got off, and maybe she'd get lucky, and they'd miss it.

The atrium was dimly lit and deserted, save for others from her train and some staff and cleaners. An overhead sign displaying a taxi icon glowed bright green. It pointed toward the main automatic doors. She walked toward it. Footsteps echoed in the high ceiling above. A middle-aged woman and the two businessmen were ahead of Olivia, all wearing thick winter coats. They seemed in a big hurry, maybe sensing there might be a shortage of cabs given the weather.

Passengers behind Olivia seemed to have the same idea. Now, everyone rushed toward the door, desperate to ride out the storm somewhere more comfortable than a train station. Despite the pain, Olivia picked up the pace. Before the two businessmen made it to the exit, the automatic doors opened. Four cops rushed into the atrium with pistols drawn in their high visibility vests.

They'd found the body, radioed from the train.

"Go, go," one of the cops shouted at two of the others, a sergeant.

Two of the cops sprinted past the crowd toward the platforms. The other two stayed blocking the door. Clearly on edge, they kept their pistols ready but not pointed at the passengers.

You can't shoot your way out. You'll never make it. Surveying the crowd, the officers looked nervous.

"Alright, everybody, form a straight line," the sergeant barked at the crowd.

Nobody argued. Olivia bunched up behind the two businessmen. The younger man with the slick hair had the pocket of his winter coat wide open. *Do it.* Hidden behind the woman and the two men, Olivia slipped her hand into her pocket. Cupping the folded bladed, she hid it as best possible in the palm of her hand.

Pain throbbed through the bullet wound, reminding her of the stakes. In one swift movement, she took the blade from her pocket and slid it softly into the young businessman's.

"Step forward, please, ma'am," the cop instructed the middle-aged woman at the front of the queue.

The woman stepped forward nervously. She wasn't carrying any luggage.

"You traveling alone, ma'am?"

"Yes."

"Can you put your hands behind your head, please? We just need to do a quick search, if that's OK,"

Frightened, the woman only nodded in approval. The officer put his pistol in its holster and frisked her. The sergeant, weapon still drawn, kept a close eye on both the woman and the rest of the crowd. Olivia waited in hope, the hope they'd do their job well for once. Thoroughly, the cop fished into every pocket, finding keys, wallets, and other detritus. It was a good sign.

As he worked, the sergeant got a message on the radio. His face lost some of its color. No more doubt now, they'd found Sara's body. Finishing the search, the cop nodded to the sergeant that the woman was clean.

"Can you step over to the right-hand side, ma'am. Don't leave the terminal. We may need to take a statement," the sergeant instructed as she shuffled off, shaken.

"Step forward, please, sir," the sergeant told the young businessman.

Doing as instructed, he came forward.

"Can you put your hands behind your head, please, sir."

He complied but gave a huff of frustration as he did. It didn't go down well with the cops.

"You traveling together?" the sergeant asked, gesturing to the other businessman.

"Yeah."

"And the girl."

Olivia shook her head.

"No," the slick-haired man replied.

"You been drinking, sir?" the sergeant asked.

"Yeah, a while ago. That a crime?"

"We'll see," the sergeant answered dead-eyed, then nodded his head to start the search.

Smug and secure in the belief they'd find nothing, the businessman rolled his eyes at the inconvenience. Olivia stood behind his friend with no such confidence, a loaded pistol in her pocket, a bullet wound in her side. The sergeant was more on edge now, pistol trained just below the man's feet, ready to be raised if needed.

Slick had given him every reason to be suspicious, a godsend for Olivia. Methodically, the cop started his search, patting the legs, checking for hidden weapons, then up to the pockets of his pants, wallet, phone. Moving up to the jacket pockets, he patted them carefully, then paused.

Bingo.

Placing one hand on his holstered pistol, the cop reached into the pocket. The sergeant seeing this trained his weapon on the man's chest. Suddenly, the cop pulled away and drew his pistol, putting distance between him the target.

"Down on the fucking ground, now," the cop roared.

"You too, on your knees over there." The sergeant trained his weapon on the businessman's partner.

Like two deer in the headlights, both men were slow to respond, only freezing. Olivia, playing coy, backed away from the second man. The cops were screaming orders. Everyone in the queue scattered, trying to get out of harm's way.

"Lie down, face down, keep your hands where I can see them," the sergeant shouted, spittle coming out of his mouth.

The two businessmen dropped face down on the freezing tiles. The officer reached into the pocket, pulled out the knife, and threw it on the tiles as the sergeant covered him. There was still some blood on the blade and handle. The crowd was frightened. They moved away from the men even farther. Some passengers moved toward the exit doors in case someone started shooting Olivia followed them.

The cops fully engaged with their prime suspects were oblivious to everyone else. As they frantically called for backup, Olivia walked out through the automatic doors into the cold night. No one tried to stop her.

Snow swirled in massive eddies and swept under the canopy of the train station. Gusts of wind almost blew Olivia off her feet. Visibility was negligible, but across the street, a few green lights could be seen, the only cab drivers brave or desperate enough to work in the storm. Olivia didn't stop. She walked as quickly as possible. Her side throbbed, but she forced through the pain. The commotion was still going on in the station, they weren't pursuing Olivia. They had their men, or so they thought, for now.

Plumes of heat poured off the engine of the taxi as it sat idling. Sturdy-looking snow chains were wrapped around the tires, and the vehicle looked well-equipped for the weather. Olivia knocked on the window, and the driver gestured to enter. She pulled the door open and climbed inside. The car was toasty warm, like an old cottage with an open fire.

"Where you headed?" the cab driver asked.

"The border station," Olivia replied.

"Sure. You work up there?"

"No, I fix network issues. I got an emergency call."

"I can drop you off, no problem, but just so you know, there's a twenty percent surcharge for severe weather."

"That's fine."

Pulling the seatbelt around herself was a struggle, but she managed it. The driver pulled out into the road. Olivia was delighted to get away from the station by any means. They had their suspects, but it might not take them long to figure out Olivia had been involved.

The waiter had seen her meet Sara on the train. Once they took a statement from him, they'd put some pieces together. Hopefully, by then, she'd have already crossed the border. Slowly, the cab made its way away from the station through the blizzard.

As they drove farther up the street, they passed a white van pulled up on the curb. Snow chains, engine idling, it could have been anyone, or it could have been Sara's van. The cab picked up a little speed as it pulled onto a larger road, but the driver was driving cautiously.

Arvin Simms, the taxi ID sat in a plastic slot on the dashboard read. He was bald with a mustache and a warm, friendly face. A face that would invite you to a pleasant neighborhood barbecue. Next to the ID was a picture of Arvin with a plump-looking woman and two young girls, all smiling, taken at the beach, somewhere far away from Overton.

"Was there some commotion in the terminal? I saw a bunch of cops rush in?" asked Arvin.

"They arrested some guy. They seemed to know who they were looking for," Olivia answered.

"Yeah, they usually get a tip-off about someone smuggling and pick 'em up when they arrive."

"Is it far to the border?"

"No, normally it's five minutes, but more like ten in this weather. You never been up there?"

"No, first time."

The car pulled out onto a large wide road. Through the rapid sweeps of the windshield wipers and the storm, Olivia could read a massive overhead LED sign.

MILITARIZED BORDER AHEAD - OFFICIAL BUSINESS AND DROP-OFF ONLY

The pain didn't matter now. The border was no longer a dream or some far-off notion. It was real, almost within touching distance. Olivia afforded herself a little smile, but then quickly suppressed it.

"They don't have someone local who could look at the problem here in Overton?"

"What?"

"The network problem? You came on the train. Just seems odd they wouldn't have someone available here in Overton."

Glancing over at Olivia, he noticed the hole in her jacket, but then returned his eyes to the road. Looking down herself, she could see blood was seeping through the hole. Not much, a tiny patch, but it was visible up close in the car. *He knows*. Olivia reached into her pocket.

"But, hey, I guess you don't care. You get the overtime either way, right?"

"Yeah," Olivia smiled as she answered.

Plowing through the night, the two didn't speak for a minute or so. Overhead, another LED sign read:

FINAL WARNING - MILITARIZED BORDER AHEAD - OFFICIAL BUSINESS AND DROP-OFF ONLY

A large arrow pointed to an off-ramp, and the cab drifted its way toward it, but Arvin hadn't put on his turn signal. Olivia took the pistol from her pocket, keeping it low, out of sight, and pointed it at Arvin's torso.

"Don't," she told him.

Arvin didn't need to be told twice. He didn't say anything, but the cab righted itself and returned to the lane it had been in. Olivia kept the pistol trained on him.

"What's down the ramp?" Olivia asked.

"Police pull-in point. If we drop someone to the border who's engaged in criminality, we can get into a lot of trouble."

"Tell them you were held at gunpoint. You'll be fine."

"Yeah, sure. I could get fined or maybe even lose my medallion."

"I don't care. I'm trying to stay alive."

"Yeah."

Livelihood possibly on the line, Arvin was more angry than intimidated. It probably wasn't the first time he'd had a gun or knife pulled on him. Cab drivers got robbed all the time. Would he try something stupid again? Maybe when they got to the border. A crackle over the radio interrupted Olivia's thought process.

"Arvin," an old, husky voice come over the radio. "You should see the shit going down back at the train station, cops everywhere. There's a rumor they found a girl’s body. They dragged away two guys. Hey, man, pick up. It's fucking nuts back here."

The atmosphere in the cab turned dark. Olivia, expressionless, just stared at Arvin. He understood now. What was a second murder when you'd already crossed the line of no return? The stare continued. She wanted to make sure Arvin knew where he stood in the pecking order.

"What can I expect when I get to the border? You drop staff up there often?" Olivia asked him, her voice low and calm.

"During the day plenty of staff and officials come and go," Arvin began, his voice shaking. "At night it's a skeleton crew."

"Much military up there?"

"Yeah, plenty, but they can't stop you crossing, not unless they suspect you of some serious crime. If they see that wound, you might have a problem. There's usually a civil rights organization that monitors the border, makes sure people like you can cross."

"You sure?"

"Yeah, sometimes they have a couple of people at the train station, too. But I don't think they have the numbers for that recently, and with the weather and everything, I guess you were just out of luck."

"Yeah, story of my life," Olivia said. "What about metal detectors? Do they frisk you?"

"It's basically a one-way border from the NSC side, so they don't really do any checks as far as I know. Once they don't see something obviously wrong, you can just walk across the line."

"Once I cross, what happens then?" Olivia asked.

"Come on. How the hell would I know how shit works once you cross that line."

"Fair point."

"So, how is this gonna go?" Arvin asked.

Olivia didn't answer immediately, pausing for a moment to look at the family photo on the dashboard. Arvin's hands trembled as he gripped the wheel, steadying the car against the battering gusts. The windshield wipers zipped back and forth, barely able to keep the snow clear from the window.

"You're gonna stop at the drop-off point and let me out, then you're gonna turn around and drive back to the station," Olivia told him. "If you try anything stupid, I can promise you two things. I won't make it across that border, and your kids won't see their father alive again."

The tone was clear and concise. Hardened by the last few days, she sounded like the kind of person who'd make good on the threat. Arvin swallowed hard again and nodded in silent agreement. The cab driver didn't need the pistol pointed at him now. He understood the situation and the kind of person he was dealing with. Putting the gun away, Olivia took out the bundle of money Angie had given her and counted out one hundred dollars.

"For your trouble." She held the money out.

"Keep it. It's harder to argue I was held at gunpoint if you paid me."

Olivia nodded and put the money away. The cab driver kept his eyes on the road. He wasn't an idiot, just afraid. But she was afraid, too, had to be ruthless. Almost there, couldn't fail now. The car kept its slow, steady pace moving through the darkness. Despite his hands shaking, Arvin managed to keep its line true. In the rearview mirror, far behind, there were the lights of another vehicle, just pinpricks in the darkness. Who else was coming to a minor border crossing at that hour, in that weather?

"Speed up," Olivia ordered.

"We go any faster, snow chains or not, we're gonna leave the road. Don't worry. Whoever they are, they're not catching up, not in this weather."

Looking behind nervously, Olivia could see the lights wavered from side to side. The driver was having difficulty staying on the road, not used to the conditions. *David.* She had to be across the border before he arrived.

"How long?" Olivia asked.

"Without the storm, you'd already see it by now."

Agonizing seconds passed as Olivia kept an eye on the rearview mirror. Finally, in the distance ahead, a series of lights appeared, tiny at first, but then they grew, floodlights illuminating the border. She could taste it now. The pain in her side was nothing, survival was within reach.

One last problem, the blood and bullet hole. Taking the inside of her jacket sleeve she wiped the blood away and flattened the hole. It covered up just fine, at a glance, nobody would know it was there. Feeling around to the exit hole the material flattened down perfectly and she couldn't feel any blood. Illuminated by the cab's headlights, a guard tower, and some small buildings came into view. Arvin's hands shook as he put on his turn signal. A sign read:

DROP-OFF AND PICKUP ONLY

The cab pulled into an area under a small awning clear of snow. The ground was marked with yellow paint. Olivia took off her seatbelt in anticipation.

"This is you," Arvin said.

Pausing for a split-second, Olivia wasn't sure. Was this it? Could she just walk up and over? Where exactly did you do it?

"Building straight ahead is the one you want."

The driver just wanted her gone without any trouble. She took a deep breath and got out of the car into the frigid night.

"Thanks," she said into the vehicle.

"Yeah."

Arvin had a look on his face that said, 'Go fuck yourself.' Olivia shut the door and walked forward, then looked back. The cab turned and drove away into the night as if nothing had happened.

The lights of the other vehicle were still coming in the distance. *No time to think, move.*

The border crossing was small. It was part of why she chose it in the first place. Spanning two thousand miles, not every crossing on the border could be a fortress, but the place looked almost ramshackle. She walked. The wound didn't matter, the biting wind and cold didn't matter, only the destination.

Approaching the border, it appeared through the blizzard. A razor-wire fence maybe twenty feet high with a large gate, a few prefabs, a guard tower on either side, and one main building that seemed to straddle the border.

Trudging through the snow, the building became clearer. A main door. It had to be the place. As she approached the door, it opened, and a soldier emerged. Dressed in thick snow camouflage fatigues and a ski mask, he cut a terrifying figure, the last thing she wanted to see. Was this even the right place? had Arvin screwed her over? Surprised to see another figure out in the elements at the lonely border post, he quickly flicked the safety off his rifle but didn't raise it.

"Can I help you, ma'am?" he asked.

Olivia froze for a moment, then reminded herself what she'd been told all along. *They can't stop you, they can't stop you.* Her feet started moving again.

"Ma'am, can I help you?" voice firmer now, he put the rifle butt to his shoulder, ready to raise it if needed.

She froze again, had to say something or he might not let her pass. Could she just come out and say it?

"I'm here to…" Olivia began.

A figure emerged to the right from a small prefab building, a woman in a thick winter coat and gloves. She walked to within a few feet of Olivia. The woman was middle-aged, her big, fat, friendly-looking moon-face was surrounded by the fur of her winter jacket.

"Are you here to present yourself?" the woman asked.

"Yes," Olivia called over the storm so both the woman and the soldier could hear.

"It's that door right there." The woman gestured to the door the soldier had just emerged from.

At a guess, the woman was one of the rights observers. She seemed to be speaking plainly, at the very least. Olivia nodded to the soldier as if to say, 'What about him?' The woman understood perfectly, and she moved closer to Olivia.

"You've just declared your intention to cross. He can't stop you. It's just intimidation. This one's bark is worse than his bite anyway."

The soldier cut the woman a look like he wanted to strangle her with her own guts. She just grinned at him in response.

"I can't go into the building with you, new laws. Observers aren't allowed. You just walk in and over the marked line. They can't stop you."

Nodding acknowledgment, Olivia walked forward. The soldier moved toward her. Heart skipping a beat, she prayed he wouldn't notice the wound. As he passed within a foot of her, he spat at her feet, then went about his patrol. Marching onward, she arrived at the windowless door, last stop. Finally, a push, and she was inside a small corridor with another door ahead. She took down the hood of the parka.

A strange fear gripped her. Was this real or some final sick joke? Maybe it was all a con. Nobody ever made it, and they just herded you like cattle into a final slaughterhouse. Reaching into her pocket, she felt the smooth steel of the pistol, cold comfort. If it had all been a trick, she'd end it before they got a chance to take her away, maybe take one or two of them with her, if she could.

Leaving the pistol in the pocket, she double-checked that the bullet holes were still hidden, and no blood was showing. *Now or never*. Taking one last breath, she pushed the door open.

Two soldiers stood posts at opposite ends of a very long room, bare concrete with laminate flooring. No windows, harsh florescent lighting, a door at the far end, same as the one she came in by. The opposite wall was made of inch-thick glass, and two men sat in small offices behind the barrier. One was near Olivia, wearing a blue uniform with an NSC flag on the shoulder.

A concrete wall behind the glass separated him from the other *man* farther in the room. The only other feature of the formless room was a perfectly straight yellow line painted halfway down it that cut it in two. Either side of the line were two arrows.

One pointing toward Olivia read 'NSC,' the other pointed to the other end of the room and read 'VU.'

The NSC soldier was only a few feet from Olivia, but he didn't make any discernible movement on her entering. Only his eyes tracked her. There it was, the border, no spectacle or grandeur, just a painted line, its only power resting in the fact the world decided it meant something.

Walk.

Her legs obeyed. The soldier didn't try to stop her. The NSC official behind the glass raised his head in curiosity but nothing more. Forward, forward, along the length of the corridor-like room, until the yellow line was at her feet. Olivia stopped before the line as if waiting for permission. After everything she'd been through to get to that point, it seemed almost comically simplistic.

Looking up, she locked eyes with the soldier on the other side of the border, desperate for someone to tell her it was OK to cross. He was young, or at least he looked it, his skin a dark shade of black. Dressed in an unusually camouflaged uniform, his rifle also of a very odd design. It was short, and the magazine lay behind the trigger. She'd never seen a weapon like it, almost like it was from some science-fiction movie.

The soldier noticing her hesitation spoke, "At this point, the only person stopping you is you," he called from the far end of the room.

Olivia nodded, took a final deep breath, and with no real ceremony, walked into the Vampire Union. Looking behind, the soldier on the NSC side hadn't moved. No one rushed to drag her back into the NSC. A non-event, as if the two and half days she'd spent fighting for her life were all a joke.

The Vampire Union soldier smiled for a second, then returned his face to flat nothingness. The official behind the glass motioned for Olivia to come forward. She stepped up to the partition. Like the soldier, he looked young too, a narrow face with jet-black hair, his uniform was a deep crimson red. A patch on his shoulder had the flag of the Vampire Union. A drop of blood and a drop of water set on a blue shield emblazoned on a red rectangle. The man was the picture of officialdom.

Stuck to the outside of the glass was a small camera. A large steel drawer was the only physical link between Olivia and the official. It slid open. Inside was what looked like a white medical device with a thick cable attached.

"Place your right index finger in the tester," he said.

Olivia complied. Almost instantly, something sharp jabbed her finger. The pain was barely noticeable over the bullet wound.

"You can remove it now."

Retracting her finger from the device, the official pulled the drawer back to his side. A larger machine sat on the desk beside him, the cable from the blood sampler connected to it. It made a gentle whirring sound as it analyzed her blood. Olivia stood waiting. The pain in her side intensified. Maybe ten seconds later, the device gave a confirmatory *beep*. It sounded like the good kind of beep to her ears.

"Your bloodwork checks out," the official informed her.

"So, what happens next?"

"Do you wish to defect to the Vampire Union?"

It was an odd turn of phrase. Olivia didn't expect it to be worded in such a way, like she was some kind of traitor. But what was she going to do, say no?

"Yes."

"Excellent. Your name for the database and paperwork?"

"Olivia Thompson…my name's Olivia Thompson."

"Face the camera please."

Standing up straight to face the camera a stabbing pain shot through Olivia's wound. A flash indicated the photo had been taken, and she relaxed her posture again. The official typed details into his computer.

"You're wounded?" he asked as low as possible over the mic.

"Yes."

"Bad?"

"Gunshot wound, tore my side. I don't think it'll be fatal once I get some treatment."

He didn't show any sign of panic but started to type at a feverish speed. After a second or two, he finished, and a printer to his right spat out a document. He put the document into the drawer and slid it over to Olivia with a clunk.

"Provisional statement of bloodwork. Think of it like your ID for now," he said. "Head through that door. I'll let them know you're injured and it's an emergency. They'll get the wound looked at."

Olivia picked up the document. The paper was thick. The bottom corner had a hologram of the flag of the Vampire Union. In the top corner was a color photograph of her face. She looked like shit. A tremble came over her hands as she looked at the document. She didn't have the time to read it before stuffing it into her bag.

"That's it?" Olivia asked.

"That's it."

She shuffled toward the door at the end of the room.

"Oh, and, Olivia," the official called after her. Olivia turned. “Welcome home."

An exhausted smile spread across her face. She hobbled toward the door at the end of the room, holding her wound. *Home. This is home now.* The Vampire Union soldier gave her a tiny sideways smile as she passed him. Hand on the door, she reached out to pull it open, but the door at the far end of the room burst open first, the door she'd come in.

A figure entered the room and pulled down its hood. David, face a burning rage, tracks of tears frozen down his cheeks. The soldier on the NSC side readied his weapon, and the Vampire Union soldier flicked the safety off his rifle. Eyes filled with hate, David spotted his quarry at the end of the room.

"Stop that woman," he shouted, pointing his finger at Olivia. "Stop her, she's a murderer."

"She's already crossed," the NSC soldier told him. "Don't do anything stupid, son, it's not worth it."

David sprinted toward the borderline. The NSC soldier slung his rifle over his shoulder and tackled David, keeping him from running toward Olivia. David reached into his pocket, desperate to grab something.

"Don't throw your life away, not on them. They're not worth it," the soldier told David, desperate to calm him.

For a second or so, there was silence. The NSC soldier kept a tight grip on David's arm. The soldier on the Vampire Union side just stared at the spectacle. Pupils as wide as saucers, weapon ready, like a trained attack dog waiting for David to cross the magic line that would cut him loose.

"Go on, do it, boy. See how far you get?" the Vampire Union soldier goaded David.

"Hey, shut your fucking mouth," the NSC soldier shouted at his counterpart.

David struggled, spittle pouring from his gritted teeth as he looked at Olivia, who silently regarded him. She could have just walked through the door. The bullet wound in her side was telling her to, but spite kept her there, taunting David with her silence, half-hoping he'd make it across the border, and the Vampire Union soldier would cut him down.

"Easy, kid, easy," the NSC soldier seemed to be calming him. He took an object from David's pocket and hid it in his own, a weapon, he was covering for him.

Unarmed now, the expression of uncontrollable rage on David's face calmed, replaced with one of more calculating malice, a somehow deeper hatred. The soldier stood him up, holding his arms back and trying to get him back out the door.

"I'll see you burn for this, you inhuman cunt," David shouted at Olivia. "With the Lord as my right hand, I swear, if it takes me a lifetime, I'll see you and your unholy land turned to ash."

Something triggered in Olivia. David's voice spitting bile, she'd heard it before, and not on the bus where they'd first met, earlier. *Amy Sandherst.* The girl burned alive in the video and into Olivia's consciousness.

"Your voice," Olivia said through the pain. "I didn't recognize it before on the bus, but now, all fire and brimstone, I know who you are, what you've done. Well, I'm not lying down for you. I'm not getting tied to a tree like some animal. If the day ever arrives that we meet again, I'll be waiting to put a knife through your heart."

The final insult had the desired effect. It was too much for David. Despite the obvious strength differential, the soldier had difficulty holding him, like trying to rein in a rabid dog.

"You heathen abomination! The Lord's sword will cut you from the womb of existence. I will—"

The soldier had had enough of the madness. David, now held in a chokehold, could barely speak or breathe. He was dragged outside. Olivia nodded to the soldier of the Vampire Union, who nodded back with admiration. The officials just looked happy the situation hadn't turned into a diplomatic incident.

No more waiting now, Olivia walked out the door.

A short corridor led to a security screening room. It didn't look any different to a security screening room anywhere in the NSC. The room must not have been permanently manned, as a massive, jolly-looking man with a big, bushy beard was busy turning on the scanner in a hurry. He wasn't wearing any kind of uniform.

"Oiche messaged me, said you're injured." the man said.

"Oiche…what?"

"Oiche, the official at the desk. I'm Jean, by the way. This wound?"

"It's a gunshot wound."

"Show me."

Olivia took off the Parka and lifted her hoodie to reveal the injury. The improvised bandage was soaked through with blood. Jean's eyes grew like saucers. He winced in empathy and came closer to take a better look.

"Looks nasty," he said. “But even accounting for you still being human right now, it doesn't look fatal. There's a medical clinic for humans up in Vampire's Rest. Let’s not roll the dice. I'll get you there ASAP. Don't take that…bandage off before we get there."

Jean returned to booting up the scanner.

"I thought we were going to Vampire's Rest?" Olivia asked.

"I still have to do a security scan. It'll take less than a minute. You're not carrying any weapons, are you?"

"If I was, would that be a massive problem?"

"No, but it would be if you didn't tell me about it and tried to sneak it through," Jean answered, holding out a plastic tray.

Reaching into her pocket, Olivia produced the unusual pistol and placed it in the tray. Jean took a look at it and whistled in surprise.

"You're not in any trouble, but you’re gonna need to answer some questions once they patch you up."

"Great."

Jean sealed the pistol in an evidence bag. The two went through the quick process of scanning her backpack and parka. Finally, Olivia hobbled through the metal detector herself. The whole procedure took less than thirty seconds.

"All good?"

"All good. Let's get you to Vampire's Rest before you fall over."

With a smile, the massive man hunched down a little, offering his shoulder for support. Apprehensive, Olivia still wasn't in a trusting mood.

"I get it, you've been through a lot, but you can barely walk."

Grudgingly, Olivia put her arm around his shoulder and the two walked across the room to an elevator door. Jean pressed the button, it opened immediately, and he helped her inside. Zero, minus one, minus two, no upper floors, protection from the sunlight.

As the elevator dropped into the basement, a small fear still gripped Olivia, but she was reassured by the confrontation with David. Nobody could fake that. This wasn't some elaborate trick. She wasn't being led to her execution. She was in a different land now, with a different people; they were her people now.

The elevator dinged, and the doors drew open to reveal a parking garage big enough for about four cars. Jean pressed a button on his keys, and the engine of a large SUV started. The lights illuminated the darkness. Olivia felt weak. The determination and adrenaline that had carried her this far faded, her body trying to shut down, thinking it was already safe. The tiny amount of Sara's blood she'd drunk might have been the only thing keeping her conscious. Jean's massive hands helped her up and into the back of the SUV.

"Try to stay conscious. If you feel sleepy, slap yourself," he told her.

"I'll be fine."

Wasting no time, Jean climbed into the driver's seat and reversed the vehicle out in an arc, then hit the gas and powered up the ramp. Ahead, an automatic gate opened just in time to let the vehicle burst out without losing any speed. The vehicle was well-built for the storm, more like a small armored car than a civilian vehicle. All the windows had shutters on the inside, even the windshield. A large viewscreen was mounted near the driver. He must have been able to drive it even during daylight hours.

The storm was so intense Olivia could make out almost nothing outside the side windows. Only thing she knew for certain was they were traveling uphill at a decent gradient. Gravity gently pushed her against the back of the seat. With the heater on full blast, she barely knew there was a storm raging outside. She could have slept for a week. Taking Jean's advice, she slapped herself across the face three times.

Don't sleep, not yet.

"Hey, you OK? We're almost there, so don't pass out."

"I won't."

She wasn't fully certain she could keep her promise. Blood leaked from the bandage and trickled down her leg. It would have been so easy to just sleep, but she refused to give in. Lights ahead, the SUV squeezed through a narrow stone archway and bounded around on cobblestones before coming to a sudden halt. Jean jumped out, opened the door for Olivia, and helped her down. He went to bang on a large wooden door with a green medical sign above it.

Snow swirled around Olivia. She stood dumbfounded in the corner of a small town square. Tall, narrow, ornate buildings with black exterior wooden frames towered above, sheltering the square from the full force of the wind and snow. Frozen over, a massive fountain sat right at the center of the square.

Across the way, one building seemed to be busy. A bar where laughter could be heard. The Vampire Union wasn't like the horror stories, it was a place people lived and laughed, the same as she'd come from. Maybe she was half-delirious from blood loss, but she decided Vampire's Rest was the most beautiful place she'd ever seen.

Jean continued to hammer on the clinic door, and it finally opened. Legs no longer able to support her weight, Olivia collapsed into the snow next to the vehicle. Slumped there in the fresh snow, and despite the pain, she laughed. A little at first, then uncontrollably.

She'd made it.